On the Couch

By Alisa Kwitney

ON THE COUCH
DOES SHE OR DOESN'T SHE?
THE DOMINANT BLONDE

On the Couch

ALISA KWITNEY

AVON
TRADE

An Imprint of HarperCollinsPublishers

HarperCollins books may be purchased for education, business, or sales promotional use. For information please write: Special Markets Department, HarperCollins Publishers Inc., 10 East 53rd Street, New York, NY 10022.

FIRST EDITION

Designed by Elizabeth M. Glover

Library of Congress Cataloging-in-Publication Data

Kwitney, Alisa, 1964–
  On the couch / by Alisa Kwitney.—1st ed.
    p. cm.
  ISBN 0-06-053079-0 (acid-free paper)
  1. Police—New York (State)—New York—Fiction. 2. Women psychologists—Fiction. 3. New York (N.Y.)—Fiction. I. Title.

PS3611.W5805 2004
813'.6—dc22   2004001016

04 05 06 07 08 JTC/RRD 10 9 8 7 6 5 4 3 2 1

For Matthew and Elinor,
who waited patiently for this book to be done
so Mommy could come out and play

thanks

My thanks to retired detective captain Salvatore Blando, for nine months of patiently explaining cop psychology, terminology, and methodology. Sal, this book could not have been written without you. To Holly Harrison and my mother, Ziva, thank you for dropping everything to be my intrepid first readers. Thanks also to detective Heidi Higgins, for introducing me to Sal, arranging for me to ride along with the officers of the 24th Precinct, and telling me some hysterical stories. My old friend Tom Smith, now a big shot Special Agent, AFOSI at the Pentagon, gave me advice and help throughout. Attorney Melinda Caplan supplied trust fund info, Dr. Shuli Kon dispensed last-minute medical advice, and my husband, Mark, kept the family sane and fed while I stayed up all night writing. And I owe a great deal of gratitude to my brilliant agent, Meg Ruley, my outrageously talented and supportive editor Lucia Macro and her assistant, the kind and capable Kelly Harms. The drinks are on me, guys.

marlowe

I woke up and discovered that the phone was ringing. I had the groggy impression that it had been ringing for some time, and that the call was probably urgent.

"Hello," I said. It came out in a throaty whisper.

"God, you sound sexy. Can I come over right now and see you?"

I rolled over to check the clock on my bedside table, accidentally kicking my cat in the head. It was one-thirty in the morning, I was barely conscious, and at some point during the night I'd managed to put my foot through my black lace nightgown, ripping it down the middle.

Of course I was going to see him.

"I'm not sure," I said slowly. "Did you have an appointment?"

There was a pause on the other end. "I thought I did. I mean, I think I do. Do I?"

I turned on the light and my cat glared at me before jumping off the bed. "I believe you had an appointment at just after one."

1

"There was a problem and I just got off work this minute."

I pulled my torn nightgown over my head. "Hmm. I don't know about this. You're not a cop, are you?"

"Do I sound like a cop?"

"You can't always go by how people sound. Talking without having to look at someone is the easiest way to lie." Rummaging through my lingerie drawer, I tossed aside twelve pairs of cotton bikini underpants and four beige brassieres before unearthing a black and pink thong and push-up bra set that looked appropriately whorish.

"So let me talk to you face-to-face."

I cradled the phone between my shoulder and chin as I hooked the bra's clasp between my breasts. "Are you willing to pay the price?"

"Abso-fucking-lutely."

"But you don't even know what that is yet."

"For you, I'll sign a blank check." I stepped into the thong panties and checked myself out in the full-length mirror on my bathroom door. Should I clean up my sleep-smeared eye makeup? Nah. So what if I looked like I was taking a brief pause between sessions of inspired debauchery?

At least I didn't look like a psychologist in private practice who was about to have sex for the first time in over a year.

As for what could motivate an attractive, financially secure woman with a Ph.D. in clinical psych to let a man think that she was a call girl, well, I could say it was just being a single thirtysomething woman in Manhattan.

Or else I could cite the fact that I'd been told that if I

wanted to publish my dissertation, I needed to spice it up with some intimate personal revelations.

The truth, of course, was messier, more complicated, and a lot less rational. Most people think that therapists are immune to the kinds of problems they treat, but the truth is, we're all motivated by the pursuit of pleasure. Not to mention occasionally blinded by it.

If Joe were a client, I'd probably diagnose him as a high-achieving, mildly obsessive type A personality with excellent coping skills and some deep, underlying insecurity. I'd also have a much better handle on what's really motivating him, because he's not the kind of guy who needs to hire a date by the hour. In fact, it's not always clear to me who's seducing whom.

"Marlowe? You still there, or did you fall asleep on me?"

"All right," I said. "You can come over. But make it snappy."

"I'm on my way."

"Oh, and Joe?"

"Yeah?"

"Bring your handcuffs."

joe

Two weeks earlier

I told myself it was a bit of covert surveillance, not eavesdropping on women's conversations while they exercised. It wasn't like I was some kind of sweaty-palmed perv who needed to get a life; I was simply gathering intelligence before deciding on the appropriate course of action.

Sometimes I had to wait awhile before talkers showed up, but today I got lucky right off the bat: Two girlfriends without headphones doing free weights.

"It's this city. It's insane. Here, you go out with a guy, the only thing he's thinking about is, How long's it gonna take me to get her into bed? Back in Atlanta, I never had this sense that the meter was running. People in New York aren't willing to take the time to look beneath the surface."

"Hold on, I need to work my inner thighs now."

The two women walked over to a machine that looked as if it belonged in a gynecologist's office and took turns squeezing their knees together.

"Do you think it's because you knew the guys in Atlanta better?"

"Thirteen, fourteen, fifteen. No, I don't know, I think
everyone here schedules everything. Even the five-year-
olds have to make playdates a month in advance."

I continued my bench presses while observing the
women from across the room. Should I make a move?
After being banished to this precinct from the Joint Organized Crime Task Force, I'd decided to avoid the station house's crummy excuse for a gym. Instead, I'd
swallowed this club's hefty initiation fee, hoping to meet
healthy, solvent, career-minded women.

In the past month, I'd managed to lose the ten pounds
I'd gained around my midsection from last year's steady
diet of stress and junk food. I'd also acquired some decent muscle definition across the shoulders and chest.
What I hadn't gotten was anyone's phone number.

The problem was, the women in this precinct were a
different species from the ones I'd grown up with—like
the one I'd dated, married, and divorced. It wasn't just a
different borough; it was a parallel universe.

But there was something about these women—a confidence that was very female but not at all feminine, at
least not in the way I was used to thinking of as feminine.
No lipstick, no high heels, no long nails or cleavage. Just
a way of meeting your eye that said, Buddy, while you
were taking criminal science classes in the evenings, I
was getting my liberal arts degree in leftist politics, Eastern religion, feminist literature, and fucking everyone in
sight.

I wanted to know what these women knew. Not just
the sex part; the Eastern religion and the feminist litera-

ture, too. I wanted a taste of a different reality from my own, one that didn't involve equal parts monotony and adrenaline.

So far, I hadn't actually spoken to anyone, but I had learned a lot about low-carbohydrate diets, divorce law, elementary school politics, and liposuction.

If God was kind, these two ladies would have no personal interest in any of the aforementioned subjects.

Reflected in the club's long mirrors, the two women were both beauty shop blondes, both attractive and in their twenties. One had a better body, the other seemed nicer and had a faint Southern accent.

Neither of them looked like she had the key to any erotic alternate reality, but then, what exactly would that look like, anyway? The Southern one seemed like a prospect, at least.

I rested my barbell on the rack and sat up, stretching my arms up over my head and swiveling my torso. Ah, there they were: The women had finished with the machines and were heading for the mat area. They were too far away for me to catch what they were saying over the piped-in pop music, but presumably, the ladies were elaborating their views of Manhattan's lust-crazed men.

Part of me wanted to go over to them and say, Listen, you think men think about sex all the time? Guess what—we don't. At least, I don't. At least, not anymore.

I thought about thinking about sex a lot, and the fact that I didn't anymore, and I thought about the fact that I was no longer in the prime 18-34 TV-watching, music-buying demographic. I thought about the fact that most of the other guys my age had begun to go soft around the edges: soft jawlines, soft middles, big, soft cars with plenty of room in the back for their big, soft wives, kids, and dogs.

At 38, I was a hell of a lot harder than I had been fifteen years ago, when I'd first joined the force. My ex-wife used to say I had the kind of looks that improve with age—but that was back before most of her comments were designed to draw blood.

I wiped down the bench with a towel and walked by the mat where the two young women were doing sit-ups. The Georgia Belle was perched awkwardly on a huge yellow medicine ball, and for a moment I considered telling her to move her legs farther apart, for traction.

But I suddenly felt that I couldn't go through it all one more time: The ritual conversation, the introductions, the gimlet-look from the busty friend, the oh-you're-a-detective, the falsely casual banter, the scribbling of the phone numbers, the test-drive lunch, the formal dinner to follow, the dancing to some ear-splitting Techno din, followed by some serious kissing, all this leading up to the great moment when, with painful self-consciousness, she takes her clothes off, lies down and gives you the smile that says, This is it, the big chance, the ultimate challenge, figure me out in the next fifteen minutes or I'll be discussing you over leg lifts in the health club tomorrow.

No thank you. No way. I cut a detour, avoiding the two women on the exercise mat, making my way past the rhythmic pounding of the treadmill runners and the pulse of synthesizer samba from the glass-walled studio. I glanced left and saw about twenty straight females and two gay males thrashing and flailing along with the instructor. As I watched, one girl smacked her arm into a support pillar. You had to know you weren't cut out for dancing if you couldn't avoid hitting a stationary object, for crying out loud.

Nice ass on her, though.

The men's locker room was blessedly silent and empty. I was pulling on my Levis when I glanced up at the clock and realized I had fourteen more gray hours of Saturday and all of Sunday to get through before it was time to report in for work again.

Since my schedule is four days on, two days off, my Saturday nights on the town are few and far between. Once upon a time, I'd plotted and schemed for those nights. You dated a girl, she wanted to go out when everyone else went out. You wanted to meet a girl, you had to go out when everyone else went out.

But the way I felt right now, the weekend was just a lottery ticket and I was sick of throwing my money at a million to one.

So what else could I do besides chase girls? My old friends were living the soft life in Long Island and Rockland County, doing whatever married people do with their kids in the suburbs in the middle of a cold April. My newer friends all seemed to have gone over to my ex-wife as part of the divorce settlement.

I contemplated my options.

1. Clean my apartment of the last few reminders of my ex-wife

2. Visit my folks so my mom can suggest a career change

3. Get in bed and fantasize about that pretty doe-
   eyed actress who plays a CIA agent on TV

Shit. Well, maybe some major case would crack and I'd
wind up going in to work today after all.

marlowe

"Okay and now step back! Step left! Mambo step and then turn right! One-two, one-two-three, turn, turn, kick and right back into the first combination!"

On the third turn, I smacked my arm into a support pillar. As the pain in my elbow subsided to a dull throbbing, I grabbed my bottle of water off the floor with my good hand and dodged past a pot-bellied man with a fierce expression and two sinewy Latinas. A statuesque woman in black dance sneakers spun into me, mumbling something that might have been either irritation or apology.

This, I knew, was the true price of living in Manhattan. If you took an aerobics class in a normal town, you'd likely find yourself surrounded by a bunch of panting suburban moms. In Manhattan, you couldn't spit without hitting two former Rockettes and the entire touring cast of *Fosse*.

So maybe you were a budding writer. The person seated next to you at Starbucks had already won a Pulitzer. Needed a pair of jeans from the Gap? The woman in the dressing room across from you was a soap opera actress with buttocks as firm as a fifteen-year-old boy's. You couldn't even order a cheeseburger from the corner diner without discovering that your waiter used to sing in '80s hair band videos.

And if you were a newly-minted psychologist like me, struggling to launch a private practice, you were in competition with the greatest concentration of psychiatrists, psychologists, and psychotherapists in the world.

I made my way past the frantically healthy treadmill runners and the gang of yoga freaks stretching in front of the aerobics studio. God, it just wasn't fair. Now it wasn't enough to be firm and toned; you also had to be as limber as a squirrel monkey.

No, no, negative thinking, flawed perception. Maybe a trip to the Met would shift my mood. Or a foreign film. Forget about the life of the body, focus on the life of the mind.

Inside the women's changing room, I had just gotten my locker open and was thinking that a dose of Impressionism would do me good, when two damp, towel-clad blondes appeared.

"Sorry, I'm right here to the left of you," said the curvier blonde. To her friend, she said, "No, Hailey, he was definitely checking you out."

"Which one?"

"Kind of lanky but muscular, very dark brown hair that kept falling in his face? He had these really intense, deep-set eyes."

"Ugh, him? You've got to be kidding. He looked like a thug." Blonde #2 had a faint Southern accent.

"Well, he certainly liked you," said the first blonde, wriggling into her thong underwear.

"Doesn't it figure? Whenever there's a good-looking guy who turns out to be some kind of decent prospect, he goes for you, Jenna. I get the losers and weirdos. What is it with this place?"

It took me a moment to realize that Southern Blonde was including me in this conversation. I had just unhooked my sport bra and was holding it in front of my breasts, stalling for time. "You mean this gym?"

"I mean this city. The men here are just unbelievable hounds, don't you find?"

"Oh, it's not so bad," I said, quickly shoving my bra into the locker and wrapping myself in a towel. I had been stalked by an emotionally dependent patient in his seventies last month, but I didn't think that counted as male attention.

"Sounds like she's found someone, huh, Hailey?" The two blondes looked at me expectantly.

"Actually, I haven't gone on a date in over a year."

"No way! But you're so pretty. A whole year?"

Come to think of it, more like fifteen months. "I just haven't found myself that attracted to anyone lately." Well, that wasn't exactly true. I'd spotted a few blue collar types around my building that appealed in a base, mammalian way, but I suspected that the attraction wouldn't outlast a first conversation; and I'd met one or two nice, soft-spoken professional men I could've taken to a foreign film festival, but who failed to rouse the beast in me.

"I don't mean to scare you, but I hear your vagina starts to fuse together after a while," said the bustier blonde.

"Oh, the vaginal walls don't start to atrophy till after

menopause," I said, realizing a beat too late that she'd been joking. I sloped off to the showers, wishing I could take a vacation and leave myself behind. How could a person who was paid for talking with people be so awkward in social situations?

But it was my feeling of not quite fitting in that had finally led me to my true calling: exploring the tangled motivations of human behavior.

Of course, other people were relatively easy to diagnose: I wasn't always so clear about what was driving my own behavior. I did know one thing, however: I wasn't coming back to this gym. Forget the fact that I'd gained seven pounds this winter. There was no way I was getting myself in the middle of a bunch of crazed ex-Broadway dancers again.

And yet it had seemed like such a healthy, life-affirming decision. Get out of the apartment! Get physically active! Meet new girlfriends to replace the ones who were all either getting married, getting pregnant, or moving to Westchester. Meet a new man with whom to get married and pregnant and move to Westchester.

But synchronized samba was not my idea of fun, and so far all the men I'd seen at the gym seemed almost maniacally focused on their Cybex machines. Besides, even if I did attend one of the club's periodic cheap wine and stale cheese socials, I knew what my fate would be: mercy conversation from the gay 22-year-old trainers.

Because on the Upper West Side, it was not enough to be an attractive, intelligent, financially solvent 36-year-old woman. No, a woman had to be a Playboy pinup with a Ph.D. to get noticed south of 96th Street. Walk me past a construction site and I'd have ten men calling me

Baby and making kissy noises, but in my own neighborhood, where single women outnumbered men three to one, I kept slipping under everyone's radar.

Had it been an option, I would've gone back to the small town that had felt so confining back when I was in high school, in order to discover that the juvenile delinquent from chem lab was now the town sheriff, still unattached and still carrying a torch for me. But this part of New York City *was* my hometown, and I couldn't imagine life as a single being easier anywhere else.

Besides, I couldn't drive, which limited my options.

Feeling a bit better from the shower, I dried myself off, pulled on a gray sweatshirt and black jeans, and dried my shoulder length hair without bothering to style it. Ten years ago, when my hair was still a soft red, I'd given it the specialized care usually lavished on wild orchids and snow leopards. These days I just scraped the whole brownish mass into a ponytail.

All around me, women were busy at the long communal mirror, moisturizing their necks, applying mascara to their lashes, brushing color into their cheeks. I didn't see the point in making myself up; in five minutes, I'd be back at home, and the chances of my bumping into the man of my dreams along the way seemed fairly slim.

Outside, I found the sky had turned the color of a used ashtray and the temperature had dropped a good ten degrees. Hard to believe that this was already the middle of April. It felt more like winter than spring.

The good-looking thug who had been checking out one of the blondes was standing outside the gym, one arm braced by the window of a police car as he talked to the driver. As my glance skimmed over the muscular way he filled out his faded jeans, he looked over his shoulder at me, then turned back to the cop as if dismissing me.

I had a sudden urge to walk up and say, "What am I, the invisible woman?" He wasn't even my type: I go for boyish, endearingly shy and outdoorsy. Which meant that I had been rejected by the kind of guy I wouldn't even have noticed ten years ago.

Dispirited, I decided to head straight home. I reviewed my options:

1. Do laundry

2. Read Michael Faber's Victorian prostitute book

3. Lie in bed and indulge in a licentious fantasy about Dennis Quaid's armadillo-like abdominals and Cheshire Cat grin

What did it say about me that I couldn't decide between #1 and #3?

joe

It started the minute I walked into the squad room. I didn't even have time to take off my jacket, much less get a chance to tackle the precariously stacked pile of reports on my desk.

"Hey, Kain, something big's just come in for you."

"Yeah, Joe, we saved it for you special."

"Just got the call and thought, this one's for Kain." Lili Gonzales, Denny Moreland, and Kito Birdwell smiled at me with identical expressions of smug, schoolyard maliciousness. The neurotic princess, the snarky nerd, and the arrogant pup, united in their dislike of me.

Christ, I could have been back in second grade: same sad beige tiled walls, same flickering fluorescent lights, same broken green shades over heavily barred windows. A layer of city grime on everything higher than your chest. A bunch of desks that smelled like disinfectant and a closet that stank of dead mouse. And most of all, the same goddamn bunch of cannibal ethics: Show no aggression, show no fear, try not to look like anyone's meat.

"Aw, shit." I tried to look amused instead of pissed off. "What have we got?"

"I've got court duty," said Kito, looking pleased with himself. Young, ambitious, and educated at City College, Kito was one of the few cops I knew who liked testifying. "Well, lucky you, lunch in Chinatown. And what do I have, Kito?"

"A DOA on a hundred and sixth."

Great. A DOA, or as one of my old sergeants used to say, decomposing odiferous artifact—AKA a dead body. "What am I, the Lone Ranger? What're you guys supposed to be doing?"

"Denny and I have to make a collar," said Lili.

Translation: We're all avoiding you like the plague. I didn't mind about the others so much, but Denny and I had gone to the Academy together. After getting flopped from the Organized Crime Task Force back to a precinct house last month, I'd figured I'd lucked out winding up with Denny at the two-four. At least until I arrived and my old friend started acting like he barely knew me.

Sometimes I wished I could just walk up to Denny and say, "Look, what is it? What did I do? Why are we on the outs?" But the first thing a police officer learns on the job is that everybody lies. To hide something. To avoid embarrassment. To make the problem go away.

And asking what had gone wrong was a fool's game. You looked at the clues and you put them together in your head. You made up a story and then tried to see if you could poke any holes in it. If it didn't fall apart, then you knew as much as you were ever going to about what the fuck went on in somebody else's head.

Besides, it wasn't exactly a mystery to me as to why I had no friends among the 24th precinct's three detective teams. On the police force, a new transfer was like a new student in high school. Everyone looked at you, wondering what you were: troublemaker, slacker, bookworm, or jerk. You had about two or three weeks to make an impression, and then whatever reputation you'd left behind at your old stomping grounds usually caught up with you.

And I knew what my rep was: fuck-up, first grade. Seems you don't get rewarded for butting heads with FBI agents. Next time some flat-eyed farm boy from the Midwest started lecturing me on apprehending criminals, I'd grin and bear it.

In the meantime, I was just going to have to put up with being this house's resident pariah.

Despite everything, I was surprised to find myself whistling as I walked up the steps to Mr. Tony Russo's fourth-floor apartment. Why was I suddenly feeling all bright-eyed and bushy-tailed? Because I had a date with a corpse, of course. Maybe a problem to discover. A puzzle to solve.

Someone to think about who wasn't me.

My good mood lasted while I spoke to the uniform who'd been first on the scene and learned that the deceased was not in an advanced state of decomposition. The body had been discovered an hour ago by the cleaning woman, who had her own key. She'd run into the street, shrieking, and had fetched a couple of patrol cops off the street.

All fairly commonplace occurrences, in my line of work. Then I walked through the yellow tape and opened the dead man's door, at which point the day took a turn for the strange.

Because this corpse had a very familiar face.

Not familiar in the sense that I knew the man, a Mr.

Russo. Familiar in the sense that the dead guy looked a hell of a lot like me—the main difference being that he was stark naked, wrapped head to toe in plastic wrap, and propped against a living room wall with a snorkel in his mouth.

The uniform came up behind me. "What kind of a sick fuck does something like that?"

I glanced at the copy of *New York* magazine on a table by the corpse's feet. It was open to the "Escorts" section. "A lonely kind of fuck," I said, taking out my notebook.

"You mean you don't think it's a homicide?"

I started to make some smart-ass remark, but the young patrol cop was looking at me as if he half expected someone to hit him. How old was this kid, twenty-one, twenty-two? He still had that gangly puppy look of not having grown into his hands and feet. "Don't worry," I told him. "It takes at least a year on the job to find out that lonely kills as least as many folks as angry does."

marlowe

Savannah LaBrecque arrived late. My first impression of my new client was that she was extremely pretty, in her early twenties, and probably an actress, as she was wearing what amounted to a costume: a black riding jacket and fox-hunting boots over slim black slacks, her light brown hair pulled back in a ponytail to show off her even-featured, exquisitely made-up face. All that was missing was the crop to beat the horse; perhaps that was stashed in the Prada bag.

Even though it was early in the afternoon, I was already cranky and tired. I'd been woken up at two A.M. by a wrong number who'd been looking for an escort service, and hadn't been able to fall back asleep.

I waited as Savannah strode in without apology, went over to the window, shrugged out of her jacket, and said how much she envied my view of Central Park.

"But it's still so brown and bleak-looking down there. That's the problem with New York. Winter just lasts forever." She had a slight Southern accent.

"I think we should get started pretty soon, because I have someone coming at twelve," I lied. I'd been sitting

20

around in a pressed white shirt and black skirt, not knowing whether or not my only appointment of the day was late or delinquent.

"Oh, right." Savanna seated herself, not on the white linen couch most of my female clients preferred, but on the big, masculine leather chair, crossing her legs with the self-conscious grace of a beauty contestant and folding her hands in her lap.

"Why don't we start with you telling me a little about why you wanted to come see me?"

"Well, Dr. Riddle, it's my mother. We usually get along really well together—I mean, we have the usual mom-daughter tussles, and then we work things out. But lately she's been driving me round the bend. She's on my case all the time—have I remembered to pay the bills, did I manage to hire a new house cleaner yet, did I put our ad into *New York* magazine this month. I feel like I'm sixteen again."

I waited a moment to see if Savannah would say more. Her eyes, I realized, were green—not hazel, like mine, but a true, clear green.

"Is that the only reason you sought some counseling?" Compared to her soft, musical voice, mine sounded dry and flat, colorless.

"Well, maybe not the only thing, but the main thing. She just keeps criticizing me, and maybe if I went to an office, I could handle it, but since we both work from home, it's just nag, nag, nag, twenty-four/seven."

"So both you and your mother live and work in the same place?"

Savannah nodded. "We run our business out of our brownstone."

I made a mental note of that. "And what kind of business are you two in?"

"The oldest kind."

"Excuse me?"

Savannah looked at me and smiled, and it was the smile—knowing, rueful, a little naughty—that clued me in. "Yep, that's it—exactly what you're thinking."

I tried not to look as surprised as I felt. "I think you'd better get explicit here, just so I'm sure we're on the same page."

"How explicit do you want? We run a top-notch house, and cater to a very exclusive clientele."

"House meaning . . . brothel?"

Savannah nodded.

"And your mother is the madame?"

"We're co-owners. She handles the phones and the figures, because she used to be a legal secretary, and I manage the girls."

"And you've been doing this for . . ."

"Two years. When I first came to New York about seven years ago, I started seeing a few guys through this one upscale service. My mother came to visit me and answered the phone one time and all hell broke loose. But after she got done telling me how I was ruining my life, I pointed out that at my age, she was living with one abusive bastard after another just so she'd have a roof over our heads. So Momma went off and thought about it, and she wound up saying, If you're going to do this, I want to be right here watching over you. Which really meant I'd be watching out for her, of course."

"So she stayed in New York?"

"And started working the phones. Shortly after that I

met this one real estate lawyer who helped us find a place of our own. Our brainstorm was settling into a brownstone right here on the Upper West Side."

"Your brothel is in this neighborhood?"

"Think about it. I mean, it's stroller city around here, isn't it? You've got a bunch of wealthy lawyers and doctors and businessmen with pregnant wives and little kids underfoot—that's exactly the kind of clientele we're looking for."

"But do men really want to . . . visit a prostitute that close to their homes?"

"Sure. This way, hubby goes out to walk the dog or go for a run and comes back an hour later and no one's the wiser."

"And nobody notices the constant stream of late-night visitors?"

"Nobody cares. Our customers are discreet, for one thing. And we don't have to contend with coop boards and nosy doormen. Although I have to say, I do envy you your view of the park."

I tried to digest all this. "Ms. LaBrecque, I'm getting the impression that you're content with the line of work you've chosen, but that your mother's involvement has made it harder for you to experience yourself as an independent adult."

"That's exactly it! I keep telling her she needs to get a life of her own, but all she thinks about is the business, me, and her Yorkshire Terriers. The minute I want to go do something on my own, she's all over me. Who am I going out with? What do I know about this guy? Is he really safe?" Savannah gave a little huff of exasperation.

"I take it you're not talking about the men you see at work."

"Oh, I don't really see guys professionally much anymore, except for a few longtime customers. And my mother doesn't care about those. She's worried about the ones I date."

"Is there someone in particular you're seeing right now?"

"Well, not exactly. I've met someone who steams my clams, but so far he's not partaking of the shellfish. The thing is, I'm not entirely sure how much of what we're doing is business and how much is pleasure, because he came to visit me in my professional capacity. But not as a client. He's doing research."

"Research? Is he an academic? A journalist?"

"He didn't say. He just wanted to know about who comes to see me, what ages and backgrounds, did I get any religious nuts, things like that."

"So you just talked?"

"Yeah, we talked, I gave him a tour . . . showed him some of the toys . . . I couldn't quite tell if he was getting turned on or not."

"Did you want him to be?"

"I guess I did, yeah. I mean, here he was, absolutely Brad Pitt-gorgeous, and so clean-cut and professional and smart, like, he'd just make some comment about how a particular device would work on the nerve endings, or say that society has a huge effect on what we consider shameful versus exciting or painful rather than pleasurable."

"So what happened?"

"I asked him if he wanted me to demonstrate anything. And he went all quiet and asked me what sort of thing, which made me think—usually it's the client that

24

comes in with the scenario. So I said, whatever you want, a little B and D, you know, tie you up, boss you around." Savannah took a deep breath. "And he said, he'd have to think about it. So he left, and really nothing out of the ordinary happened, except for the fact that by the time he walked out the door, my panties were soaking wet."

As Savannah launched into the many carnal fantasies this man's visit had engendered, I realized that this was the kind of conversation I could never have with a therapist of my own, for fear we'd meet up at some professional function and have to stand around making small talk and pretending we'd never discussed my lubricious secretions. Of course, I'd stopped seeing my therapist, as I'd begun to feel like a sitcom in its sixth season: I was rehashing all my old themes and providing very little in the way of new material.

I looked up; Savannah had completed her whole earth catalogue of sexual pleasures.

"You sound really taken with this man."

"I am completely, utterly over the moon. But I don't even know if he'll call me again."

It took the rest of the session for us to work through what Savannah could do to impact on the development of this nascent relationship. I kept trying to move her past her focus on this mystery man and to think about what it meant that she was beginning to want romance in her life, which might help her become more independent from her mother. But Savannah wasn't going to be seduced into having any personal insights. I did touch briefly on the possibility that Savannah's preoccupation with this new man might be making her mother uneasy.

"I guess I should be thinking about all this, but really all I want to know is how I can get him to call me," Savannah said, in a wail that was meant to be half ironic. "I'm desperate."

We sat for a moment, listening to the echo of her words in the quiet apartment, and then, from behind my closed bedroom door, we both heard my cat give a long, disgruntled howl.

Savannah laughed. "I guess my time must be up."

I glanced at the clock; we'd run over. "So, will I see you next week?"

"I'm not sure. I have to keep my schedule a bit free in case he calls and wants to get together. How about I ring you later on and let you know?"

I think I succeeded in keeping my feelings from showing on my face. It seemed to me that most of my clients paid me to help them arrive at the most painfully obvious of insights. Such as, do not spend twenty-four hours a day, seven days a week with three children under the age of three. Or, of course you should leave your alcoholic, three-timing girlfriend.

In this case, I wondered how long it would take Savannah to realize that getting involved with a guy whose main attraction was his seeming indifference to her was a truly awful idea.

We finished the session with my assigning Savannah the task of writing a list of goals she wanted to achieve. With any luck, it would get her thinking about the advisability of chasing after a man who might just be viewing her as a case study.

See, I told myself, there are worse things than feeling a complete lack of desire for all the men you meet.

26

I opened the door to my bedroom, and Burt, my very vocal sable Burmese, bounded out and then skidded to a halt, looking up at me balefully with his very round, golden eyes. I didn't have to look to know there would be new claw marks on my wicker rocking chair. I was just happy that, since putting Burt on kitty Prozac, there wouldn't be cat piss on my 1940s patchwork quilt.

"Sorry, Burt, I'd have let you out sooner, but you're a distraction when I'm working."

Burt made a sound like a teething baby and I picked him up. "It's okay, boy, yes it is." I had purchased Burt in England, where breeders specialize in producing needy felines for emotionally contained owners. No one had warned me about willful incontinence, but then, as my father had taught me, the British tend to say things by implication. Perhaps in East Sussex "needs a lot of attention" means "will spray your fine linens whenever you go out for groceries."

I let the cat stroke his cheek against my chin as I carried him into my study and settled down on my favorite cigar-brown leather chair. This was the room where I was supposed to be turning my dissertation into a book. The problem was, I'd grown bored with it.

Four years ago, when I began writing my paper on The Mardi Gras Phenomenon: Behavioral Effects of Masking Identity, I'd had waist-length hair and an active membership in the Society for Creative Anachronism.

I'd never pretended that the exercise was purely intellectual; I admitted that I felt a yearning for a secret identity. Well, why wouldn't I want to be some other version of myself from time to time? In my regular life, as a twenty-first–century Ph.D. candidate, I knew that I had acquired a reputation for being serious and self-contained and a bit unapproachable.

(I was made aware of this by Nitsa, a woman in my program who had short curly black hair and the trace of a mustache. Nitsa said she felt I should know that our classmates considered me emotionally aloof, because it might have bearing on my future success as a clinician. I wanted to ask my friends if she was right, but realized I didn't actually know anyone well enough to initiate that kind of conversation.)

I wasn't completely sure why people perceived me this way; in high school, I had been considered cool and unflappable, rather than flat and affectless.

Maybe the difference was attributable to the fact that as a teenager, my social life had consisted mainly of drinking, smoking pot, dancing, and fooling around. When you're a teenager, no one minds if you're more of a listener than a talker, but by the time you reach your thirties, you're supposed to have mastered the art of rendering your life history into easily digestible sound bites. I had never managed to turn myself into cocktail conversation, and the truth was, I didn't really want to serve myself up as an hors d'oeuvre.

As a sixteenth-century Italian courtesan and poet, however, I was free to invent my own reputation as an erudite wanton. I didn't have to offer any proof of my wantonness or wit; I just told people in my bio that this is who I was, and they agreed to see me as I wished to be seen. It gave me a delicious feeling of freedom to be able to research and write my own character, and at first I assumed that there was no limit to the power of my imagination. I thought that in my remarkably cleavage-enhancing gowns, I would be able to attract a Renaissance man with sword-wielding muscles and a basic understanding of the longbow's role in England's rise to power—someone clever enough to appeal to Marlowe Riddle's intellectual taste and masculine enough to satisfy Tullia d'Aragona's wayward appetites.

But after a year of attending bi-monthly meetings of the costuming guild and tramping around various muddy Medieval Faires, I gave up on my vague hope of meeting a knight errant. The Society, it seemed, tended to attract obsessional types who were fascinated by arcane rules of falconry or sword fighting or the minutiae of horse armour.

In the end, I decided to concentrate on the Internet instead, where it was easy to find people using assumed screen names and personae that granted them license to speak and act as they pleased.

By the time I handed in my paper, I was bored with my own findings. Yes, it was true that people behaved differently when their identities were concealed, but so what? Back in the days when I corseted myself up for a field trip, the whole concept seemed fun and even a bit titillating. If there was something fun or titillating about the Internet, I had yet to discover it—it all reeked of laziness and desperation to me. How could you suspend disbelief and imagine that any man who e-mailed you ten times a day had any kind of life outside his apartment?

Burt shifted in my lap and began cleaning his left paw. I couldn't bring myself to turn my computer on. Instead, I found myself sitting by the window in a patch of sunlight as a breeze fluttered through the gauzy curtains, thinking of Savannah. Despite all she knew about men, she had managed to develop a crush. My job, if she permitted me to perform it, would be to walk her around her dream man, leading her up to the places where termites had eaten through the foundation and damp had rotted the roof. Someday, with the tools I could give her, she would be able to detect the flaws in a relationship from a block away, and read the end of the affair into the opening lines.

Where ignorance is bliss, the poet said, tis folly to be wise. Could there be such a thing as growing too evolved for romance?

Burt, neutered and content, began to purr.

joe

After a night spent on a lumpy mattress in the precinct and then eight hours on duty, the only thing I wanted to do was go home and collapse in front of the TV set with a bottle of beer and a bowl of chips. Instead, I took the subway one stop past my building and got out at 181st Street before walking up the steep incline that leads to Overlook Terrace.

It was the first night of Passover, and even bacon-eating Jews like myself were expected to show up for the ritual meal and argument.

Why is this night different from all other nights? Because the TV set's not on and we have to talk to each other.

At least seeing my folks got me out of my own head a bit. I wasn't about to admit it to anyone, but I'd gotten a little creeped out this afternoon. I mean, I was aware that my post-divorce decorating was pretty generic, but still, Tony Russo's apartment had been decorated in the exact same IKEA furnishings as mine—he'd even had the same pattern on his plates, for Chrissake.

I wasn't sure why, but something about the whole case

was bugging me. But what? I knew this wasn't a homicide. I'd taken photos of the scene and copied down the last numbers called from his cellphone, but those were just formalities. There hadn't been any blood inside the plastic wrap, but there had been evidence of another kind of bodily fluid. Seems Mr. Russo had achieved his intended goal—before accidentally dislodging his snorkel and suffocating.

Maybe it was just the sheer, wasteful stupidity of the man's death. Nowadays doctors don't believe that masturbation makes you mentally defective, but how else do you explain a guy who decides to wrap himself up like a big zucchini in order to deprive himself of oxygen? Even if starving yourself of air does intensify orgasm, how fucking intense does it have to be?

I turned right just before I reached the top of the hill. To my left were the gates that led to Fort Tryon Park, where I used to ride my skateboard all the way up to the entrance of the Cloisters until the guard chased me away. My parents' apartment building was only half a block away, with faux medieval doors that always reminded me of a dungeon.

I climbed the four flights of stairs instead of taking the elevator, to avoid getting trapped with a neighbor who wanted to know how I was doing after the divorce.

I knocked twice and my mother opened the door without checking who it was through the peephole.

"Ma, what do I always tell you about asking who it is?"

"I know your knock. Let me look at you, Yossi." My mother gave me a long look as I hung up my coat, and she didn't look happy. "You're too thin."

32

"I was getting a stomach, Ma."

"You were a healthy-looking man. Now you're a stick."

I leaned down to kiss my mother on her disapproving chipmunk cheek.

"With kisses you think you'll shut me up? Go. Go wash your hands and then say hello to your father." My mother may stand five foot two from the toes of her orthopedic pumps to the top of her dyed beige hair, but she could teach Lieutenant Franks a thing or two about handling yourself with authority. "And use antibacterial soap!"

I stopped in the hallway, where a parade of dead relatives glowered down at me from picture frames. "Ma, I took a shower back at the precinct and I also wore gloves when I touched the body."

"A body? You touched a body? Do me a favor. Take another shower. I have enough medical problems without you bringing some exotic flesh-eating bacteria into the house."

"Ma." As far as I could tell, the only thing my mother was suffering from was acute hypochondria.

"Besides, our shower is better than the precinct's. We have a massage setting. Reduces stress."

No way to explain to my mother that seeing her was the most stressful part of my life. Mr. Russo, on the other hand, had been as cooperative as a dead person could be. He'd even left his copy of *New York* magazine out, open to the classifieds section. Clearly he'd been trying to decide whether or not to call for some professional assistance, and then thought, Hey, why not save the money and do it myself?

I turned off the shower and decided I might as well get out my dad's disposable razor and have a shave.

"Yossi, what are you doing in there?"

"Making myself presentable. Ma, please do not open the bathroom door." I leaned my weight against the wood.

"What, you've grown something new I haven't seen before? The food is getting cold."

"I'll be out in a sec."

Of course the food wasn't getting cold, it was getting dried out in the oven. There was a good smell of dill and chicken in the air, because even my mother couldn't manage to cook all the flavor out of soup.

"Smells great, Ma."

"Go tell your father to come to the table."

As if they didn't live in a tiny apartment where everything anyone said was perfectly audible. Growing up, I'd had to listen to my father's snores from two doors down. I'm pretty sure my parents never had sex while I was in the house, because if they had, quite frankly, I would've known about it.

I went over to say hi to my father, who was watching the TV as if it were personally delivering bad news to him. He shook his head, clucked in disapproval one last time, and turned CNN off.

"How's it going, Dad? Business okay?" Dad owned Kain's Kribs, a baby furniture store, and until I was twelve years old, I'd believed that his was one of the world's most challenging professions.

"We're surviving. I just got another recall for a stroller and tomorrow I'm going to have a mob of angry women at my door, but what can I do?" My father, lean and neat in a pressed white shirt, looked at my newly shaven face. "You used my razor?"

"You're the one who bequeathed me five o'clock shadow genes." Unlike most of the other Jewish men in their building, my dad didn't grow his beard. He and my mother belonged to a Conservative synagogue, which meant that as a kid, I was too religious to fit in with the kids who could eat at McDonalds and watch TV on Saturday but not observant enough to fit in with any of the other Jewish boys in the neighborhood.

To make matters worse, my Mom had suffered two miscarriages after having me, so I was the full recipient of what would have been enough Jewish mothering for at least three or four.

We sat down at the table and my father cleared his throat and began reading from his beautifully illustrated Passover Haggadah. When I realized that he was intending to go through each and every section of the book, I cleared my throat.

"Dad, I'm running on almost no sleep here and there aren't any kids at the table. You think maybe we could speed this up?"

"What do you mean, speed it up? These are the traditions of our people, handed down from time immemorial . . ."

"Yeah, I know, but let's face it, this show's for the benefit of kids, and we don't have any here. So let's just do the edited version, sing a few songs, and get to eating before I keel over, all right?"

My father said something in Yiddish that I thought might have meant "thing from the nether regions," but I wasn't sure. My mother intervened and they argued for a few minutes before settling on an abbreviated run through the ritual.

I tried to ignore the waves of disapproval emanating from my father as my mother served up the soup in Blue Willow bowls. There was a chicken neck in mine, complete with skin.

"So, Yossi," said my mother, "are you studying?"

I swallowed my soup and tore off a chunk of matzoh. "I'm not having this conversation again, Ma."

"So many cops become lawyers these days. All the criminal science classes you took? With the grades you had, you could be ready to take the bar exam in a month."

"Ettie, stop it." My father gestured with his spoon. "First you complain he never comes to dinner and then you give him *muser* with his meal. Leave the boy alone."

"And if I leave him alone, then what? He dies on the street, Hyman, bleeding like a dog. Do you know what happens to police officers? If a bullet doesn't get them, a heart attack will, and let's not even talk about the divorce rate."

"I thought you were happy he got divorced." My father had finished his soup during my mother's tirade; now she stood up to collect the blue-and-white dishes with their delicate Chinese pastoral designs.

"Happy? I haven't been happy since he came home with that *shiksa* with her hair down to her *tuchus*. Leave him alone, you said, don't hound him into marrying her. So I left him alone. And what did he do? He married her. What was wrong with that nice Jewish hairdresser you were dating, I'd like to know."

"Lydia? Oh, Ma, please, she was a nervous *choleria*."

"She called me, you know. You broke her heart." My mother paused, standing behind me. "You not eating the neck, Yossi? You love necks."

I pulled the neck out of my bowl and started eating. My mother swept the bowl out from under me and, still muttering about my ex-wife and chicken necks, disappeared into the kitchen.

My father and I took deep breaths, not quite meeting the other's eye. "So." My father cleared his throat. "How is business by you?"

An image of Tony Russo, wrapped like a mummy in clear plastic up to his ears, flashed in front of me. I put the chicken neck down on a napkin: Autoerotic asphyxiation cases tend to ruin the appetite for such things.

"Well, it's quieter than my last assignment," I said, but my father was already perusing the TV listings with a pen in hand, circling the programs he didn't want to miss.

"Why so quiet?" My mother came out with dishes of pot roast, potatoes, and the desiccated remains of a green vegetable. And then it hit me: That magazine I'd seen next to the body. Had any of the ads been circled? Because even though I'd seen slides of just how creative some of these guys could be, how fucking likely was it that the man just rolled himself up in Saran Wrap? I mean, it could probably be done, but it sure as hell wasn't as easy as wrapping a noose around your neck and sticking a tangerine in your mouth. So could Mr. Russo have called a pro to come over for a little technical support?

Maybe it wasn't accidental suicide. Maybe it was accidental manslaughter. Or maybe the call girl had decided that a dead john wouldn't object to paying the entire contents of his wallet and then some. Jesus, maybe the goddamn uniforms had been right and it was a homicide.

"Shit," I said, and then looked up into my mother's shocked face. "Ma, I'm so sorry. I just remembered something and it's urgent."

"You don't use language like that in this house," said my father. "Apologize."

"I already did." I was pulling on my coat, and my mother was standing there with my plate in her hands, looking like she was about to cry. "But all this food I made. You want me to wrap it up in a little plastic for you?"

I gave that suggestion a snort of laughter, kissed my mother, and said, "I'll come back next week and I promise I'll stay for at least two hours."

"Oh, fine, and what about the rest of the seder?"

"Come on, Dad, it's too late for me." I pulled on my jacket, feeling a sinful surge of exhilaration at the thought of getting out of there. "How about I promise that when I have kids I'll force them to sit through the whole thing?"

"With the girls you date? You'll probably invite us to eat a roast pig for Easter." My father's jowls were quivering. "Your children will ask me why I'm wearing a coaster on my head."

"No, Dad, I swear, if I ever get married again, she'll be Jewish." I was inching toward the door. Easy enough thing to say, when I had no intention of ever tying the knot again. "Love you, Ma. Love you, Dad." As I raced down the stairs, I heard my mother's voice echoing after me.

"Wait, Yossi! Are you coming back tomorrow for the second night's seder?"

"I have to work late, Ma!"

Freed from bondage and those terrible little yeast-free honey cakes and macaroons, I flipped open my cell and called the coroner's office.

marlowe

It was 7 P.M., and even though the lecture didn't begin for an hour, there was already a line outside the entrance to the 92nd Street Y. Like everyone else, I was there to hear Eliane LeFevre speak about "Sexual Personae: The Influence of Hollywood on Erotic Identity."

"I can't believe this is the crowd for a Monday," said my friend Claudia, pulling her shearling closed and stamping her stiletto-booted feet. There was a hint of snow in the air, and if the sun hadn't just begun to sink between the high rises, I would've thought I was back in February.

"I think they were sold out the first day tickets went on sale," I said, wishing we'd had time for an after-dinner coffee. "God, I hope we go in soon. Some idiot phoned me at two in the morning and I'm exhausted. "

"You look it." Actually, calling Claudia my friend was inaccurate. Since college, she had been my friendly rival, Ginger to my Mary Anne, Veronica to my Betty. In our junior year, Claudia had beaten me out for a semester in Paris and had come back wearing her silky dark hair so

40

that it fell over one eye and speaking with the faintest hint of a French accent.

"So," Claudia said, turning back to me with the air of someone remembering her social duty, "who called you in the middle of the night?"

"I don't know. A wrong number." Still dazed from sleep, I'd assumed the man was in crisis when he said he wanted to make an appointment.

But then he'd refused to give me more than his first name—Tony—and couldn't say who had referred him. Instead, he said he'd seen my ad.

That had been my first indication that something was wrong here. "My ad?"

"In *New York* magazine."

I had put a personals ad in once, but that had been over a year ago. "An old issue?"

"A new one." The man had begun to sound impatient. "Look, can we make an appointment or not?"

"Of course we can. I just want to understand which ad . . ."

"Look, are we doing this or not?"

"I think you've got the wrong number . . ." Before I'd been able to finish my sentence, he'd hung up again.

When I finished relating this story to Claudia, she started laughing. "Oh, that's too funny, Marlowe. So he thought you were a call girl?"

"I can't think what else he'd be trying to book at that hour."

"I think you should string him along if he calls back."

"And do what? Offer him an introductory session of free therapy?"

"It might be amusing."

I didn't see what was funny about pretending to be a prostitute, but then I wasn't walking around pretending to be French. Of course it was also possible that I was missing something here. One boyfriend admitted he'd found me a bit intimidating at first, which he amended a few weeks later to "you're not really a humorless android."

I glanced up to find that Claudia was looking at me with irritation thinly disguised as concern. "Well, I don't know, Marlowe. If you're really upset, why not get caller ID?"

"What for, so I can call the guy back?"

Claudia moved her head so that her dark hair swung over one side of her face. "If you ask me, the whole thing sounds kind of sexy. Very *Belle de Jour.*"

All right, I could accept that there might be a comical aspect to this situation, but what was sexy about some man thinking he could buy his way out of establishing personal rapport, let alone providing decent foreplay?

I'd never really bought the idea that Catherine Deneuve's exquisitely repressed Parisian housewife would want to work as a high-priced call girl. I wondered what Savannah the Upper West Side madame would have to say about the film—probably that it was a typically male fantasy.

"Oh, thank God, the line is moving," said Claudia. "I'm supposed to be talking with an editor tomorrow, so I do not want to be up all night."

"You're talking with an editor?"

"Farrar Straus Giroux is publishing my dissertation."

"That's great, Claudia." I'd never gotten to that stage. In fact, I hadn't gotten to the stage before the editor stage, although there was an agent who said she'd be interested in looking at my work again after I'd made extensive revisions and additions.

Meaning, I had to make my manuscript a whole lot juicier. "What was your dissertation title again, Claudia?"

"The New Europeans: A Study in Post-Historical Psychology."

"And the publisher thinks that will sell?"

"They must—they gave me a hefty advance. But that was probably because of the bidding war. In any case, we're changing the title to 'International Relations: Europe and America Between the Sheets.' "

I tried to think of something to say other than, But my idea is inherently sexier than yours, why am I being rejected while you're getting the star treatment?

Finally, I thought of something. "Who's your agent?"

"Debra Gordon. Hey, want me to introduce you?"

"She's already met me." She'd been the agent who had asked for extensive revisions and additions on my proposal. She'd suggested that I throw in some personal accounts of my more amusing sexual misadventures and add some intimate details about a few close female friends, which was when I'd realized that I didn't have amusing sexual misadventures or intimate female friends.

Claudia let her slippery hair fall into her eyes and then flipped it back with one hand. "Oh, well, never mind, Marlowe, there's sure to be—hey, that's Eliane over there!"

I turned and there she was on the stairs leading to the front doors, dressed in a sleeveless turtleneck, tight wool skirt and stiletto boots, smoking a cigarette and laughing at something a uniformed guard was saying. Her hair, as short as a boy's, made her seem both mischievous and rakishly elegant. I could see now that others had noticed her, too, though no one said anything; there was simply no way to approach her without appearing gauche.

Suddenly, she looked up and noticed Claudia. Striding toward us, she said something rapidly in French that I didn't understand, but which sounded both pretty and clever. Then she kissed Claudia rapidly on her cheeks, and Claudia responded with a French phrase that sounded not quite as pretty or clever.

"So, Claudia." Up close, Eliane was older and handsomer than in her publicity photos. "I hear a big book deal's in the works. If you are going to be famous, you must go to Didier's salon for a chic cut. This peek-a-boo hair in your eyes is a little *jejeune,* non?" And with that parting shot, Eliane was off, ready to give us our money's worth of academic sex talk.

The lecture was excellent but halfway through I read Eliane's bio and discovered that she was only thirty-one and had recently married a prominent French film director. After years of switching disciplines in college and grad school, I was only now professionally where I should have been five years earlier.

Which is also when I should have met a great man.

By the time I arrived home, I was feeling both sexless and unintelligent and had begun half-contemplating another career change: Pastry chef? Landscape designer? Something manual but requiring a degree of skill.

I distractedly comforted my howling feline, prepared the coffee for tomorrow, and brushed my teeth while pulling my hair back with my left hand. Maybe it wasn't too late to reinvent myself. How would I look in a gamine cut, roguishly insulting men into my bed?

I fell asleep thinking about Eliane's assertion that in the heavily censored Hollywood of the forties and fifties, sex infused every cinematic word and action.

I started dreaming that I was climbing the stairs to a brownstone, dressed in a chic navy dress coat. As I knocked at the door, Eliane LeFevre's voice came on.

"In these classic American films, everything became a code which suggested something else," she said as my dream self was let into the apartment. "You had to assume a huge level of sophistication in your audience, to trust that they understood that people do not always say what they mean or mean what they say."

I was ushered into a Parisian room with a four-poster bed, and I began to disrobe as a breeze from the open window made the gauzy curtains dance.

"Ironically, it is American culture that has now lost the ability to speak the language of contradiction, to parse the honest lie." Underneath Eliane's narration, a jazzy, '60s tune began to play as I got down to my black lace demi-bra and panties. I looked down, my thick black eyeliner and false eyelashes making the look less one of modesty than of flirtation. The door opened, my startled gaze flew up: It was a man, the handsome thug from the gym who hadn't noticed I was alive.

"As any European can tell you, you cannot legislate flirtation in the workplace. You cannot even always be sure what is flirtation and what is work. Business is sometimes pleasure, and pleasure is sometimes reduced to a duty and a chore."

I unhooked my bra, my eyes riveted on the frank certainty in the stranger's face. It was a look I'd never seen
on a man's face before. Not arrogance, not tenderness,
but a straightforward hunger without irony or apology.
In the moment before he reached for me with an athlete's
fluid, muscular confidence, our eyes met, and I recognized his shaggy, leonine face: This wasn't the guy from
the gym! My very first customer was Burt Lancaster in
his prime, and that clench of muscles low in my abdomen was definitely not caused by fear. As Burt
crowded me up against the wall, I heard Eliane's voice
reaching for her summation.

"Sexual fantasy is not subject to the rules of political
correctness, and the secret of desire is that we must always . . ."

In the little room, a phone began to ring. And ring.
And ring, casting me out of Burt's arms and back into my
own bed.

"Hello?" My voice came out in a husky rasp.

"Are you available?"

"What?"

"Available for tonight?" A different voice this time, not
the same man as last night. I glanced at the clock: Three
A.M., and I didn't think sleep was going to be my friend
again tonight.

"Wrong number." I slammed the phone down and
flung myself back on the bed. After a moment's consideration, I leaned over and yanked the cord out of the
wall.

But just as I'd anticipated, I never fell back asleep.

joe

Where the fuck did the day go? It was after four and I was still sitting at my desk, stuck in a chair with a broken back, staring at a cold cup of coffee and the petrified remains of my bagel breakfast.

"You still here, Joe?"

I looked up and waved at Denny. "Yeah, I just need to hear the autopsy report."

Denny rolled his eyes. "Jesus, give it a rest. You put in your eight hours. Go on home already before it starts raining again."

"Yeah, you're right."

"Take it easy." Denny pulled on his jacket, and for a moment, I thought about heading out with him, maybe asking him if he wanted to get a beer. But two seconds of friendly didn't mean Denny was my pal again, and in any case, I hadn't eaten lunch, so maybe a drink wasn't such a hot idea. God knows I didn't feel in any blind rush to get home after last night.

After leaving my folks, I'd asked the coroner's office to get back to me as soon as possible with the results on

Russo. Then, unable to do anything else on the case, I'd gone home and started looking through my music for something to suit my mood.

Unfortunately, this led to my getting into a foul mood and calling my ex-wife, Paolina, to yell at her for taking most of my CDs when she'd moved out. I kept saying that I shouldn't have to go buy another copy of *Hall and Oates' Greatest Hits* just because she'd decided to loot the apartment for whatever she felt like having, and she kept saying that I needed to figure out what was really bothering me.

I later found the CD in my Walkman, which I hadn't used since October.

I tried to call back to apologize, but Paolina wouldn't answer, clearly because she thought I'd become some kind of needy head case. This from a girl who used to ask my opinion on everything.

Maybe I needed to get a dog. Loyal companion. Faithful sidekick. Except how could I leave a dog alone all day while I was at work? I could get a cat, but that would just be like a woman—fickle, finicky, full of shit. I'm so independent but you have to feed me.

I stretched my arms over my head until my spine cracked. Come on, phone, ring and let me have the autopsy report.

The phone rang. "Yeah, Kain here. What's up?"

"Yossi, my friend Natalya just called me because her niece is visiting from Israel."

I covered my face with my hands. "Ma, you're killing me."

"But she's only here for a few days!"

"I'm hanging up now, Ma." I put the phone back on

the receiver and instantly regretted it. Maybe I should've said yes?

No, I wasn't that desperate yet. But my head was beginning to hurt, which probably meant I'd forgotten to consume my daily four-cup requirement of caffeine. As I stood up to go, the phone rang again.

This time, it was the autopsy report: Nothing in Tony Russo's bloodstream but some margaritas and a partially digested burrito.

I hung up the phone and realized my left foot had fallen asleep. Time to go home. On my way out, Lieutenant Franks rolled his chair out of his office. "So, tell me something I want to hear."

"No, I didn't close the case yet. I get two days off the chart for a homicide, remember?"

Franks gave me a look. "And exactly which homicide would that be, Joe? Last I heard, autoerotic implies a party of one. What are you looking for, a note that says, Whoops, guess I tied it a little too tight? It's a fucking gift. Take it. I know you may think we're a cupcake of a house here, but there's still a shitload of other work to be done."

I gave a couple of little nods, as if it was all starting to make sense to me now. "Okay, but let me just make sure the guy went on his sloppy snorkeling trip solo, all right?"

Franks shook a DD5 form in his hand. "I want this in, Joe. How you going to prove probable cause when a few hundred white guys kill themselves each year by choking the monkey a little too hard?"

"Look, all I want to do is find out if the guy made any calls to an escort service that night."

"You're not going back to the crime scene."

Alisa Kwitney

"He had the magazine out, for Chrissake. Open to the page and everything."

Franks smiled his gym teacher's smile at me, clumsy condescension passing as wit. "So you ought to have been more thorough the first time. Kain, you're grasping at straws here. What are you going to do, get a subpoena to get Mr. Russo's official phone records? We get bomb threats at the 96th street subway station every other day. I don't have the time for you to spend on this shit."

I held up my little red notebook. "Okay, so no subpoena. But I got a record of the guy's last cell phone calls. Let me check this out, Lieutenant."

Franks just looked at me with an expression of pure exasperation on his vulpine little face. There was no law preventing a detective at a crime scene from pressing a button on a guy's cell phone and retrieving the numbers of all the calls he'd made in the past twenty-four hours. "So check it out if you want," he said, "but the apartment's already been cleaned out by the next of kin."

"No problem." At least, no problem if the copy of the magazine that Mr. Russo had been reading happened to be this month's issue. I stopped off at the newspaper stand near the subway and picked up a copy of *New York* magazine, where you could browse film, theater, and restaurant reviews; locate the perfect entertainer for your six-year-old's party; find a soul mate in the personals; or just locate a pricey hole for hire.

It didn't matter whether or not Franks was pissed at me. I needed to know for my own peace of mind whether or not the guy who'd looked like me, in the apartment that looked like mine, had died because he couldn't find a woman that night . . . or because he'd found the wrong one.

On the ride home, I gave up my seat to a very pretty pregnant lady in a tight white shirt and wrap skirt. When did expectant mothers start dressing like pirate wenches? It was so damn appealing it made me want to go out and get myself a pregnant woman of my own.

Of course, that had been the idea with marrying Paolina, so maybe I was better off admiring the process from the sidelines.

Bracing myself against the rattling, rolling motion of the train, I glanced at the short list of numbers in my red notebook. Maybe I'd luck out and find a match for one of Mr. Russo's cell phone calls. Flipping to the adult section, sandwiched between health and fitness and the personals, I scanned the ads. The range of styles was impressive.

Pure Bliss from Coed Miss.
Major credit cards accepted.

Naughty Victorian.
Strict elegance on the Upper West Side.

Exclusive European Shemale.
Fetishes done right.

Mature blonde, speaks Russian and Yiddish.
Oy what a woman!

International Models, Inc.
Social functions/intimate encounters.

"Hey, mistah, don't do it."

I glanced at the white college boy straphanging on my right. He appeared to be about twenty, with a bad complexion, a scruffy beard, and dreadlocks. Another trust fund kid laboring under the misapprehension that he was a Rastafarian.

I ignored him.

"You go to those girls, your dick gonna fall off."

"Hmm."

"Besides, mon, you got to make love, not buy it."

I leaned in close to the boy's scruffy, red-eyed face. "You got to smoke less dope, mon, before getting on the train, 'cause you might just find yourself sitting next to a cop."

The Trustafarian just smiled back at me. "You ain't no cop, mon."

"And why is that?"

" 'Cause I got the eye for people, and I know you is okay."

I sighed, very much aware that we had an audience and that the pretty pregnant woman, three middle-aged Mexican ladies, and an Orthodox Jew were all smirking at us. Now everyone on the 1/9 thought I was looking to hire an escort. Well, screw them.

I turned back to my magazine.

Fleur de Lips: Let us pamper you.

California Blonde: For an organic experience.

Muscle Bound: Bodywork for men.

Shit. I could feel the white Rasta reading over my shoulder again. Turning my head, I beamed some irritation his way. "Anything else to say?"

"Well, if you're dedicated to the idea, I'd pick that one, mon." His hemp-braceleted wrist shot out and he indicated a boxed ad that contained, instead of a description, a poem.

> Change in a trice
> The lilies and languors of virtue
> For the raptures and roses of vice.
> —Swinburne

I checked the poetic pro's telephone number and—bingo—it matched the last digits dialed by Mr. Tony Russo. I had to tip my hat to the man. Interesting choice, Tony. You might have gone for the cheap particle board furniture, but you've redeemed yourself here. I mean, with each of the other ads, you knew what you were getting yourself into, but Swinburne here could prove to be anything—a dog, a knockout, a serial killer. I started smiling to myself, always a mistake in a public place.

The pimple-faced idiot smiled back at me, revealing the perfect teeth of modern American orthodontics. "Whoever that lady is, she got to be cool to quote the old mon."

"I'll take it under advisement." When the train stopped I stood up, too excited to wait out the last two stations, and walked home clutching my magazine under my left arm.

marlowe

I watched the three inches of my hair fall to the ground and tried to smile at my reflection.

My mouth managed it, but my eyes kept watering, making the room swim into a blur of shiny black surfaces and huge mounted mirrors.

"Turn your head to the left a little." I did, and some more hair fell. I didn't protest. It was too late for that. I'd been feeling boring and unsexy and I'd remembered Eliane LeFevre's advice to Claudia and thought, I need a new look for spring. Didier was too expensive for me, and also booked till next year, so I'd taken an appointment with his assistant, a Japanese woman named Onyx who looked as if she never smiled. There were tattoos of dragons and butterflies on her arms, and her own hair was long and pulled back in a ponytail.

But she charged $200 and was pretty booked up herself, so I'd felt lucky to get an appointment.

The problem was, I didn't look French or chic or even gamine.

I looked like an anemic boy.

I looked like Mia Farrow in *Rosemary's Baby*, being drained by the devil spawn in her belly.

I looked like I'd joined the Marines.

I closed my eyes and smelled hairspray and let the babble of female voices wash over me. I was in hairdressing hell. One moment of bad judgment and an eternity of punishment. Or at least twelve months, which could feel pretty damn eternal when you were going through ponytail withdrawal.

"So, this style is very versatile. You can do it like this," The hairdresser combed my hair down like an artichoke. "Or you can do it like this." My hair was brushed straight back, making me look almost hairless. "What do you think?"

"I think," I said slowly, staring at the few dark strands framing my pasty face in the mirror, "that maybe we should brighten my color a bit. What do you think?"

For the first time, my hairdresser smiled. "You betcha," she said.

"Okay, Marlowe, so, how bad is it?"

I rolled over onto my back, moving the phone to my other ear. "Well, Amanda, it's not so much bad as it is different. It's very red." Amanda had been my closest friend, until marriage and pregnancy had overtaken her. Now she lived in another planet, in a house in Westchester, with a husband who could never quite remember my name and three seriously charmless children.

"Red like you used to be or red like Annie Lennox in her 'Sweet Dreams' video?"

I swallowed hard, looking up at my framed English landscape painting, a thirtieth birthday gift from my mother. "Well, it's not orange. Red like Ann-Margret."

"You're strawberry blonde? You're telling me that you now possess no more than an inch of hair and it's strawberry blonde?"

"More than an inch, really. It's, you know, a pixie, but there's at least . . ." I measured it with my fingers. "At least two inches in most places. Three in others."

"Oh my God, Marlowe, hang on a moment." In the background I could hear the sound of a crash, children wailing, Amanda saying, "How many times have I told you not to do that?"

"Sorry," she said when she came back. "It's just a madhouse here sometimes. Are you going to head home for Easter?"

"No, my mother and I have an unspoken agreement. I'll visit in October, when the leaves are at their prettiest and I can go horseback riding a lot, and by the end of a week we will still both have depleted our annual reserves of goodwill toward each other."

Ever since my mother moved upstate full time and opened a Thoroughbred breeding farm, horses had become her religion. Like a lot of horsey women, she had discovered that apparently well-behaved husbands could suddenly reveal an appalling propensity for running off in search of greener pastures, while children either seemed to require too much care and attention or too little. Horses, which were large and powerful (like husbands) and yet in need of guidance and training (like children) had the added advantage of providing one with an alternative social life.

My mother hadn't been particularly maternal when my brother Tanner and I were little; by the time I was an irritable, sooty-eyed teenager, she was too busy breeding and training her Thoroughbreds to notice my various acts of rebellion. Her friends thought she was remarkably tolerant; I felt she was so egocentric my adolescence barely registered.

"So you're going to be all by yourself, Marlowe?"

"Well, my older brother invited me, but I'm not up for his family's version of Easter. He's one of those bland white guys who marries ethnic and disappears like a slice of Wonder Bread beneath a mountain of Chimichangas. Whenever I see him I feel like Cat Stevens's sister at Ramadan—an unwelcome reminder of his family of origin."

"What about your father? Are you in touch with him at all?"

"I haven't spoken to him since 1982, when he celebrated the two million–dollar sale of his book, *The Princess of Maybe*, by running off with my babysitter."

"Well, do you want to come over to spend Easter Sunday with Michael and me? The only thing is, his folks are coming, so you'll have to rent your own car."

"Mandy, I'm not desperate for someplace to go. I don't need rescuing." I could tell she didn't believe me; she had built her life around the belief that solitude was a sign that something was missing. When her children were at school and her husband was at work, Amanda filled her days with projects, committees, classes and, I suspected, affairs. She thought my life was empty; I thought she lacked internal resources.

We said our good-byes and I hung up the phone, and there I was again, staring at my naked face in the mirror. "It's not so bad," I told myself. My reflection wasn't buying it. Such a little thing, a bad haircut. But I felt as if I'd just sabotaged myself, I felt like a teenager again, and I had a whole month's worth of "oh, you cut your hair" to get through before I could just get on with the tedious business of returning to my old status quo.

The phone rang and I picked it up. "Hello?" I was going to have to spend the next three months indoors. No singles events. No chance of impromptu sex in the near future, let alone any hope of meeting someone serious.

"Hi." The voice was male, warm, low. "I was calling to see about making an appointment."

"What do you want?" This guy, whoever he was, had a serious New York accent, and that meant that the odds were good that the next words out of his mouth were going to be "a hot chick like you." I'd been fielding wrong numbers all day.

"What do I want?" The caller sounded surprised, possibly a little amused. Maybe he wasn't used to working girls with attitude. "I'm not sure. Your ad was intriguing. Maybe what I want is to quote a little Swinburne with you. Maybe more."

Swinburne? He wanted Swinburne?

"I am tired of tears and laughter," I recited softly, making it sound like a complaint. "And men that laugh and weep, of what may come hereafter for men that sow to reap."

"Wait a minute. Are there men that don't sow to reap? I mean, what's the point of sowing, if not reaping?"

"You ever kiss just for the sake of kissing?"

He paused. "Not recently, but yes."

I didn't say anything.

"All right. Yeah, I get it. Okay, keep going."

58

Keep going? This guy was weirder than I'd thought. "I am weary of days and hours, blown buds of barren flowers, desires and dreams and powers, and everything but . . . sleep." I drew the last word out. I waited, listening to the sound of soft breathing on the other end. "That'll be twenty-nine dollars." I glanced up and was surprised to see myself in the mirror. With my face wearing a less woebegone expression, the hair didn't look quite so bad.

"But I haven't come yet," he said, and I laughed. "No, seriously, I'd like to continue this conversation."

"What do you want me to do next? Start quoting Yeats? 'How can those terrified vague fingers push the feathered glory from her loosening thighs? And how can body, laid in that white rush, but feel the strange heart beating where it lies?' "

"I think I'm getting a little confused here. Did you say something about feathers?" His New York accent made it sound like "fedders."

"It's from Leda and the Swan." There was amusement in my voice now, not irritation. I tried to put the irritation back. "I'm hanging up now."

"Wait!"

"What for?" I pulled the silk of my kimono back down where it had ridden up my thighs. I was still on my stomach, swinging my leg back and forth, like a teenager talking with her boyfriend.

"So is this what you do? You recite poetry?"

"Why, what were you looking for?"

"I wasn't sure. Now maybe I'm thinking, poetry's good. What else you got for me?"

What else did I have? Before I'd decided on going into

psychology, I'd gotten my Masters in English. Like a lot of trust fund babies, I'd accumulated degrees while trying to figure out what I really wanted to do. But I didn't have anything else memorized, except some of the dialogue from "The Taming of The Shrew." Did I want to tell him his tongue was in my tail? No, I wasn't getting that bawdy with strangers.

"Hang on," I said, walking over to my bookcase.

"Do I get to ask what you're wearing?"

I glanced down at my short red silk bathrobe, which no longer went well with my hair. "A baggy terrycloth robe with spit-up stains."

"Fair enough. What do you look like?"

"Old and fat."

"You don't sound old and fat."

"That's because I'm lying."

"Oh." The caller hesitated. "Just about being old and fat, or also about the bathrobe?"

I located my poetry book. "All of it," I said. "What do you look like?"

There was another pause. "If I tell you, promise not to hang up?"

"Mm hm." I was flipping through the index.

"I look like a cop."

Found it. "What, bald and potbellied?"

"Like a TV cop. Very rugged. Flat stomach. Deep, intense eyes."

I turned to the right page. "You're lying, right?"

"Nope."

"Got one for you."

"I'm waiting."

" 'Let us go then, you and I, when the evening is

spread out against the sky like a patient etherized upon a table . . .' "

"You're making that up."

"That's 'The Love Song of J. Alfred Prufrock' by T.S. Elliot. It's famous."

"Okay, read on."

"Let us go, through certain half-deserted streets, the muttering retreats of restless nights in one-night cheap hotels . . ."

"This one's depressing." The guy, whoever he was, sounded as if he might've been a little depressed himself.

"It is. Do you want more of it, or do you want fake happy?"

"Depressing, I guess. Or real and pleasurable."

"Or fake and pleasurable?"

Another silence, the longest one yet, but I was a psychologist and I knew how to wait. "No," came the answer. "I'd rather you be honest and let me know when you're lying to me."

"Red silk."

"What?"

"I'm wearing a red silk kimono. But it clashes with my hair." My heart pounding, I slammed the phone down. After a moment, it rang again.

joe

It wasn't like I had a hard-on or anything, but the sick thing was, I was definitely getting turned on. By a professional. By a poetry-reading professional. By a high-priced call girl who just might have had something to do with Tony Russo's untimely demise.

I couldn't remember the last time I'd been turned on by anyone other than Paolina. It was like I'd gotten imprinted on her, like a gosling will get imprinted on an airplane or a cat and spend all its time wanting the impossible.

But at least *this* attraction was something I could use. Verbal seduction is as much a part of a detective's arsenal as intimidation; interviewing subjects, as opposed to interrogating them in a police station, usually involves a fair amount of flattery, cajolery, charm. I stripped off my jeans and work shirt and changed into gray sweats and a white T-shirt. Uncapping a beer, I hit redial.

"Hello?" She sounded cautious. Also a little breathless. Or maybe she always sounded like that, like you'd caught her in the middle of sex.

"It's me," I said. "Joe."

"Joe."

"The guy you just hung up on . . ."

"I know who you are." She paused, and I took a swig of cold beer. "Listen," she began, but I was already talking.

"Look, I've never done this before." Of course, she probably got that all the time. "I mean, I never called a service before." Now it sounded like I was putting her down. "Not that there's anything wrong with your profession, just that I haven't availed myself of it."

"Joe," she said again, but I'd been around enough women to know what that tone of voice meant. So I started thinking: Why would she refuse a potential client? Maybe the ad was partly a screening device. She was extremely selective, and the Swinburne reference was meant to throw off the riff raff. Was I coming across as riff raff? Well, cultured I was not, but I did know how to establish trust, create rapport.

"You're about to tell me to get lost, I know, but before you do, I want you to know something."

"What?" She sounded almost alarmed.

"This is the first time I've felt interested in anyone except for my ex-wife." And there it was, a big hunk of truth lying flat out there at her feet, because there's no better way to craft a lie than starting with something real.

I eased my legs straight till they were stretched out on my windowsill and stared out at the fire escape across the way, where a cat was sitting. "I got divorced about six months ago, and I was separated about four months before that, and every time I look at a girl, I think, I'll say hello and she'll say hello and then, if we connect enough, there will be the first testing-the-waters date, and if I pass that test we'll start to feel out what movies we like, what books we have in common—I like biographies, by the way. Maybe she'll pretend to like basketball for a month or two. We'll start to have sex and it'll be fun and reckless and her legs will always be smooth and she'll wear mascara until the last possible moment at night. And we'll build trust and we'll start hanging out with each other's friends, and the next thing you know, I'm seeing a future here, I'm seeing coffee tables and vacations in Italy and even, you know, babies."

I stopped and raked my hand through my hair. The tabby cat on the fire escape was making his move, walking on a ledge over a drop so sheer it made the skin on the back of my neck crawl.

"Joe." Her voice was soft.

"And then she'll tell me she wasn't being real. She was just being some version of herself designed to please me. Never liked those comic book movies. Never wanted those hula girl cocktail glasses. Didn't really enjoy hiking or camping." The cat has made it safely to an open window.

"I'm listening."

"So I figured, maybe it's better to have it all on the level, you know? I'm paying, you're pretending, everybody's clear and no one gets hurt." Jeez, I'd made such a good case for it, I'd nearly convinced myself. It wasn't the first time I'd opened myself up to get a subject to do the same, but it was the first time I'd done it since my life imploded.

I put one hand on the back of my neck and looked at my fourth-floor apartment, decorated in pale particle wood furniture in shades of navy and green. Tony Russo had at least put up some prints on the wall. All I had was white walls with cracks on them.

"Are you hairy, Joe?"

"What?"

"Your back. Is it hairy?"

My hand, which was massaging some of the tension out of my right shoulder, stilled. "Do you mean, is there hair on my neck, or is there hair growing out of my neck?"

"The latter."

"My hair's kind of in need of a cut, but I don't have back hair. Why?"

"Because if I'm going to get into some long flirtatious conversation with you, I need to know what I'm dealing with. I'm not going to pretend and I don't like hairy backs."

"You're not going to pretend?"

"No."

I thought about it. "So what am I paying for?"

"If you were paying me for something, which you're not, you'd be paying me for honesty. Seems to me you get pretense for free, so what you want, what you really desire, is honesty."

Damn, she was good. "Damn," I said, "you're good. What else do you want to know before you can flirt with me?"

"How old are you, Joe?"

"Thirty-eight."

"Height?"

"Six feet, two inches. One hundred and seventy-eight pounds."

"What do you do for a living?"

"What do you need to know that for?"

"Because some professions are just inherently unsexy to me. If you're a dog groomer, I'm sorry, but I don't want you. I could probably handle your being a lawyer or an accountant, but not an actor."

"I'm a firefighter. Does that work for you?"

"I find that extremely attractive."

"Yeah, all the girls always go for the firefighters. Well, let me tell you, after the first five years of sitting around the station house eating chili, most of those guys look like Fred Flintstone."

"You're not really a firefighter, are you?"

"I'm a cop." I don't know why, but it had to be said. If I was playing a part and the part was supposed to be me, then I couldn't be anything else but a cop.

"What kind of cop?"

I finished the bottle of beer and walked to the kitchen. "Not vice. I'm a detective with the two-four."

"The what?"

"The twenty-fourth precinct. I used to work on the Organized Crime Task Force with the FBI." Why was I telling her this, to impress her? *Shmuck.* "Don't worry, you don't have a case."

"Excuse me?"

"I'm not going to arrest you." And then, because I wished it was the truth, I said: "I'm in the business of catching real bad guys, not naughty girls."

"Then why aren't you on the Task Force anymore?"

Christ, this one was sharp. What story to tell her? "Because of what I just told you."

"About naughty girls?" She sounded confused.

"Let's just say that I suggested to the agent in charge that we rethink the allocation of our resources."

"So as to focus less on naughty girls and more on real bad guys?"

"Exactly."

She chewed that over for a minute. "So what happened?"

"He reallocated me." Even though telling her all this was a calculated move, a disclosure of insider information to create a sense of alliance, saying it gave me a little illicit thrill. This freewheeling conversation was as close as I'd ever get to borrowing a car and indulging in the kind of wild vehicular chase you see in the movies.

And it was working: On the other end of the line, she gave a lovely, deep laugh. "Joe, you don't need to pay anyone for anything."

"Swinburne, this is New York. Everyone pays someone for something. Things people used to do for their family, for their friends, for their neighbors, these days, you got to pay someone. I know people who pay someone to walk their dog, feed their cat, water their plants, and play catch with their kid. I know people who pay for some shmuck with a degree to advise them on how to lift weights, shop for dinner, decorate their apartment, and choose a school for their kid, who they do not know because they paid someone to take care of him since he was born. And don't get me started on the shrinks! There are so many shrinks on the Upper West Side of Manhattan that the only explanation I can find is that everyone is paying everyone else for the privilege of sitting down and listening without answering the phone for an hour."

I took a breath. "You still there, Swinburne?"

"Still here."

"Sorry about that. I got a little carried away."

"That's all right. Although I usually charge extra for ranting."

I laughed. "What's your name, anyhow?"

She hesitated. "Sydney."

"No it's not.

"Spencer."

"Give me your real name."

"I don't want you to keep calling me."

"Why not?" I looked inside my fridge. One beer, one carton of orange juice, two dead apples, and some old Chinese food. Paolina used to fill our fridge with green grapes, olive and rosemary bread, zucchini, and the kind of tomatoes with some vine still attached. We used to have these stinky cheeses that melted on your tongue, and a skinny, garlicky sausage that I kept eating before she could use it in a sauce.

"Because I'm retiring."

"You are?" For a minute I was still seeing the ghosts of pasta dinners past. Then I started paying attention again.

"I'm not really a call girl."

"I get you." Now, this was interesting. What had happened since she'd put the ad in to make her want to give up being on the game? Had Tony Russo's death been an accident? "But can't you make one last exception for me?"

"I wish I could."

"Has something happened with a client that upset you?"

"No."

"Some other life-altering event, like a death?"

"It's not that anything's happened per se, so much as . . ."

"You gotten religion?"

"No!" She laughed. "It's just . . . just give it up, Joe. You're not going to manipulate me into seeing you."

A-hah, so she was thinking about seeing me. I could work with that. Face to face, it would be a hell of a lot easier to tell when she was lying. "Even if we don't sow to reap?"

"Excuse me?"

"We could just get together and continue our conversation, no expectation of more." I'd started out on pure instinct, but now I knew what I was doing. She'd figured out that I wanted honesty; I'd figured out that what she wanted was to be courted. "We could meet in a public place, where you would be safe from any possibility of it going any further. And if you didn't like the look of me, you could walk away, and if you did, I'd just . . ."

"I'm sorry, Joe, but I'm not going to meet you."

"Why not?"

"Just not."

"But you've made me realize that I've forgotten how to kiss for the sake of kissing. I need to become less goal-oriented." Christ, why'd the woman put the ad in if she was going to play this hard to get? Something must have happened to make her so spookish about taking on a new client.

"Are you one of those guys that sticks your tongue in right away?"

Now this was more like it. "Depends. Not usually. But if there's enough tension built up, then yes."

"And what do you do with your hands?"

I looked down at them. "I don't know. Maybe hold

your head. Maybe under your chin . . ." She inhaled, an audible intake of air. "You okay?"

"I'm fine."

A thought occurred to me. "How fine?"

"Fine." She was aiming for matter-of-fact, which told me everything I needed to know.

"You're thinking about kissing me, aren't you? You're considering it."

"No, Joe, I'm not."

"But you like the idea of it, don't you?" I was pacing the floor. "Tell me your name."

"You can't call me anymore."

"When I hang up, though, I can think about you. And I want to know your name. Because I am. Going. To think about you."

"Oh."

"I'm going to think really hard about kissing you."

"Oh."

"Are you, uh, getting turned on by this?"

"Yes." She sounded embarrassed.

"Thank God, because I am, too." Charged with restless energy, I walked myself into my bedroom. "So how about getting together?"

She hung up on me. Again. It didn't matter. I forced myself to lie down on my bed and waited, and then I called her back.

"Me again."

"You can't call me anymore."

"I'm not some wack job. I swear it."

"I can't have you calling me all the time."

Fucking hell, were we breaking up already? "Like I

told you, Swinburne, I'm a cop. I don't have all the time. I barely have some of the time."

"Marlowe."

"Excuse me?"

"Marlowe, like the playwright."

"The play what?"

"Like the detective." She sounded exasperated. Shit. I was failing a girl test again. "I must be crazy."

"You're a very cautious kind of crazy."

"Good night, Joe. No calling me back. If you call me back again tonight, I'm changing my number."

Girl tests. You could never get away from them. "555-4333."

"What's that?"

"My number. You call me back." This time, I hung up on her.

It took her fifteen minutes, during which time I looked up Marlowe and learned a little about Renaissance poetry. I let the phone ring only once before answering. "So he died young, this Marlowe. Did you know there might even be a murder mystery involved?"

"Like this you answer the phone?"

"Hi, Ma." I dropped down into a chair and my call-waiting beeped. "Hang on," I said, and switched to the second line.

"Joe?"

Jesus. "Don't hang up." I went back to the first line. "Ma, I gotta run. It's a work call."

"I don't care, I'm not hanging up. I have something to tell you, Yossi."

"Hang on, Ma." I returned to Marlowe. "You still there?"

"I'm here." She took a breath. "Joe, you seem like a nice guy, and . . . I don't think you need a call girl. I think you could probably use a few sessions of therapy . . ."

She thought I was nuts? The phone beeped. "Don't hang up," I said, pressing call waiting.

"Yossi, are you there? I just had to hang up and call you again. Can I talk now? Because I've been thinking about your life and I've come to a conclusion. You deliberately chose a wife who was going to dump you. All this moping, shmoping, and deep down, you know you got exactly what you wanted."

"Ma, not now. I'm going to the other line, which is, as I told you, a work call." I pressed the call waiting button again. "Marlowe?"

"Joe, I'm glad you have other people to talk to. Because going through a divorce can be incredibly stressful."

"That's my mother on the other line. She's incredibly stressful. Listen," I said, improvising, "you're right about my needing someone to talk to. Doesn't anyone ever pay you just to talk to you? Maybe I could do that?" The phone was beeping again. I ignored it.

"I don't know . . ."

"But you'll think about it?"

"I'll think about it."

She hung up, and then so did I. After a moment, the phone rang.

"Hello, Ma."

"You can try to ignore me, Yossi, but somewhere you must know I'm right. This thing with Paolina is an excuse. So the next time I come to you with the number of a nice, Jewish girl who'd be only too happy to meet you,

you think about what's really going on. Have you considered therapy?"

"I gotta go now, Ma." I hung up the phone and discovered that my left ear was sore from being pressed against the plastic. Unfortunately, I still needed dinner and there was no food in the house. I picked up the phone one last time, ordered myself some Chinese food, watched talking heads on CNN, and put myself to bed an hour early.

And woke up at two A.M. with a vague memory of a dream about doing something I shouldn't have and wet, sticky sheets.

marlowe

It was eight o'clock on a Saturday night and I was wearing a little black dress, a lot of hair gel, and two-inch heels. It wasn't my idea; my old high school friend Melissa had insisted.

"Come on," Melissa had said, "what are you going to do, sit at home watching your hair grow?"

Not watching. Waiting for.

"I'll come over first and fix you up," she'd promised. Melissa worked as a magazine editor for *Curve*, the Voluptuous Woman's magazine, and dressed with an insider's attention to detail.

Back at Gotham Prep, where most of the students had been a bunch of self-satisfied snobs in their pastel Izod shirts and ostentatious hickeys, Melissa and I had been part of a small and exuberant group of Rocky Horror fans. Our clique had been basically an alliance of outcasts, and Melissa's and my friendship had been partly based on the rather superficial fact that we'd both adopted versions of the '80s New Wave look.

She'd dyed her wavy, dark brown hair magenta and worn row upon row of little black rubber bracelets on both arms. I'd cut my hair short on the sides and but kept it long in front, and wore black Lycra mid-calf leggings with matching mini skirts and ankle boots. We both smoked Dunhill blue cigarettes, liked Sting best and, by junior year, were both dating Eurotrash boys who didn't speak English very well.

Over the years, Melissa and I had drifted in and out of contact. We probably had nothing left in common, except for both still being single.

Melissa and I were trying to think of things to say to each other. We'd already discussed my difficulty in finding a publisher for my dissertation. She'd suggested the same thing that Claudia's agent had: For this to sell, I needed to spice up the text with more personal revelations. But so far, my research into the behavioral impact of concealing identity hadn't produced one juicy anecdote, let alone a book's worth of intellectual naughtiness.

Melissa remained irritatingly upbeat about my prospects. "Well, Marlowe, maybe you'll meet someone interesting tonight. Why not make up some story to tell him and see what happens?"

I stared at her in disbelief. "Because interesting and attractive are not synonymous terms."

Ten women and five men had shown up for this swing dancing lesson. The ten women all looked fairly attractive. The five men looked like escapees from a mental institution.

"I mean, really," I said, "what is this, One Flew Over the Learning Annex? I figured swing dancing might attract a less desperate crowd than the Successful Singles Cocktail Party or the Evening of Speed Dating and Wine Tasting."

Melissa raised her perfectly plucked eyebrows. "I don't think it's desperate to make an effort. Even you can't expect to be mobbed by guys every Saturday night anymore."

"When was I ever mobbed? If you mean the drunk teenagers that used to hit on me, they hit on you, too, Melissa."

"Come on, Marlowe, I was the girl the other guy got stuck with while the cute boy was hitting on you. But age levels the playing field." I started to say something but Melissa wasn't done yet. "Most of the guys that wanted to get married already are, and it's too early for the first crop of divorces. So you can't think of meeting a guy every time you go out. You just have to try different activities and trust that one day, serendipity will strike."

I looked at Melissa, trying to think of a way to respond. Had she always sounded like a women's magazine article? I'd met Ethan, the last man I'd dated, through an Internet personals ad, so I didn't think I needed the lecture on not expecting men to just drop into my lap.

On paper, Ethan had looked great. Thirty-six, favorite film *Casablanca*, favorite book *Our Man in Havana*; liked hiking, cycling, baseball, travel, both cats and dogs. He was an actuary, which I discovered meant he was part of the accounting aristocracy that designs insurance tables. In person, he'd been startlingly handsome, in an unknowing, Midwestern way. But as well as Ethan and I had fit in the computer, we failed to connect in person. He was fine company as long as we were doing something—playing tennis, skiing, watching a play. But sitting across from him in a restaurant I sometimes felt he was following a script, and in bed, he generated localized pleasure, but no bliss. I realized I could see myself married to him, but couldn't imagine falling in love. After three months, I broke up with him explaining I needed a relationship that spoke to my subconscious. I wanted to want someone in a more unreasonable way. Ethan had been disappointed, but not distressed. Until recently, I hadn't second-guessed my decision to end the relationship.

But at the moment, I was finding it hard to maintain the correct "open to whatever the evening brings" attitude in the face of the strange, death row atmosphere in the room, made up of equal parts desperation, boredom, and misplaced arrogance. The guy standing on my left was wearing a matted toupee and what appeared to be tissue paper in his ears; every time the birdlike fellow on my right turned, I caught a whiff of his sour breath.

"I also do a lot of Cajun dancing," he said. "Do you know the derivation of the word 'Cajun'?"

I leaned back. "Yes," I said, "I do."

"It's from the word Acadian, which is another word for paradise . . ."

I diagnosed him as deficient in reading social cues and turned to Melissa, who was resolutely looking away from me, as if willing the instruction to begin.

"All right," said the female instructor, who was really too far into her forties for her high ponytail and 1940s cheerleader-style skirt. "I'm Merry, your dance instructor. Before we begin we're going to need a couple of you ladies to volunteer to dance the gentlemen's part."

My hand shot up; no way was I going to pass up a chance to avoid physical contact with the Bellevue Male

Dancers' Revue. Besides, maybe being a guy would stop Melissa from glowering at me. Across from me, a plumply pretty blonde in a tight black sweater and floral skirt and a sinewy brunette who appeared to be in her early sixties jockeyed for position.

Melissa moved farther down the line on the women's side.

No one wanted to be paired with me. Any man, it seemed, no matter how repulsive, was preferable to being partnered by another woman.

"Okay," said Merry, "you girls are going to follow me. Boys, follow Pedro." Pedro was muscular and beautiful in black trousers and a black sleeveless T-shirt.

The first step we learned was the basic lindy hop; step on the right foot, step on the left foot, swing the right foot back, step on the left foot again. The four other women dancing men's parts got it right away; I got it on the third try. The five men, whom I'd mentally dubbed Hairy, Beady, Sweaty, Horny, and Needy, took much longer.

"All right," said Pedro, "shall we try this with music?" I took the blond woman's hand, and put my other arm at her waist. We managed to move through the steps while the CD player blared a Big Band tune.

"I hear they open it up at nine, after the lesson," she said. "All the real swing dancers show up then."

"Uh huh." I had to watch my feet. Being the man meant making everything happen; I couldn't talk and steer at the same time.

"And there's live music, too," she said.

"Okay," yelled our Merry instructor, "now couples switch!"

I found myself in the arms of the man I'd dubbed

Beady. He had sharp, dark eyes and was wearing a white, short-sleeved business shirt and an attitude. "You're in the wrong position," he said.

"I'm supposed to be a man."

"Here, stand on the other side." He moved me around and began dancing me backwards, which I hadn't practiced.

"Sorry," I said when I stepped on his foot.

"You're not doing it right. Left, right, left, right. What if I pound on your shoulder like this whenever you're supposed to step back?"

"Please stop hitting me."

"Switch partners," shouted the instructors. I turned into the arms of a tall redhead in platforms. My eyes were level with her neck: She had an Adam's apple.

"I think I'd better be the man," she said, and for a moment I wasn't sure how to react. "It's not like I haven't been there before."

We both laughed. She kicked off her shoes and danced the man's role so well that I managed a turn. "Oh, my Lord, we are swingin'," she said. "My name's Rita, and I cannot believe the men in this place."

"I hear more people come in at nine," I said.

"Switch partners," bellowed the instructors.

"I don't want to," I said. "Rita, how about we just . . ."

"Hello," said a good-looking man with tousled, prematurely silver hair, wire-rimmed spectacles, and a Stray Cats T-shirt. He gestured with the vodka miniature in his hand. "Who's my lady?" He took a quick swig off the bottle and gave me an up-and-down look that suggested I was his first choice, but I ducked to the side and he took Rita's hand instead.

I turned and found myself face to face with Needy. "Hi," he said quickly. "I'm Greg. I'm not sure I'm doing this right, but if you'll give me a moment, I think we can muddle through."

"Tell you what," I said. "You let me lead." I grabbed him around the waist and steered him across the floor. He looked dumbfounded. "Well, this is certainly different," he said. "What's your name? Have you been here before?"

"Shh," I said. "I have to concentrate."

"Switch partners!"

And I was alone, the last kid left standing in musical chairs. Everyone else was dancing. Melissa was laughing animatedly at something Needy had said; I had a feeling she'd make damn sure that serendipity struck tonight.

Well, good for her, but I needed the illusion that a man's attraction to me was more than a generic desire for female companionship.

Suddenly a male voice, lightly accented, spoke next to my ear. "May I have the pleasure?"

It was Pedro. I put my hand in his dry, capable grasp, and he spun me out, in, and back out again. His body moved and mine followed, easy as breathing.

"Very good," he said approvingly. "Why, with just a few more lessons, you could really start to take off."

"You really think so?" Okay, so it was a sales pitch, but I was beginning to think it would be worth paying for the sheer physical joy of moving well with a partner who looked and danced as well as Pedro did.

"I know so." Pedro whipped me around again, and then there was a commotion at the door: the band, arriving with the serious swing dancers, everyone laughing and shouting and calling out "Pedro" and "Merry" and talking about some big event out in Philadelphia.

As the band set up, someone put on a CD that had a rockier, faster edge than the Big Band music we'd been hearing all evening. Two dancers in their twenties began to practice, pulling back on each other's arms, swiveling on the balls of their feet, filling their moves with the promise of athletic sex and a hint of abandon. Other dancers slipped on saddle shoes, hanging their feet off their partner's laps as they chatted away with our instructors.

"Well," said Rita, coming up behind me, "I guess that's that. I have a feeling those boys will not be dancing with the likes of us."

I had to agree, though the blonde and the other women from our class were looking at the newcomers with untempered enthusiasm.

"So, what do you think? Do we dare display our less than spectacular form out on the floor?"

I looked up at Rita. She must have been a handsome man at some point; as a woman, however, there was something a little disconcerting about the length of her jaw.

"On one condition," I said, as the band began to launch into "Bei Mir Bist Du Schön." "You have to let me lead."

"You got it, girl. But try to dance us to the left. I want to get another look at that Pedro in action." We attempted a few careful spins until we were near the center of the floor, where Pedro was energetically sliding Merry through his legs, swinging her across his waist, hoisting her over his head.

"For twelve dollars an hour, Rita, he could be yours."

Rita smiled at me a little crookedly. "And don't you know, I almost think it would be worth it."

We watched Pedro as he slid across the dance floor on his knees. "Well, I have to admit, in all my Dirty Dancing fantasies, I don't wind up having to shell out for Johnny to teach me the mambo."

Rita laughed. "Oh, darling, I'd gladly pay for Patrick Swayze."

The music stopped, which was for the best, as Rita and I were doing more talking than dancing and more active couples kept bumping into us. I waited a moment for the applause to die down. "Would you really pay for a man you found attractive, Rita?"

"Any man, no. Patrick Swayze, yes. Why? Wouldn't you?"

I shrugged. The truth was, my libido had become a bit of a hothouse plant; I required just the right conditions to make my desire grow. "I guess a big part of what I want is to be the object of someone's specific desire, so the idea of paying for it just doesn't work for me." As a feminist, I felt embarrassed, but one's erotic imagination is seldom politically correct.

"Interesting," said Rita, as the band began to play again. "Shall we?" She gestured toward the now crowded dance floor, where my friend Melissa and Needy were twirling, having found their rhythm.

"Actually," I said, "I think I'm done for the evening. But it was really nice meeting you." In a moment, she was gone, heading for Horny with a determined look in her eye.

As I got my shawl, I wondered if my real problem was that I wasn't European. Europeans know that passion is quirky, ephemeral, a happy collusion of madnesses. A woman my age living in Paris or Florence or Barcelona wouldn't take swing dancing lessons to meet men. She would go stylishly along with the business of living her life.

And when passion arrived, a European woman would understand it for the runaway balloon it was—a bit of magic, never meant to last.

On the other hand, a European woman would probably have married Ethan the compatible actuary and remained open to the possibility of a little magic on the side. Maybe I needed to get clearer on what I really wanted—a committed, mature relationship or a red balloon that defied the laws of gravity until it burst.

I arrived home and Burt leapt down from the linen closet and padded over to me, howling all the while about my neglect of him. I served him up a portion of guilt food before I'd even kicked off my heels. Then I fixed myself a Black Forest ham sandwich, made from a spring care package my mother had sent along with a picture of her newest foal.

There was one message on my machine. Another wrong number, wanting to make an appointment.

Not Joe.

I glanced at the clock. Half past nine. I picked up the phone and dialed my mother's number.

"Stable Environment, Marnie speaking."

"Hi, Marnie."

"Marlowe?"

"No, your other daughter."

"Very funny. Did you get my package?"

"I'm eating the ham right now and it's . . . ugh, wait,

something tastes strange." I opened the sandwich. "Marnie, some of this meat has mold on it."

"You're kidding me! I only bought that last week. Maybe I didn't refrigerate it fast enough. Oh, well. Hey, I'm down at the barn right now, looking at Singapore Sling's new baby."

Singapore Sling was my mother's most valuable mare. "Everything all right?"

"Well, basically." My mother went on to recite a typical array of Thoroughbred misadventures: a stallion who'd bitten a stablehand's thumb, a mare with a stomach complaint, a long and difficult day of trying to breed Reckless Driving to Lady Muck. After a while she remembered to ask, "How are you?"

"Fine."

"Well, that's good. Have you spoken to your brother? He's planning on coming up here for an Easter egg hunt with his entire pack of Mexican savages."

"Those are your grandchildren."

"I'm not saying there's anything wrong with their being Mexican. They're all short enough to be jockeys, if they'd stop eating so damn much."

"Going to hang up now, Marnie." I did, then stared at the phone for a moment, trying to decide whether or not to call Tanner. In the end, it didn't seem worth the bother; it was hard to complain to my brother because he liked to believe that despite all evidence to the contrary, our mother really cared for us.

And all at once, I knew what I wanted. I wanted to be fiercely, intimately connected to someone, even if it was only for a little while. Because when you came right down to it, everything was temporary, not just passion and balloons.

joe

It was shaping up to be one of the worst Saturday nights of my life, up there with the time when I was in the Air Force reserves and took a double dose of antihistamine right before my first jump.

Since then, I've tended to avoid medication, even when the pollen count was as high as it was right now. As a result, my eyes were swollen up like a boxer's. Had I been working a case, I probably would have soldiered on, but it had been my second lousy day off. With nothing to distract me from myself, I found I was turning into an old man—bitching about the talky shit they call music on the radio, wondering why pretty girls on TV want to tattoo and pierce themselves like sailors, depressed to see that the rock stars of my youth were doddering around like premature geriatrics, while all the new rock stars looked like somebody's whiney kid.

The last thing on earth I felt like doing was going out on the town. But I'd made it through childhood and basic training, and I was going to make it through my pal Lurch's fucking bachelor party without wimping out.

Juan Garcia walked by, saw my face. "Jeez, Joe, you look like you got into something."

"Not a fight, just apple blossoms."

Juan gave a low whistle. "Looks painful, man. Your eyes is all red and shit."

"Tell me something I don't know. What're you working on these days?"

"Same old case. The chatter at the Brownstone Brothel's that Big Daddy's due in by the end of the month, so we're figuring this whole thing's about ready to pop."

"Come on, Juan, you guys still really think you're going to get a racketeering charge to stick? This was no damn RICO case, this was just your basic mother and daughter twat shop." Big Daddy was a Russian mobster who'd managed to eliminate his competitors by informing for the FBI. The feds caught wise and started closing in on him four years ago in Miami, when Big Daddy fled with the only person in his organization he had to report to—his scary ass wife, Marusa. Nowadays, with the FBI's new priority of dealing with international terrorism, it wasn't too hard to run a crime network while on the move, and that's what Big Daddy was doing.

As for what the hell the task force was doing, that was another question. The way I saw it, Big Daddy had made a fool of the feds and that was why there was a special task force of agents and cops over at 135th Street in Detective Bureau Manhattan South, spinning their wheels over a bunch of women whose biggest crime was probably overcharging for furry handcuffs.

Loosened by a second beer, I said as much to Juan.

"We have reason to believe that there are some major in-

ternational narcotics deals being made out of this house."
Juan looked almost prim; I couldn't help grinning.

"You mean you found some coke in a whorehouse?
Shocking!"

"Come on, man, let's not go over that old shit again.
Besides, who need to be talking shop when there's naked
girls walking around?" Juan glanced over his shoulder.
"Hey, there's Keith. I'll be back in a minute."

I remember when Juan's defense was that at least he
was getting paid to listen to pretty girls talk dirty. Either
he'd gotten religion or he just didn't feel like letting an
outsider bitch about his job. I took a long swallow of beer
and Lurch came up beside me.

"Having a good time, Joe?"

I toasted Lurch with my bottle but didn't say anything.
I thought about saying I was enjoying myself fine because asshole Dave, the fed who'd gotten me flopped
from the task force, was not going to pollute the temple
of his body by showing up at the Go-Go Club. But the
truth was, I didn't much go for upscale strip joints, even
ones that looked like old-style men's clubs with over-
stuffed leather chairs and snooker tables. I couldn't put
my finger on the bad; I mean, the waitresses were pretty
and the drinks were served in oversized glasses. No one
was paying attention to the no-smoking rule and there
was some kind of Rat Pack song on the sound system,
just loud enough to drown out conversation.

But it all felt just a little too trendy for a bunch of off-
duty cops, and we all looked a little out of place, even me
in my black on black jeans, shirt and jacket. Paolina had
made me aware of how people labeled you according to
the nuances of what you wore, but no amount of careful

tailoring could make me fit in with this hip downtown crowd.

On the whole I would have preferred a bar with some peanut shells and sawdust on the floor.

And, to be perfectly honest, I could've done without having to make conversation with a bunch of guys who'd all witnessed my defeat at the hands of the Evil Preppie.

Lurch ordered another martini and put his hand on my shoulder. A slow-moving six-foot-four, he was one of the few guys I knew who could make me feel short and speedy.

"So, what're you working on these days? Got anything good?"

I took a cigarette from Lurch's pack, just for something to do. "Well, I got this one autoerotic case that's just fucking unbelievable."

Lurch lit my cigarette, which I could've done without. Now I had to actually smoke it. "Yeah? What's so special about it?"

"About six feet of Saran wrap and a snorkel."

Lurch snorted, his version of a laugh. "Hey, look, show's about to begin."

I took an absent-minded drag on the cigarette in my hand and turned to the stage, where a redheaded girl in go-go boots and a miniskirt was striding out as the music changed to a Tom Jones tune. It was a small club, and we were close enough that I could see the sheen of sweat on the dancer's forehead.

"Man," said Lurch as the stripper ripped off her top and began to do the frug, "I love this retro shit. Go, Pussycat, go."

Whatever.

Lurch and I'd gotten to know each other three years ago, when he'd been working up near where I lived in Washington Heights. The three-four was a heavy house, and if it hadn't been my home turf, I would've enjoyed the challenge of rock around the clock action. But no cop ever works where he lives—otherwise, you wouldn't have a life.

Anyway, Lurch and I discovered we had a few things in common—we were both Democrats in a sea of Republicanism, we both tended to destroy the cars we drove, and we'd both spent time in the armed forces.

When I first got assigned to Organized Crime, Lurch and I celebrated. Six months later, after 9/11, I was mouthing off to anyone who would listen about how we were wasting our time wiretapping brothels when we should've been chasing down Al Qaeda.

I told Lurch right before I asked to be transferred to the Joint Terrorist Task Force, where I could check on crime patterns in London, Hamburg, and Tel Aviv. Instead, Dave the creep made sure that I got stuck in the two-four, writing up reports on stolen laptops and TV sets and investigating every homebound geezer who kicked the bucket between 86th Street and 110th.

And Lurch got to take my place on the task force.

Of course, all of this might not have hit me so hard if Paolina hadn't decided that with *her* career going into overdrive, this was the perfect time to leave her dumb shmo of a husband.

"Hey, Dude—you think those are real?" Lurch's question snapped me out of my pityfest. He was talking about the dancer's large, firm, globular breasts. She'd stripped down to a G-string that revealed she took her hair removal seriously. Everyone else was applauding.

I started clapping, but not before I saw the dancer give me a long, disapproving look. God, I hate a front row seat. "Lurch, old buddy, nothing that looks that good is ever real."

"You're just saying that to make me feel better." Lurch was marrying a war bride—a gorgeous girl he'd met in the Heights. I figured she'd get her citizenship and then Adios, muchacho, but what did I know?

"Listen, Joe, I wanted to tell you I'm sorry about the whole wedding thing, but Talia insisted, so what could I do?"

I looked at Lurch. "Backstory?"

"Oh, man, you mean you didn't know Paolina was designing Tina's gown? Shit."

"Oh, that, yeah, I'd just forgotten. Course I knew." And I had known, I'd just put it out of my mind. "Don't sweat it. What'd you think, I was going to freak out because Paolina's hands had touched the wedding dress? Rest easy, Lurch. I'm not hung up on my ex-wife anymore."

Lurch was watching me closely, his long face as serious as I'd ever seen it. "Well, that's great, Joe, 'cause you do know she's going to be at the reception?"

"I assumed she might be."

"With her new boyfriend." Lurch had the loyalty to make the last word sound whiny and sarcastic. It didn't help, though I appreciated the effort.

"She's dating someone?"

Lurch raised his arm and ordered me another beer. "Some actor."

"Great. No, really, I mean it. What," I said, as Lurch gave me the fishy eyeball. "You think *I'm* not dating?"

At that moment, the red-headed dancer came over, dressed in her little G-string and go-go boots. She'd brought my beer.

"Are you Benicio Del Toro, or just look like him?"

"I don't even look like him," I said. "It's allergies."

"So you just didn't like my act, hotshot?"

The guys were all watching, nudging and elbowing each other.

"I liked it fine."

"Didn't look like it. Maybe you can't see too well with your eyes all puffed up? Maybe you want to see me—up close and personal?"

"Thanks but no thanks."

"What are you, gay?" Up close, she was model pretty, and probably ten years younger than me. Her breasts were the size of cantaloupes and sparkled with gold glitter. I suspected I'd be seeing them in my dreams.

"No," said Lurch, "he's just gotten his heart broke by his ex-wife."

The dancer looked interested. "That true?"

Jesus. "Look," I said, spreading my hands wide, "I just don't see the point in getting a lap dance. You grind on me, I get a boner but I can't touch you, and either I wind up with sticky shorts or I walk around funny for the rest of the evening."

"I'm not a prostitute," she said.

"Did I say you were?"

"You're a funny one." There was something different in the way she was looking at me now. I knew the guys saw it too, and were impressed, but I also knew it had very little to do with me. She was young, was all, and not used to guys saying no.

"So why don't you ask her to dance, Joe?" Lurch elbowed me in the ribs.

I looked up at her from my chair and some of the day's misery must have shown in my face. She reached out a hand. "You're a cop, right?"

"We're all cops," said Juan, but she wasn't paying attention.

"I'm not what you're thinking I am," I said. "If you let me, I'll take total advantage of this situation. Give me your number, I'll call it. Go home with me, I'll do my best to put a smile on your face."

"You think a lot of yourself." But all this lack of trying was clearly new to her; she looked fascinated.

"I'm just another asshole in a bar," I told her.

"At least you admit it," she said, chucking me under the chin. She'd finally gotten close enough that I could look right into her shiny, too-bright eyes, the pupils huge, too huge to be accounted for by anything natural, even by the dimly lit room and all the physical attraction in the world.

I could also see that, underneath the pancake makeup, she was probably closer to eighteen than to twenty-eight.

She leaned in and whispered her number in my ear. My body responded, but it was just a single note of interest, not that screaming chorus of want that drowns out all your other thoughts. As she walked away, Lurch and Juan started laughing and joking and asking me was I aware that I had just done the impossible.

And bastard that I was, I let them think what they liked. Because it didn't matter that I wasn't going to take advantage of a teenager on Ecstasy.

My pals thought I was, and that meant they weren't

feeling so damn sorry for me anymore. Feeling better than I had all night, I turned to say something to Juan and then froze.

Because there, walking toward us with a tight smile, was Dave the FBI asshole, prepped out in his powder blue golf shirt and khakis.

"Hello, guys," he said. "Joe." He nodded his head in my direction.

"Hey, Davey, you made it." Lurch raised his hand to get a waitress's attention. "What can I get you? Beer? Scotch?"

"Just a Coke, please." Asshole. Dave turned to me. "How are you, Joe?" There was a pleasant but firm kindergarten teacher's expression on his blond-haired, blue-eyed, corn-fed baby face, and I wanted to sock him so bad my right hand was tingling.

"Just peachy. And yourself? Fire anyone lately?"

Dave took his soda from the waitress and thanked her. "I don't make a habit of removing people from the team."

"Of course you don't, Dave. That was just a little sarcastic humor. Speak the unspeakable, you know? Clears the air."

Dave blinked. "You know that I did respect your abilities, Joe. But you were not a team player."

Out of the corner of my eye I saw Lurch and Juan exchange a quick look.

"That's a matter of opinion." I tipped my bottle and starting swallowing down beer and angry words. Barely thirty years old and just because this kid had more degrees than a thermometer, he figured he was the boss of me. The other guys had humored him when he talked about "reliable information" pointing to some little brownstone brothel being the center of a major international drug ring, or started up with "in my experience" as if he had twenty years of it.

"Well, Joe, it wasn't just my opinion or you'd still be on the task force." Dave took a sip of his Coke and a surge of adrenaline, of rage, poured through me, and I had to work at keeping everything I was feeling tucked inside.

"If you'd spent any time in your short, spoon-fed life listening to guys who had experience on the street, Davey, you'd know that I was just telling you to your face what everyone was saying behind your back." Okay, so I was leaking a little hostility. At least I wasn't punching the guy.

Dave, on the other hand, was managing to hold onto his steady, deliberate Mr. Rogers voice. "You kept challenging my authority, Joe, which was a shame. Not only for you, but for the team. You had some good qualities."

"You know, Dave, you do a good imitation of an all-around nice guy, but there's something wrong with you. I just haven't figured out what it is yet."

Dave the reptile didn't even blink. "I'd say the problem's yours then, Joe."

Nice comeback. I guess it would've been too much to ask for him to lose his cool and throw the first punch.

"Hey, guys," said Juan, "come on, now. Lighten up."

I kept looking at Dave. With most folks, I could mentally peel back the years and see the kid underneath. For example, it was clear to me that slick Juan Garcia had been a momma's boy and that my buddy Lurch had been one of those kids that always look a year or so older than they really are, and get punished for not being as mature as they appear. Once I figured out the kid part, I pretty much had a handle on the adult man or woman.

"Joe," Lurch said in a loud voice, "Tell us about that stiff you had, you know, the snorkel guy."

"Fred," I said, "you're not going to distract me from the peckerhead who ruined my career by getting me to tell the funny story of the bullshit I spend my days on now."

"We all spend our days on bullshit," said Lurch, pretending not to hear the way I'd said his real name. "But that bullshit of yours was a candidate for the Darwin awards."

Dave held up a hand. "Hang on, the *what* awards?"

"You know, for the person who kills himself in the most extraordinarily stupid way. Like there's this one guy who gets off on his wife stomping on small rodents, and then he decides that it's not enough, now he wants to be stomped . . ."

I watched Dave as he listened to Lurch, laughing in all the right places, and knew it was a performance, but it was a good one, almost impossible to penetrate.

The music struck up again, an old Dusty Springfield song, and I watched the slow flush on Davey boy's cheeks as a new stripper took to the stage.

"Well, I think that's it for me," he said to Lurch and Juan and the others, who made the requisite protests as Davey shook their hands and made his farewells. Watching him go, I felt my stomach start to burn with all the sour asides and bitter comments I hadn't made.

"I'm leaving, too," I told Lurch.

"We were going to get some ribs later at Dixie's."

My heartburn made the prospect sound less than inviting. I imagined a platter of ulcer-causing propor-

Alisa Kwitney

tions, with six cops all jockeying for the corner seat so as not to leave their backs exposed. "Maybe at your next bachelor party."

I said my own good-byes to the others and hurried out just in time to see Dave hail a cab. The night air was cool and a little damp, and there were wet puddles on the dark street, reflecting the club's neon lights.

"Hey, Dave."

He looked at me, his hand on the taxi door's handle, clearly searching his mental rulebook for the right thing to say. I decided to make up his mind for him.

"Tell me something, Davey. When you had me kicked off the task force, you knew it was a petty bullshit move, right?"

His eyes narrowed. "I guess you have to keep telling yourself that." Behind Dave, a couple got out of another taxi and moved quickly away from us, the woman's heels clicking rapidly over the damp pavement.

"So you think eavesdropping on Yuppies in search of blondes with nice tits is really going to lead us to some major mob figures?"

"You know what Porky Malloy said . . ."

"Porky Malloy is full of shit. He's probably just mad at the madame for not giving him three girls for the price of one."

"And that theory is based on what, your gut feeling? This isn't just about instincts, Joe. A task force doesn't need hunches. It needs calculated assessments and a coherent plan." Dave opened the taxi's rear door and climbed into the backseat. "Look, you made a power play, and you lost." He paused for a moment, as if about to say something else, then closed the door.

"I wasn't jockeying for position, Agent Bellamy. That's your game."

Dave leaned his head out the window. "Why don't you just admit that you lost, instead of pretending you weren't competing?"

I stared him down. "Bet you were one snotty little kindergarten kid. Bet everyone wanted to beat you up when teacher wasn't looking."

"I wouldn't know," said Dave. "I skipped kindergarten, along with a bunch of other grades." Then he said something to the driver and his cab drove off before I could say anything more.

A prodigy. A fucking socially retarded goody two shoes child prodigy. No wonder I couldn't see him as a child—he'd never been one. Figure he was three or four years ahead of all his peers in school, which means he made it through high school without ever getting laid. No wonder Davey boy worried about my propensity for questioning rules.

He'd probably never even been on a team in his whole miserable, high-achieving life until he'd been asked to take charge of one.

marlowe

I put down *The Crimson Petal and the White*, wondering why I wasn't getting into the book when all my friends had loved it. I kept getting distracted by the prostitute heroine's flaking skin and the fact that her smugly arrogant client had lost control of his bladder one drunken night. It wasn't that I was prudish, I thought, but did I really want to read in such detail about soiled sheets?

I was flossing my teeth when the phone rang. At first, I thought it might be Melissa, too excited from swinging with Needy to sleep.

"Swinburne? Am I bothering you?"

"Joe?"

"You remembered my name."

"Joe, it's after one in the morning."

"You alone?"

"That's not the point." I walked back into my bedroom, looking at the row of stuffed animals on my dresser, each one originally intended as a gift for some boyfriend on Valentine's Day. Gorilla, pig, weasel, frog, snake, and sad-eyed puppy. I'd decided to lose the boys and keep the critters, a bit like Circe, the enchantress who turned all her disappointing ex-lovers into beasts.

"I just got off my tour and I had this feeling you'd be awake. I love it that you remembered my name."

"Unlike some."

"You kidding, Marlowe? I even looked you up."

"You did what?" I sat down on my bed next to my cat. Burt half opened one golden eye and began to purr.

"Looked up the poet Marlowe. Only from what I read, he's more of a playwright."

"Oh, great, I have a literary critic stalking me."

"I'm not stalking you, M. I'm courting you. 'Come live with me and be my love, and we will all the pleasures prove,' right? 'And I will make thee beds of roses and a thousand fragrant posies.' "

I curled my feet under me. "Beds of roses always sounded painful to me."

"Maybe he meant just the petals. How come you're alone on Saturday night, Marlowe?"

I stroked Burt's smooth brown head and he lifted his chin, his two small front fangs sticking out of his mouth like a vampire's. What could I say? I'm alone because the only men who were interested in me were the walking wounded. I took a breath. "I told you—I'm retired."

"Yeah, me too, M. I could've gotten laid tonight, but the thing is, I've retired."

I turned over on my stomach and Burt closed his eyes again. "Retired from women?"

"From dating."

"What happened?"

"Strip club. Not my idea—a buddy's bachelor party. The stripper liked me."

"But?"

There was a long sigh on the other end. "You think maybe there's something wrong with me? What's it called, where you stop feeling things so sharply and everything you used to enjoy seems like too much trouble?"

"Depression." I kept stroking Burt, who ignored me. "Were you physically attracted to this woman?"

"She had great breasts. But. I don't know." Another sigh.

"Let yourself know."

Joe laughed, a deep, masculine sound. "Anyone ever tell you that you sound like a shrink? Okay, so maybe this girl was too young and too doped up on something and maybe if I took her home I wouldn't be able to think of myself as one of the good guys anymore."

"There you go," I said. "That's your answer."

"Except now I'm alone again. And my wife's got a new boyfriend."

"Here's where I use my shrink voice to say a-hah."

"And I have to go to this wedding and probably see her with her new guy. Shit. I sound like a mope, don't I? Never mind. Let's drop that subject. Tell me something, Marlowe. What were you doing when I called?"

"Reading a book." Which sounded better than flossing.

"I used to read all the time, but these days I can't seem to focus. I've got this book going about that FBI mole, the one they called the Mortician?"

"I've heard of it."

"I'm stuck on chapter three."

"I've been having trouble getting through my book, too." It occurred to me that if Joe was depressed, then maybe I was, too.

"Marlowe. Something I'm itching to ask you, but if it offends you . . ."

"Go ahead."

"If you do it for money, then does it spoil doing it for fun?"

What could I say to that? I'm not a call girl, Joe. You called a wrong number. It's what I meant to say, but the words stuck in my throat. All I had to say was the word "psychologist" and Joe would apologize, hang up the phone, stop bothering me.

On the other hand, all I had to do was play along, and I could discover for myself whether concealing my identity would have any real impact on how I behaved. Dear God, it was so obvious, how could I not have seen it before? Joe could provide the charge of sexual interest that my dissertation had been lacking. How far would I let this flirtation go? My heart gave a flutter of excitement. This was the kind of tension that could turn an academic paper into a page turner.

"Actually," I said slowly, "I haven't had that kind of fun in a long time."

"Some of the guys you see must be real assholes."

I glanced at my menagerie of ex-boyfriend toys. "Some."

"I mean, you get to see human nature at its worst, don't you? Kind of like a cop."

"I hear some of the secrets people don't ordinarily reveal, but I haven't had . . . I don't cater to just anyone." This was actually true. According to my former clinical supervisor, I was operating a boutique practice, by which he meant I was turning down the more seriously unstable patients he referred.

Alisa Kwitney

"Meaning you avoid sociopaths?"

"Exactly." God, he was smart. Imagine how insightful he'd be if he knew what I was talking about.

"So, is there any type of guy that just disgusts you?"

"I'm not sure I understand what you mean . . ." What would repulse a call girl? Dirty fingernails? Flatulence? Comb-overs?

"Guys into all that kinky bondage stuff. Wanting you to tie them up, say, or choke them a little . . ."

"I actually did have one client who was interested in autoerotic asphyxiation." Handsome guy, an actor in his midtwenties.

"What happened?"

"He didn't stay with me long." The client in question was very sweet and charming and essentially immature. In the end, I referred him on to a sexual surrogate who worked with his kind of dysfunction.

"What happened to him?"

"I passed him on to someone else."

"Why some guys can't just beat off to *Penthouse*, I'll never understand. I mean, being a cop, I've seen how easy it is for a guy to have a fatal accident without dressing up in women's underwear and sticking his head in a noose."

I laughed. "Yes, masturbation is supposed to be safe sex."

"Does your profession have its own sick humor, like mine? You must, right? Tell me something outrageous, some story you'd tell a fellow . . . colleague."

I stretched out my legs and realized it was time to get waxed—the hairs on my calves wouldn't bear close scrutiny. "I guess this sounds prissy, Joe, but I don't tell stories about my clients. Some of my . . . colleagues do, but I wouldn't want to be talked about like that. It's disrespectful."

I could feel Joe considering this on the other line. "So you'd feel uncomfortable telling me any more about this autoerotic case?"

"It's not just you. I wouldn't want to turn someone's intimate life into cocktail conversation. No pun intended."

"I didn't mean to sound like my interest was just . . .

"Prurient?"

"Okay, I'll just whip out my pocket dictionary here."

"Unwholesome sexual interest."

"That works. Although the word I was going to use was *schadenfreude*."

"Ooh, satisfaction in someone else's misfortune. Very good word. How do you know it?"

"What, you think cops are stupid? I took Abnormal Psych. Anyway, I didn't mean to make it sound as if I was getting my rocks off, asking you this stuff. The truth is, I knew someone who died like that."

"A friend?"

"Yeah. I just feel so guilty about it. If only I'd known why he wanted to borrow the Saran Wrap . . ."

"He used Saran Wrap?"

"And a snorkel. Is that unusual? Your client, for example . . ."

"Let's just say I've heard of using an orange segment . . . yes, I do think that's a bit unusual."

"So you've never encountered that particular method?"

"I've never even heard of that method. Although I know that men can get very creative when left to their own devices."

"I never got more creative than Vaseline and girly magazines."

I laughed.

"Hey, Marlowe. Do *you* masturbate?"

I got the feeling he was trying to catch me off guard. "Everyone masturbates."

"None of the girls I've been with."

"Of course they do. They're just not admitting it."

"I'm not saying they never did it, M, I'm saying that they stopped doing it after high school."

"You mean, once they graduated, they stopped playing varsity?"

He laughed. "Yeah, that's what I mean."

"You don't think they self-pleasured when they were in between relationships?" Oh, yikes, where did that phrase come from? I sounded like some seventies sex ed text.

"I know Paolina didn't do her own toenails, cleaning or laundry, so I suspect she didn't do that herself, either. Alexa—she was sort of a friend I fooled around with when I was doing my stint as a weekend warrior—I could see her doing it, yeah, but only when she wasn't with someone. I mean, not involved with someone."

"Let me just say, speaking from professional experience, that you might be surprised."

"Get out of here!"

"Well, sometimes Harry doesn't give Sally what she needs, so she sneaks off to remedy the situation."

"So, next time I hear the electric toothbrush going, I should go investigate?"

I laughed, but didn't reassure him that I was certain he'd never left a woman unsatisfied. I was going to be as honest a liar as I could be with this man. "Joe, what did you mean when you said you were a weekend warrior?"

"Air force reserve. I met Alexa at McGuire, over in New Jersey. So you—how'd you put it—self-pleasure?"

Yes, while wearing my mood ring and getting in touch with my inner child. "Of course."

"Because you don't get a lot of pleasure from the men you see?"

I thought about the men I no longer saw: There was Ethan, my most recent, computer-matched boyfriend. Before him there had been a brief fling with a guy who'd owned a succession of schnauzers, each one named Happy. There'd been a morning coffee shop flirtation with an English guy who turned out to have a wife back in Sussex, but he didn't count, as we'd never done more than discuss the news.

Before that, things got a little hairier, both literally and figuratively. Benoit, Lorenzo, Alfredo, Etienne, Bruno, Stavros, Tomer, and that U.N. guy I nicknamed Goliath flashed through my memory, a beery parade of spring breaks and summer holidays spent in the South of France, Tuscany, Barcelona, Israel, and Greece. Had I gotten pleasure from them during our brief, postcard unions? Yes, but not that kind that survived even a brief layover in Manhattan. What feels like hedonism on the island of Ibiza smacks of obligation when it lands in your apartment, wearing strangely fitted jeans, wanting to see the Statue of Liberty and only able to speak in the present tense.

A breeze blew in from my open window, rustling the curtains. From somewhere down the street, a siren wailed past. I had always been convinced that I was by nature a deeply sexual person, capable of wild, carnal abandon, but this really hadn't translated into any bona fide carnally abandoned experience. When it came right down to it, I didn't even masturbate that much anymore.

"Marlowe?"

"Mm hm." I realized I hadn't answered his question, which, I supposed, was its own answer.

"Would you do something for me?"

"What?"

"Touch your breasts."

Okay, this was the reason I couldn't take this long distance *Belle de Jour* game any farther. Because now he was taking it to a direction that I had absolutely no interest in pursuing. Did I?

I did if I wanted to publish my damn dissertation.

I cleared my throat. "How?"

"Just cup them in your hands."

I did, wondering if other women were turned on by this kind of thing.

"How do they feel?" His voice was huskier than before.

"Full. A little tender."

"You expecting your period?"

"Not yet." I felt my cheeks flush. "I'm about a week away."

"You have underwear on?"

"Yes."

"Describe." He said it like a cop, I thought.

"Pink. Cotton. Bikini." I laughed a little, embarrassed. "Saturday underwear."

"You wear the same underwear every Saturday?"

"No, well, they say Saturday." I took a breath. "What about you?"

"What kind of underwear do I wear or am I wearing any?"

"Both."

"I'm wearing navy combos. Those things that are snug but as long as boxers. Want me to take them off?"

"No."

"I want to make fun with you. Will you touch yourself for me?"

"I'm hanging up the phone now." My heart was pounding hard and fast and I couldn't have said if I was aroused or alarmed or repelled or some uneasy combination of all three.

"Wait."

I hesitated. "What is it, Joe?"

"You upset?"

"I don't know what I am." I replaced the receiver and sat there for a moment before turning out the light. In the darkness, I could hear Burt stretch before thumping down to the floor, his claws clicking as he walked across the wood. Alone in bed, I reached between my legs, slipping my fingers through the elastic waistband of my underwear.

Somewhere else in the city, I knew Joe was doing the same, and thinking of me. I thought about him in his bed, imagining me touching myself, and my fingers quickened and my breath came faster and then the phone rang.

Damn. I fumbled, reached for it.

"Yes?"

"Um. Are you pissed off at me now?"

"This isn't a good time."

"Sorry. Good night."

"Wait." My heart had started beating as if it were trying to knock out a rib.

"I'm still here."

I could barely get the words out. "I'm touching myself."

He sucked in a sharp breath. "Okay, does this mean . . . you mean you were . . . can I touch myself too?"

"Yes. It's, uh, it's what I was imagining you doing. Before."

He made a sound, and I felt the climb begin again. I closed my eyes and imagined him holding me the way Pedro had, but with his hand between my legs. On the other end of the line, his breathing quickened and suddenly I whimpered as I felt myself pulse once, twice, three times, a quick release, leaving me panting and somehow unsatisfied. I wrapped my arms around myself as I heard the faint sound of flesh against flesh, faster now.

"Joe," I said, wishing this didn't feel so pathetic now, wishing that he were a real lover beside me, holding me.

He gave a low moan and I felt another little throb between my legs. "God."

"Goddess."

He laughed. "Jeez. Well. That was . . ."

"Unsatisfying."

"Absolutely. What the hell is all the fuss about, I'd like to know?"

So it had been his first time long distance, too. "Can you sleep now?"

"Holding a pillow. Pretending it's you."

Wow. Okay. Deep breath. Don't say anything you'll regret. "Good night, Joe. No more calls."

"No more calls. Tonight."

I hung up and turned on the light so I could see the clock. Two A.M., and I had early clients in the morning.

I fell asleep with my arms around the pillow, and dreamt about having sex with a stranger who seemed very familiar and dear, but kept having to get up and leave before I was satisfied.

joe

There's a belief in law enforcement that the first hours after a homicide are the critical ones. If you're going to have a decent chance to solve a murder, you have to get going before the bloodstains get laundered, the weapons get discarded, and the perps and witnesses have time to rewrite the story of what happened.

Of course, I wasn't all that sure that Tony Russo was the victim of anything other than his own stupidity, but at this rate, I was never going to find out. Time was passing, other cases kept piling up on my desk, and all I'd learned about Mr. Russo in the past four days was that he'd worked for three years as an account manager at a local bank and didn't have a regular girlfriend—or boyfriend, for that matter.

He did have a personal ad in one of those Internet singles sites—a special one for sufferers of genital herpes. That, at least, was one thing he and I definitely did *not* have in common.

His neighbors said they weren't aware of his ever having any friends over.

I probably would've made the lieutenant happy and

let the case drop, except that I seemed on the verge of getting involved with the pro who might have contributed to his untimely demise.

Did I have great taste in women, or what?

In any event, I'd been too busy to call for another dirty poetry reading.

Monday, my turnaround day, I worked from four P.M. till one A.M. on a bomb threat from a disgruntled teenager, then slept for six hours on a bunk bed in the precinct locker room. Theoretically, this was supposed to help me wake up bright and early to start work at 8 A.M. on Tuesday. In reality, it made me feel like crap.

But yesterday was definitely the icing on my cake: I'd had to spend most of the day talking to a hysterical crackhead who said he'd been robbed and his old lady abducted. Turned out he'd killed her; while Denny brought in a sketch artist to draw the imaginary kidnapper, I got a warrant and discovered that our man had gone Sweeny Todd, stashing bits of wife in the fridge behind a bucket of Kansas Fried.

I stumbled home at five P.M., conked out on the couch around six and then woke up at two A.M. and couldn't fall asleep again. I spent the rest of the night watching reruns of *Three's Company* and wondering if my body was just getting too fucking old to keep switching from day to night tours. Married guys usually got the regular slots, but I was beginning to think I'd never make it to retirement if I didn't do something about my lack of sleep.

I could've called Marlowe this morning, but figured I'd do something healthy instead. I was spending far too much time brooding in my apartment. Today was a beautiful fucking spring day and I was going to fucking well enjoy it.

Life really wasn't so bad. I was still pleasantly full from a full Irish heart-attack breakfast from the deli and there was enough coffee in me to keep me rolling till I hit the Palisades. A nice sixty-mile ride, that's what I needed, fresh air and the good rush and muscle fatigue of a workout.

As I walked my bike toward the park, I noticed that some of the trees on Broadway had budded. Other trees were already in leaf, and a breeze brought the improbable scent of apple blossoms. In just eight weeks, the city would smell like sweat, exhaust, and rotting garbage, and in twelve, the only people left in the city would be the ones who couldn't afford to escape. But for the moment, you could catch a glimpse of the elegant Manhattan of old movies, the one where the colors were sharp and the people were stylish and just a little fast.

If the weather held, Lurch was going to have one hell of a wedding this Sunday.

Two young girls passed by me in sleeveless flowered dresses, and I heard one say something about my bike shorts that made them both laugh low in their throats.

Well, glad my butt still passed muster with the under-twenties.

I passed the newsstand and was just glancing at the day's headlines when I saw it: my wife's face, on the cover of a magazine. Draped around some young actor. I picked it up, read:

Does She Have Designs on Him?

Hot young designer Paolina Kane has been seen out with Mario Vendrame, the up-and-coming star of *Soldier of Fortune.*

Flipping open the magazine, I found a photo of myself, no bigger than a dime:

Paolina's first husband, NYPD cop Joe Kane, lasted four years. Lucas Smythe, the baseball player, was her previous boyfriend and lasted only a few months.

Shit, my name was misspelled. And Lucas's picture got at least two more inches than mine did.

"It was the best sex I ever had," Paolina said at the time of Lucas, "but in the end, we didn't have what it takes to make a relationship work long term."

"Three dollars," said the newsstand guy. "I'll give you a fresh one."

Now Paolina says of girl-magnet Mario, who is just beginning to extend his fame to this side of the Atlantic, "it's not just the physical connection—although we can't keep our hands off of each other. It's also a meeting of the minds." As for whether she regrets calling Lucas "the best," Paolina says, "All I can say is, I didn't know what I was talking about. When Mario makes love to me, I want to shout Hallelujah and make babies."

There was more drivel about her family originally coming from some small village in Italy not far from where Mario's family still lived. I put the magazine down and rolled my bike away. The best sex she ever had was me, she'd said. She'd even said it after we'd broken up. Well, she'd implied it.

We were sitting in one of those Columbus Avenue restaurants where a burger costs $20 and she put her hand over mine and said, "You know, I still miss it." And I'd said, "What, the sex?" Kind of half joking. And she said, I remember it, "No, the sex with you. The fun of sex with you."

That was only, what, a month ago. She'd just broken up with the baseball player, who'd been cheating, and had called me up to see if I wanted to get together as friends. I said sure, wondering if we might wind up in the sack, half hoping we might be getting back together.

So when she put her hand on mine, I was already mentally undressing her, and she knew me well enough to know that's what I was doing. I'm pretty sure now that's what she was there for in the first place—someone crazy about her to restore her confidence. She'd picked a restaurant around the corner from her studio apartment and the excuse we hit upon was that I was going to make sure her locks were strong enough.

We barely got through the door and we were at it, but it was definitely not the best sex either of us had ever had.

Married, we'd been good together in bed. Paolina was one of those women that required a lot of foreplay every time, but I didn't mind; I'm a guy that likes foreplay. Divorced, we seemed to have fallen out of sync. I kept getting distracted by the fact that some other guy had been touching her, had been inside her.

She didn't feel as tight as she used to; I wondered if Lucas the baseball player was bigger than me.

I'd never been so relieved to come. I don't know how much she enjoyed it, either; I started to touch her afterward, but she said she was getting sore. When it was time for me to report to the precinct, I checked the locks on her door and kissed her good-bye.

Now I regretted the whole thing. People always judge stories by the way they end, and that lousy last screw was the epitaph to my marriage.

I was on my bike now, body moving along Riverside Drive while my mind went in an opposite direction. People are like dominoes, my mother used to say. You think your dots line up with someone else's and you've found a good fit, but just wait till you encounter their other side. It was her argument for why I should've married a nice, Jewish girl with all her dots in the right place, but now I was wondering whether it was a good argument for never hooking up seriously with anyone.

The traffic light turned yellow and, like all cops everywhere, I sped up. I didn't see the car change lanes without signaling until I was flipping over its hood.

For a moment, I was stunned, on my back. And then I saw the car start backing up at an angle. I realized the sonofabitch who'd clipped me was about to drive off.

"Hey!" I was on my feet now. "You asshole! You nearly fucking took my head off!" I pounded on the man's windshield and the driver stuck his head out.

"Why don't you back off, mister, and count yourself lucky you're not dead? Next time keep your mind on the road." He was young and neat and had an accent. I realized his car was a gypsy cab and figured I knew how to get his attention.

"Hey asshole, next time you nearly run over a cop, you might just want to . . ."

"Yeah, right." The look on the guy's face said it all. He thought I was making it up. "I'm so scared, I'm shaking."

I grabbed him by the front of his shirt with one hand, opened the car door with the other, and hauled him out of the driver's seat. "Scared yet?"

"Get the hell off of me. This is New York, man. You don't look out, you get run over. Learn to deal."

I sucker punched him in the chin. Ever notice how, in the movies, guys are always trading witty comebacks while they fight? That's 'cause they know the other guy's a stuntman. I was busy trying to keep this jerk from opening up the cut over my eye, and he was busy getting his switchblade out of his back pocket.

I used to take lessons in Krav Maga, a martial arts form that's big in Israel. Krav Maga doesn't involve a lot of flying through the air or fancy moves. It might not have looked good on a big screen, but it only took me about a minute to get the knife out of my assailant's hand and less than a minute to have him backed up against his car with his own blade at his throat. Which was, of course, the moment when the uniforms rolled in with lights flashing and sirens wailing.

"Okay, buddy, drop the weapon," said the first uniform.

I did, holding my hands up. "The knife's his, by the way. I'm a detective."

"Hold on a moment, sir, while we verify what's going on here."

It took twenty embarrassing minutes and then I was free to limp back to my apartment, my broken bike in tow.

I got myself a beer from the fridge and discovered I

couldn't manage to get the cap off the bottle. My right hand had started to swell up, so I wrapped a bag of frozen peas around my knuckles and started to dial Paolina's number with my left. Then I hung up, and called Marlowe instead.

marlowe

"And then he put his hand on my thigh and said, 'I've been thinking about you for months.' "

I glanced at my Madison Avenue client's firm thighs, which were encased in a double armor of pantyhose and light wool trousers. What subtle signal made her legs approachable to an attractive male, while mine remained untouched, even when displayed in short skirts?

"So now I'm having affairs with two different married men and I still can't find anyone to go to my twentieth high school reunion with me."

And here we had it, a classic case of doorknob therapy. Why was it that some clients had to wait until the last five minutes to drop the bombshell? For fifty minutes, Nancy Boyle had been discussing her mild anxiety about giving a speech during her business retreat next week and her lingering concern that her dog Quigley was unhappy with his new walker. We'd touched on the status of her year-long affair with a married man, and now, all of a sudden, with two minutes to go, she'd started talking about her personal trainer and burst into tears.

I should've been feeling compassion, not irritation, but the truth was I'd just gotten my period last night and needed this session to end so I could get to the bathroom.

The phone rang twice and the answering machine clicked on. I could hear my own voice, explaining with irritating deliberateness that I couldn't come to the phone right now. I tried to concentrate on my client.

"And the worst part is, I know I shouldn't keep calling him, I've made a complete fool of myself, and since he's also my son's s-s-soccer coach I have to see him this weekend. What should I do?"

Nancy raked her hands through her three-hundred dollar brown bob and I was about to answer when I heard Joe's voice leaving a message.

I'd forgotten to press the damn mute button.

"Marlowe? You there? This is Joe and I've got a business proposition for you. Don't worry, it doesn't involve any se . . ." I picked up the phone.

"Joe? I can't talk right now, I'm in session." I covered the mouthpiece and said to my client, "Sorry, it's an emergency, he's in crisis." Nancy nodded, dabbing at her eyes with a tissue.

"You're in session? But I thought you said . . ."

"Joe, I can call you back in a little while."

"So what's the deal, when you said you weren't seeing any clients, that was just bullshit?"

I made an apologetic face at Nancy. "We can discuss this in ten minutes, all right?"

"So you're just not seeing new clients?"

"I'm hanging up now, Joe."

"Oh please," said Nancy. "If he's that desperate, I can wait."

"Hang on, is your client a woman, Marlowe?"

"Yes. Now I'm saying good-bye." I hung up the phone and tried to compose myself. Nancy looked more curious than distraught.

"You know," she said, "it's kind of nice to be reminded that men can be out of control and keep phoning, too. I mean, sometimes I tell myself that it's men, men are all cold, unavailable bastards, but really, it's the men I'm choosing, isn't it?" Her eyes widened. "That's it, isn't it? I'm choosing a certain kind of man, the kind that's emotionally unavailable."

Good Lord, Joe had triggered a therapeutic breakthrough. "And why do you think you've been selecting unavailable men?"

"Because I'm ambivalent! Because this way I'm prepared for the guy to disappoint me, but if I let myself want someone who's really there . . ."

"Keep going."

"Then I'm taking a chance on being really disappointed. Then I'm risking being completely wiped out."

"That's your fear, Nancy. That's what's been keeping you locked in an unsatisfactory relationship all these months."

"I'm scared of taking a chance on a real contender."

I leaned back in my chair and smiled at her, thinking, And if I'm so damn smart, how come I'm not taking any romantic chances at all?

"Wow." Nancy wiped the smear of mascara under her eyes. "I think that's probably a good place to stop for today. Can I see you on Monday?"

"Absolutely." I took out my appointment book.

"And one more thing?"

"Yes?"

Nancy stood up and started pulling on her camel blazer. "Is Joe available?"

Five minutes later I found Joe's number and called it. "Joe?"

I heard the click of the phone being dropped and then picked up. "Yeah?"

"It's me. Are you all right?"

"My right hand's busted up."

"Oh, Jesus. Have you seen a doctor?"

"It's not broken, I just bruised the knuckles and banged the rest of it up a bit."

"How did you do that?"

He chuckled, a lovely masculine sound. "By connecting my fist with someone's face."

"Oh."

"It's my day off and I feel like shit. I got a mouse in a glue trap that I can't release, I can't get to any of the food in my fridge, and I don't have any cash for delivery. And in case I haven't mentioned it, I'm sick to death of my own company."

"How'd you get into a fight?"

"Not only will I tell you the whole story, I will pay you a hundred dollars to come over here and bring me some food. Bring a pack of cards and a video and I'll make it one-fifty."

God, cops were cheap. "Don't you have any friends you can call, Joe?"

"Nobody I care to see right now." He was silent for a moment. "Did you do her? The client?"

"No," I said. "We just talked."

"Like you talked to me?"

It took me a moment, and then I realized what he meant. My face got hot. "No, not like that."

"Come over, Marlowe."

"I can't." I hugged my knees to my chest.

"A hundred eighty-sixth and the corner of Bennet. It's right opposite a Yeshiva, you know, a Jewish school. You take the Broadway local to a hundred sixty-eighth and then switch to the C train."

"Joe, you're not listening."

"Bring me something classic, like an old Cary Grant, okay? And pasta. I need carbs. All right? Apartment 4C. It's unmarked, just buzz and I'll let you in."

"Joe!"

"I'm hanging up now, Marlowe. I'll be expecting you in about an hour. I won't take a painkiller till you get here, even though my hand is killing me. If you don't show . . ."

"This is blackmail."

"Yeah, but I can't stop thinking about you, so whatever it takes, I'm doing." I heard the click on the other end and he was gone.

Oh, God. What was I going to do now?

And more to the point, bloated as I was, what was I going to wear?

joe

She showed at three o'clock. It had taken her two hours instead of one. I was exhausted from sitting around trying not to think *ow* every time my hand throbbed, but it had been worth it because here she was, delivering herself straight to my doorstep.

Of course, the constant discomfort had kept me from thinking too hard about what I was really planning on getting accomplished here. Was I pursuing a case? Was I trying to get laid? Or was I exactly what I was pretending to be, a guy whose social life was so fucking miserable he'd pay for a pretty girl to cook him dinner and keep him company.

And she was pretty, a petite, delicate-featured redhead with sharp eyes, small, well-shaped ears, and a long neck. Short hair suited her fine.

"Swinburne."

"Marlowe." She smiled, a nervous, crooked smile that skewed left. She had a dimple in her left cheek. It annoyed me. She probably banked on that goddamn dimple, that deceptive look of innocence.

"You take a wrong train or something?" I took the bag

of groceries from her with my left hand, then turned and let her follow me into my kitchen, the same as I would do with a skittish stray.

Okay, so I didn't really care all that much about Tony Russo. My own health, however, was a different matter. Before I started getting squelchy with the lady, I figured I'd better make sure that she wasn't going to kill me accidentally or on purpose while perfecting her bondage techniques.

"There was some kind of construction going on in the subway."

I eased the shopping bag onto the counter and took a better look at my suspect. She was smaller than I'd expected, only five-foot-two or so. Trim but not athletic, a real female body under that loose, white, man's shirt and black denim skirt. Her skirt ended just above the knees, and if she'd undone one more button and been wearing higher heels, she might've looked the tiniest bit sexy.

She didn't look like a pro. She looked like a lawyer on her day off: prim, businesslike, trying to remember how to spend her time when someone wasn't paying her top dollar for it.

She needed to stop thinking so much. I had to get her reacting, not reasoning things out.

"You want something to drink? Here, let me take your . . ." I deliberately allowed her arm to brush my bad hand when I reached for her handbag. As I had anticipated, pain spangled through my nervous system, temporarily shorting out my speech centers.

"Oh my God, Joe, your hand." She reached out and I let her.

"Are you sure this isn't broken?"

"Pretty sure."

She looked like she was about to say something and then our eyes met. I became conscious of the way my hand seemed huge, cradled in her two small palms. I was close enough to smell her perfume, something clean and citrusy with an undertone of musk and woman. It occurred to me that if I reached up three inches, I'd be cupping her left breast. Too bad I'd decided I was going to question her about Tony Russo; I was closer to getting my oats rolled than I'd been in almost a year.

Think of something to say, Joe.

Problem was, everything that came to mind seemed to have overtones. Even the way she was looking at my bare arms had overtones. Suddenly I flashed back on our phone call the other night—*"I'm touching myself"*—and thought, I've made this woman come.

Marlowe met my eyes and I felt a rush of heat.

"Does it hurt, Joe?"

Yes, but you can make it better by putting your hand right here, Miss. "It's kind of sore." I belatedly realized I hadn't showered after my ride and fight; if she got too close to my armpits, she'd probably pass out.

"Did you take your painkillers yet, Joe?"

I shook my head.

"How stupid is that?" She turned away and started taking things out of her shopping bag. A box of pasta, a jar of sauce. A bottle of red wine. Trying not to look at me, but sneaking glances.

"I was waiting for you." A bottle of red wine. That meant romance, didn't it? Friends didn't bring over red wine. Lovers did. I glanced at the label; French. Oh, yeah, she was definitely planning some hands-on nursing.

Below my waist, I felt my mood indicator shift from "somewhat interested" to "interested."

"Okay, Mr. Macho, so how about popping a pill now?" She glanced over her shoulder at me, and her face was flaming. How the hell could she work as a prostitute if she was getting embarrassed just standing with me in my kitchen?

And then I got it; she wasn't being a professional. Whatever was going on here, it was personal.

And that made my job easier, if I didn't mind a faint nagging twinge from old Jiminy Cricket, telling me that nice guys didn't interrogate on the first date.

"I wasn't exactly being macho. I just can't get the jar open with one hand."

I handed her the bottle of ibuprofen, enjoying the play of emotions flitting across her face. She shook out a pill and was handing it to me when I saw her eyes flicker down.

Oh, shit, no wonder she was blushing. I wasn't completely erect, but bicycle shorts don't leave much to the imagination.

"Here," she said, giving me the pill.

"Marlowe . . ."

What was I going to say? I haven't a clue, because in the next moment she reached out and put her hand on my dick. Just like that. As all the blood in my brain rushed south, it occurred to me that the lady looked almost as surprised by what she'd done as I was.

And then she squeezed, and I pretty much stopped thinking altogether.

marlowe

The problem with acting on impulse, I discovered, was that impulses didn't come with a plan of action. Behaving in a manner that was out of character for me would eventually make a great new chapter for my book, but in the meanwhile I had my hand on the man's erection. What now?

I could grab him and kiss him until we were horizontal, except that I had my period and that complicated everything.

I could yank my fingers back and say, woops.

I could give him a hand job, as Nora Barnacle did for James Joyce on their first date, seizing his erotic literary imagination in a grip that lasted decades.

"Marlowe." Joe's voice sounded slightly strangled. "What're we doing here?"

"Not sure." I wasn't ready for sex, but I didn't want to be a coward or a tease. I wasn't sure what had made me seize the moment, as it were, except for the fact that Joe had turned out to be so attractive I couldn't think straight and I was playing a part here. I tightened my fingers, and beneath the slick black nylon of his shorts, I felt him harden even more. He seemed to have a definite curve to him, and I slid my hand down, trying to determine its exact shape.

"Whoa, hold on there." He put his hand over mine and I could feel the tremor in his taut stomach muscles. "I didn't invite you here to service me, M."

At that, I did pull my hand away, but he grabbed my fingers and brought them to his lips. "Not trying to insult you, darlin'."

Our eyes met. Oh boy, was I in trouble here. Back when we'd been talking on the phone, I'd definitely had the power in this strange, quasi-relationship we had going on. But the moment I'd actually seen the man, I felt the kind of knee-trembling lust that I'd last felt at the age of sixteen.

Because Joe had the good/bad boy thing going for him. Not just the look, either, but the whole package: the way he stood, loose-limbed and easy in his body, the way his dark hair fell over his forehead in a cowlick wave, the watchful, ironic amusement in his deep-set eyes. When I'd grabbed his injured hand, I'd caught the pheromone-rich scent of healthy, sweaty male, and suddenly the years fell away and I was a teenager again, driven by hormones and the primal urge to connect somewhere, anywhere, with someone who wasn't family.

Think of something to say, Marlowe.

But all I could do was stand there, my hand held to his mouth, in stupefied silence. I didn't know what to say to him. I wanted to back out the door. I wanted to undo the last two minutes and be a woman of mystery again. I wanted to trace the shape of his lips with my fingers.

I traced the shape of his lips with my fingers. Thin

upper lip, fuller on bottom, bracketed by smile lines. The skin on his jaw was rough with the beginnings of his beard.

I watched his face change. His eyes went from guarded to surprised, and then, when my fingers slipped inside his mouth, to something that almost resembled anger.

He pulled my hand away, and I wobbled, righting myself with my other hand on the padded muscle of his shoulder. Our bodies brushed—my breasts to his chest, his erection against my stomach—and one of us made a sound, a wince—and we were pressed up against each other, my hand at the back of his neck, in his thick hair, his hand braced against my lower back and rear, pushing me into him while our mouths fed off of each other.

It happened so fast I barely had time to think about it. While we kissed like soldiers on the eve of battle, eyes closed, his tongue plunging into my mouth as if he could find satisfaction there, my skirt got rucked up to my waist. It registered that we were the wrong heights—he nipped me and I stopped kissing him long enough for him to lift me one-handed onto the kitchen counter. Then he came back and his hands were on my breasts, slipping under my shirt, over my ribcage. I spread my thighs, and he stepped closer; I grabbed his rear and he started moving against me in long slides. He stopped to insinuate his hand between our bodies, moving his long, slightly calloused fingers up my leg, toward my panties. I yanked his hair, hard, bringing his head up.

"Not that."

"What?"

"I, uh, have my period."

"Doesn't bother me." His eyes were so dark, it was impossible to tell what he was thinking.

"It bothers me."

His hand moved under my shirt, toward my breast, and suddenly I remembered that the brassiere I was wearing was of the ugly white cotton variety.

"Wait."

"What now?"

"Over the clothes only."

Joe looked confused and just the tiniest bit exasperated. "Did you or did you not just grab my dick?"

"Maybe this was a bad idea, Joe . . ."

"No, no, I can live with over the clothes only. Any other restrictions I should know about?"

"Not that I can think of . . ."

This time when our eyes met he grabbed my wrists and slammed them back against the wall behind me.

"Good," he said, in a clipped, gruff voice I hadn't heard from him before. His cop voice, I guessed. "So no more talking."

"Or what—you'll arrest me?" I rocked my hips and watched his eyes half close.

There was a sheen of sweat on his upper lip. "Or maybe I'll tie you up."

"Then maybe I won't stop talking." Wow. I hadn't realized I had cop fantasies. Funny how true lust casts a spotlight on all your unexplored shadow parts.

Something flickered in Joe's eyes and he smiled, a slow, carnal, knowing smile. "Oh, it's like that, is it?" He tightened his fingers on my wrists. Without another word, he began moving against me, so erect I could see the tip of his penis over his shorts when he pulled back.

And then he was pressed to me and it was like high school again, desperate friction as he slid his Lycra-encased erection over my panties again and again, and without warning I felt myself come, a sudden shock of an orgasm. I fell forward, my wrists still held prisoner, and bit into the warm muscle of his shoulder.

Joe made a sound low in his throat.

I leaned back, inhaling deeply as I slid my hands out of Joe's grasp. I was still tingling between my legs, and, if anything, more turned on than before, but when I looked up at Joe I saw that his face was still taut, intent; he almost appeared to be in pain. For a moment I considered slipping into the bathroom and getting a towel, but I wasn't sure that I was ready for intercourse, let alone messy intercourse, with a relative stranger.

On the other hand, I couldn't just leave him like this. I watched his eyes as I insinuated my hand into his shorts. His eyes shuttered closed as I slid my fist over his shaft once, twice, three times before he grunted and I felt him contract and pulse.

And then Joe was leaning over me, his forehead against the kitchen cabinet. My right hand was still down his shorts. I waited a moment, and then another moment. I began to suspect something was wrong.

I had no idea what to do next. Joe was still half slumped between my legs, his eyes closed. "Joe?" No answer. Oh, hell, was this going to be one of those absolutely miserable aftermaths, where the guy was all guilty and regretful? I released my grip on his penis, which was still surprisingly hard. "You okay, Joe?"

He opened his eyes and they were bright with tears. Oh, hell, this was about the ex-wife, wasn't it? Or else it was his ambivalence about having sex with someone he thought was a call girl. I summoned my reserves and said, softly but firmly, "Joe, I don't know what's going on in your head right now, but if you're thinking that what just happened is wrong or dirty, then you should . . ."

"My hand." His voice was barely audible. "I think I've broken it."

joe

"You sure you don't want me to come along to the emergency room with you?" Marlowe leaned into the open rear window of the cab where I was sitting, her head blotting out the sun. Jesus, how could it still be so early—I felt like I'd lived this day twice already. I moved my right hand away from the sill and wished myself back to this lovely, crisp spring morning, on a bike heading up the Palisades. Away from people.

I attempted a smile. "Nah, no need to turn this into the lousiest date you ever had. You go on home, Marlowe."

"I don't mind. Really." Some mascara had smeared under her hazel-green eyes, making her look less like a prim lawyer and more like a girl who'd been up to no good. "I'd like to help if I can."

Jesus, what did it take to convince her to leave me alone? "That's really nice of you, but you don't need to sit around for hours in some hospital."

"I could bring a book."

"No, really, I'll be fine. I'm not much for being fussed over."

"Oh." She straightened and a shaft of sunlight struck

the sidewalk around her, making it glitter. I had to squint now, and talk to the shadowy outline of Marlowe.

"So I'll call you soon, all right. Thanks for dropping by, M." I sank back into the seat, closed my eyes, and thought, Come on, driver, drive, drive, drive.

But Marlowe wasn't done with me.

"Hey, Joe? I think you're forgetting something." I opened my eyes; her voice and face were in neutral, but if she'd been a perp I would've cuffed her as a precaution. What was I supposed to do, kiss her, make another firm date, tell her I loved her? "I'm sorry, but I'm not sure what you . . ."

"That'll be one hundred and fifty dollars."

Quick as a flash, I said, "Huh?"

Marlowe leaned back down to the window, and this time there was no mistaking the anger in her eyes. "You called me over and told me you were willing to pay one hundred and fifty dollars. Which, for the record, is way below my usual fee for house calls."

Oh, Christ. I was way too tired to deal with this, especially with the taxi driver watching us in the rearview mirror and my hand throbbing like a son of a bitch. "Listen," I said, "I'm sorry to end things like this, but in case you forgot, I just broke my goddamn hand."

Marlowe smiled the way women do when they're about to slide the knife in. "Don't worry, Joe, I'm not a girlfriend feeling upset because you're treating her like a whore the moment you're finished with sex. I'm a whore and I couldn't care less about whether or not I'm going to see you again. What I do care about is the fact that you owe me one hundred and fifty dollars."

"First of all, if it's about the money, then why do you

sound so ticked off, Marlow? Now cut this bullshit. You know that I did not call you over to fuck you. Christ, I didn't fuck you, so what exactly am I supposed to be paying for?"

Marlowe narrowed her eyes. "And you know," she said, "that you called me over to take care of you, and that the hand is just a convenient excuse for your going into full emotional retreat. Or is it just that you're cheap?"

Now there was a word to slap you in the face. I fumbled in my back pocket for my wallet, clumsy with anger. "I'm afraid that at the moment, all I have on me is forty in bills." I stuck it out for her to take.

"You'll need that for cabs."

"So what do you want—a check? My credit card number?" I watched her face, but she had that wasp impassive thing down to an art. "Oh, hey, I've got it, maybe you'd like the password to my savings account?"

"You know what? I don't want a thing from you, Joe."

"A hooker who doesn't want money! I'll bet it's Julia Roberts and she really just wants to save my miserable ass. Why didn't you say so in the first place, pretty woman?"

"Get lost, Joe." And with that, she walked away, sensible pumps clicking on the pavement.

The cab driver met my eyes in his mirror. "She a hooker?"

"Yeah."

"She don't look like a hooker."

I tuned the driver out for the rest of the ride as he told me some long story about his wife and money. There was a moral, but I got out and tipped him through the window before he could relate it.

At the emergency room, a nurse with a lot of large, dark freckles took the briefest of looks at my hand and told me to take a seat.

It was clear to me that it was going to be a long wait. There were four cases ahead of me, none of them emergencies. I was betting that the fat guy with the putrid bandages on his foot, the ancient lady with shingles, the pregnant teenager with the screaming toddler, and the emaciated man didn't know what medical insurance was, let alone possess it. So they bought a few pills off their block's resident witch doctor, bred themselves some hearty, antibiotic resistant germs, then raced off to their local E.R. to spread the joy.

Jesus, my hand hurt. How long before they amputated fatty's foot, cleaned up the old lady's bloody forehead, gave the kid a shot of amoxicillin, and . . . I had no idea what the thin man needed, but the way he kept convulsing with uncontrollable, hacking coughs made everyone else sit as far from him as possible.

No one wanted to sit next to me, either, which reminded me how long it had been since I'd had a shower.

In the absence of any distractions, I seriously considered thinking about what had just happened with Marlowe, but I couldn't find the energy, what with my hand swelling up like a Macy's balloon and all. So I shoved our little friction fiesta to the side of my brain, along with the Tony Russo case, the state of my relationship with the other detectives in my precinct, my prospects for getting back on a task force, and having to see my ex-wife next week at Lurch's wedding.

All in all, I had a lot to not think about.

I tried to sleep, but the minute I nodded off my name

was called. It turned out that in addition to my seriously bruised knuckles, I'd dislocated two fingers and strained my wrist. I went home with my hand in a removable cast and a bottle of Codeine Tylenol and resolved to call Marlowe in the morning. But I knew that the odds of my actually taking the pills or picking up the phone were equally slim. It just all felt like too much. Maybe what Marlowe had said the other night was correct; maybe I was depressed. Or maybe I knew that getting involved with a woman who clearly had problems of her own was not the brightest of ideas.

My last thought before going to bed at the ridiculous hour of nine P.M. was that the lieutenant was probably right: Tony Russo's death had been an accident. What was improbable about a horny guy ending his life by lying on the floor and rolling himself up in plastic wrap? After all, I'd managed to dry hump my way to a bum hand. The way I saw it, all it took to be a dangerous idiot was a stiff dick and a little spare time.

From now on, I was going to work on whatever cases I was given and not go looking for trouble. I was going to quit the Upper West Side millionaire's health club and start playing basketball in the park again.

And if I got lonely, I was going to buy myself a fucking cat.

marlowe

Sitting in the midst of the muted earth tones of my office, Savannah LaBrecque looked out of place, like a carefully cultivated rose in a rock garden. She was wearing a cheerful pink spring halter dress but as she sat down in the same leather chair she'd chosen last time, I noticed that there were dark shadows under her eyes.

"How have you been?"

"Great now that we're getting some nice weather. Hey, you've cut your hair."

"Yes, I decided to try something new."

Savannah cocked her head to one side, considering my shorn state. "Y'know, I can never do that—go real short and sassy. Most men really prefer longer hair. But that look really suits you."

"Why don't you tell me what's been going on with you since we last met?"

Savannah's own light brown hair had been pinned up into a loose chignon, and she wore it with the same casual elegance as the kitten-heeled sandal she swung back and forth. "Well. Let's see. My momma's still acting kind of strange. She says she hears clicks on the phone and gets real paranoid about taking any new clients on."

"Do you think she's being paranoid?" Emphasis on the you.

"I think she's losing it. She says she thinks there's something suspicious about that guy I told you about last time. She says that any man who doesn't want to get laid the conventional way ought to come with a great big warning sign: I am a potential axe murderer."

Savannah leaned forward. "She keeps going on and on about how she figured I'd know better than to go trusting a man, after what we went through when I was growing up. It's like I'm offending her sensibilities by having normal female desires. She wants me to live in a little bubble with her and those damn yappy little dogs of hers, but I can't help the way I feel about this guy."

I tried to figure out which part of this to respond to first: The hint of some possible domestic strife in Savannah's childhood, the mother's possessiveness, or this new, potential romance.

"So your mother seems both generally more suspicious and specifically more suspicious of this man. Savannah, just for convenience, let's think of something to call him—it doesn't have to be his real name." Like many of my clients, Savannah seemed reluctant to name the current object of her affections. With some people, it was an unconscious desire to keep a relatively minor player from appearing too important in therapy; with others, it was a reluctance to expose an affair that had some element of secrecy to it.

"We could call him Brad. After Brad Pitt."

"All right. So, have you seen Brad?"

"Just once. Other than that, we've talked on the phone. Mainly personal stuff about me—where I grew up, what it's like doing what I do. Which is funny—most men only want to talk about themselves. But I guess in his case it's the research he's doing."

It struck me that Savannah had lost some weight since I'd seen her two weeks earlier. She'd been slender before; now her fine-boned arms seemed alarmingly fragile despite their golden tan. Of course, I'd already surmised that Savannah might not be leading the healthiest of lifestyles, but did that mean she was using drugs? Dieting in some extreme fashion? Might she have an eating disorder?

Aware that confronting these issues directly might elicit defensiveness, perhaps even deception, I decided to just focus on the man for the moment. "Remind me what he's working on."

"Will you believe I still don't know? He just keeps asking me things before I can think what to ask him back. Sometimes I can get him to open up a little—for example, I found out that he's so smart he skipped a bunch of grades."

I wasn't sure what was normal behavior for a man flirting with a prostitute, but if Joe was anything to go by, they weren't all complete ciphers. "So how do you check out your potential clients? Do you get recommendations? Did someone vouch for Brad?"

Savannah jiggled her sandaled foot. Was she annoyed by the question? "Of course. A very highly connected someone in politics vouched for him."

I waited.

"And I have an instinct about him. A good one."

She was lying. "What happened when you saw him in person?"

Savannah's smile was a schoolgirl mixture of embarrassment and pride. "Well. We stayed downstairs, in the library. He asked me about guys who are into choking—you know, cutting off the oxygen to heighten sensation? What was safe, what wasn't. He told me some stuff I didn't know—some Greek or Latin words that meant the desire for sex and the desire for death, and how one desire could get caught up in the other."

Eros and thanatos, the impulse to lose oneself in pleasure and the impulse to lose oneself in oblivion. Maybe Brad was a sex researcher doing a book on autoerotic practices. Maybe Brad was a social-working minister trying to understand the physiological bases of aberrant behavior. Maybe he was an inveterate masturbator looking for a new thrill.

But a nasty little shiver went down my back, all the same. I focused on Savannah, who had finally started talking more freely.

"So then I got to talking to Brad about stuff that I like, and how I was thinking about him when I did it, and . . ." She lowered her chin and grinned, theatrically sly. "Let's just say I think we both enjoyed ourselves. Even though he didn't actually get off. I actually kind of liked the fact that he wouldn't touch himself in front of me. He's a real boy scout, which makes him a challenge. And yes, I am aware that that's a big part of the attraction for me."

I knew without looking at the clock that we were running out of time. I thought for a moment—I didn't want to wade in wearing galoshes here, but sometimes being direct worked. "Is there something you're not telling me today, Savannah?"

She paused. "Well, it's funny, but . . . I keep bursting into tears. Yesterday I couldn't find a lipstick I liked, an old one, and all of a sudden I'm thinking what's the point, I'm out of control, I can't hold on to anything. I don't know why I'm so unhappy. I don't know why I care so much about this. I love it when he calls and then when he doesn't it's like I sink into this pit. I keep feeling like everything is hinging on whether or not I get to speak with him. And I keep wanting more and knowing I can't ask for more, because that's not the game we're playing." There was a sheen of tears in her eyes. "Am I in love?"

You're in transference, I thought. Love requires knowing at least something about the other person. All transference requires is that you imagine you know something. Longing for Daddy? Why not just transfer all that long-buried emotion to some new authority figure— a doctor, a researcher, a cop. It's not a bad thing, in and of itself; without it, therapy would be far less effective.

"I wouldn't call it love, because you don't really know this man," I said. "What you're feeling is powerful, though. I think because Brad is the first man you have a feeling of mystery about, you're granting him a significance that's out of all proportion to the role he really plays in your life."

"I don't get you."

"I think you're in love with the idea of Brad."

This, I could see she understood. "So what do I do— just convince myself I'm not falling in love?"

"I'd say just be aware that some of this man's magical

142

qualities are ones you're investing him with. Don't give all your power away, Savannah. Pay attention to what you really know and don't know about him."

"You'd think I'd know better, wouldn't you? Given my profession and all?"

I thought about Joe, who hadn't called since he'd basically told me to get lost three days ago, and thought, you and me both, Sister. And then I thought, when it came to the perverse logic of men, Savannah was the expert here.

"Let me ask you a question, Savannah. In your experience, what does it mean when a man needs to set and maintain clear boundaries at all times? If you looked at Brad for a moment as a client, what could you tell me about him? What could you surmise about him given the fact that although he is interested, he does not seem to want to explore a physical relationship with you, or at least not yet?"

Savannah straightened in her chair, suddenly more self-assured. "When a guy has to set down a lot of rules about how you get together, I'd say it means that he has control issues. Which means that he'd probably like to be tied up or to tie someone up, depending."

"Depending on what?"

"On whether or not he's got power in real life. Your average Joes with control issues, your construction workers or sales guys or computer techs, they all want to tie you up. But if the guy's a big businessman in real life, then what he really gets off on is the woman taking charge."

I tried not to think about my average Joe with control issues. "What's your guess about Brad, Savannah? Does he hold a position of power or not?"

A small crease appeared between Savannah's green

eyes. "It's funny. Something about the way he talks—the words he uses, the way he phrases things—almost makes me think lawyer or cop."

My brain was buzzing. I'd need time to go over this session, because something was bothering me, although I couldn't put my finger on it quite yet. Some connection I wasn't making.

In the meantime, I thought of one last question I had to ask. "So when it comes to cops with control issues and bondage—who ties whom up?"

It had occurred to me that Marlowe was probably pissed off because I still hadn't called her. That didn't mean I was about to go apologize, however. The way I figured it, it was me who really should have been mad. I felt she'd shown a rather startling lack of empathy for a man in extreme physical pain.

But if I knew women, she'd be all bent out of shape about the way I'd pushed off her attempts to mother me— in other words, If I wanted to see her again, I'd have to eat a fucking double-decker feeling sandwich first.

So now I was facing the age-old male dilemma: To call or not to call? On the whole, I was thinking that it might be better to let the whole thing drop, when the phone rang.

"Hello." The phone said private caller, but I didn't need caller ID to know it was going to be Marlowe. I had a cop's sixth sense about these things. I felt a little surge of adrenaline and realized I was glad. "I knew it was going to be you."

"That is amazing, Joseph."

"Paolina?" Great fucking ESP I had.

"I just wanted a chance to talk to you before the wedding."

"I'm listening." My voice was steady but my heart was slamming. What the hell was going on here? Was she going to explain that damn newspaper article? Apologize for forgetting to include me in her "best undressed" list? Was she breaking up with pretty actor boy and needing me to cheer her up?

"Joseph, I . . . how are you?"

"Fine."

"Really fine?"

"Paolina, what is this?"

"I'm just a little concerned about you. You know, after we had that lunch last month, I um, realized that neither of us had been prepared for what happened, and uh, I was just dealing with discovering that Lucas had been screwing around on me, and . . ."

"Oh, please. What do I look like, the walking wounded? Don't worry, I'm not going to fall apart at the sight of you. Or has the new guy just dumped you or fucked around on you already? You calling to see if I'm still available?"

"Mario and I are very happy."

"Well, mazel tov, sweetheart. I'm so glad your search for true love has come to yet another speedy conclusion."

"Joe, you're making this very difficult for me."

"Aw, baby, that's awful. But I'm sure you can console yourself with the best sex you ever had. Oh, wait, no, that was the other one. What's this one, the meeting of minds?"

"Don't be such a bastard, Joe."

I took a deep breath. So what if she'd left me to concentrate on her career and had wound up concentrating on famous men? Maybe it was all one and the same. "Sorry," I said. I wanted to say, So Lucas is second runner-up and Mario is the best, what the hell was four years of sex with me like, chopped liver? Instead I leaned my head down and pinched the bridge of my nose hard, trying to ward off a headache.

"Go on. Tell me why you called."

Silence.

"You're not pregnant, are you?"

"No, but I did see my gynecologist lately, because I . . ."

"Jeez, Paolina, you think you could spare me the details of your incredibly busy love life?"

I heard her start to say something, stop, start again.

"Spit it out."

"Did you—you found what you were looking for the other day? The Hall and Oates CD?"

The way she said it let me know what this was really all about—a fucking sympathy call just in case I couldn't keep it together, seeing her with the new guy.

"Yeah, sorry about that, Paolina. Listen, I've got to get going here. I'm picking my girlfriend up on the way to the church."

"You're bringing a girlfriend?" She sounded surprised, but not unhappy.

"Yeah, I'm bringing her. She started complaining that we spend all our dates at home."

Long pause as Paolina processed that report. "So are you two serious?"

"Yeah," I said. "I think she's it. The one. I can talk to her like no one I've ever met before. And touching her makes me feel like a fucking teenager."

"It'll be nice to meet her."

"Gotta run, Paolina. Thanks for calling." I hung up the phone before she could say good-bye. Shit. Shit, shit, shit. What the fuck had I been thinking, that I could bring my imaginary girlfriend to Lurch's wedding?

And then a split second later, I knew exactly what the fuck I had been thinking. That, if by some miracle she was available and had a formal dress ready, I could bring Marlowe. Except for the slight complication that I wasn't quite sure what the going rate for pissed-off call girls was.

Whatever the price was, I suspected the down payment would be a piece of my hide.

marlowe

The moment he phoned I changed my mind. Up until his call, I'd been positive that I was too irritated with him to want to continue this game. Whether or not I was playing a part, that had been my body rubbing up against his, and the rejection of my offer of help had felt personal enough.

It would make for a nice closing essay for my book: Lie all you want to, but when you're flirting with intimacy, you don't really get to leave yourself at home, out of harm's way. That was magazine worthy, wasn't it? So I had what I'd come for.

So what if I was spending another weekend on my own? I had facial masques to apply, sit-ups to attempt, my toes to paint. Maybe I'd adopt a kitten to keep Burt and me company. Even if Joe never called again, it wouldn't matter, because I wasn't intending to see him again regardless.

And then I picked up the phone and heard his voice—wry, self-assured, with that godawful New York accent—and felt an instant wash of relief that it wasn't all over. "Marlowe? It's Joe."

What to say? How to sound? Cool, angry, friendly, neutral? "Hello," I said. Damn it. Too tentative. Almost a question.

"You still pissed off at me?"

Yes, incredibly. Why didn't you call earlier? No, I don't give any man that kind of power over me. I twisted a silver and gold ring on my finger and went into reflexive therapy mode. "What do you think, Joe?"

"I think maybe you're a little oversensitive, given your profession . . . your former profession, I should say. But I wasn't treating you like I'd paid for it, Marlowe. I'd fucked . . . I'd hurt my hand pretty badly and I'm not the greatest patient in the world. So you don't have any reason to be hurt."

"Joe, that is the biggest load of bull. What I did . . . I mean, what I, when I . . ."

"Put your hand on my dick."

"Yes. When I . . . took charge that night, you lost control of the situation. And while I am aware that you were in some serious physical discomfort there, tell me the thought never crossed your mind that now you wouldn't have to worry about what came after the sticky part."

There was a pause. "Yeah," Joe said. "Maybe I did need a little time to regroup. I wasn't really planning on what happened happening."

Oh, God, I'd ambushed him. He didn't want me. I'd forced myself on him. No, that was ridiculous. "And you don't like giving up control."

Another pause, longer than the first. "You might have something there."

I waited, as I'd been trained to do, but he didn't say

On the Couch

anything else. Of course, he was a cop; he knew how to use silence as well as I did. Maybe better.

"Marlowe. One other thing."

"Yes."

"Don't ever call a Jewish guy cheap."

For a full beat and a half, I had no idea what he was talking about. Then I remembered standing in front of his taxi, arguing about money. "You're Jewish?"

"You got a problem with that?"

"I didn't know there were Jewish cops."

"Sweetheart, there are Jewish cops, Jewish thieves, Jewish good guys, and Jewish creeps. The only thing there is not that is Jewish is a fucking worldwide Jewish conspiracy, because no three Jews ever agreed on anything."

What did he think I was, some redneck hillbilly? "I grew up in Manhattan, Joe, not some small town where they've never heard of bagels and lox. And I am not prejudiced."

He snorted. "I grew up in Manhattan, too, M, and everyone's prejudiced."

"Okay, that may be true, but I'm prejudiced in your favor. I find your being Jewish attractive. I was born into a family that didn't do a lot of talking or touching—I like that whole big, fat, ethnic wedding thing." I listened to myself and felt a wave of embarrassed heat. "Not that I'm thinking about marriage or relationships here. I mean, I know that I kind of forced what happened between us and that your response was a purely physical one." Oh, God, strike me down now and spare me the rest of this conversation.

"Ah, jeez, you're killing me here. Listen, Marlowe. It

151

was good. What we did. What you started." He took a breath. "It was dangerously good."

Why was I on the verge of crying? He was admitting things. This was what I'd hoped he would do. "Why dangerous, Joe?"

His voice was so low it took me a moment to make out what he'd said. "Because I don't really want to get involved right now. I mean, you're an amazingly attractive woman, but I really don't think I'm up for the whole dating thing right now."

Which would explain why you were calling a prostitute, I thought. No surprises here, no reason for me to be getting all weepy. Get it together, Marlowe! I inhaled sharply. "Okay," I said.

"You crying, Marlowe?"

"Allergies."

"I get those. Hay? Pollen? Cats?"

Men. "Something like that."

"So, uh, I don't suppose, now that we've worked all this out, that you would consent to meet me as my escort to a wedding."

What? "What?"

"My, uh, ex-wife is dating an actor . . . Mario somebody . . . and she just called to rub it in, and we're meeting up in about half an hour at my buddy Lurch's wedding, and I thought, if you were willing . . . you see, the thing is, when she broke up with me, she said it was about needing the time to focus on her goddamn career, but here she is, seeing this other guy she just told a newspaper is the best sex she ever had, which leaves me feeling, like, what the hell was going on between us for four years, 'cause I thought that was the best sex I ever had, and I guess what I'm trying to say here is . . . do you want to come along?"

"Are you paying me?" My voice was as neutral as I could make it.

"I, uh, sure."

"You don't sound sure, Joe, even though you've just finished telling me that you do not want to get involved with me. Am I wrong in assuming that you're calling and asking me to pose as your girlfriend?"

"I didn't say I didn't want to get involved with you, I said I'm not up for dating."

"So you'd like to hire me as a professional escort for the day."

"I guess you could put it like that."

"Were you thinking of this as something else, Joe?"

"To be perfectly honest, I wasn't so much thinking as reacting out of instinct."

"Uh-huh."

"How much would you charge?"

"For you? Two-fifty. Plus what you owe me." I'd never realized how empowering asking for money could be. I felt stronger, more desirable, and strangely enough, more worthy now that I'd put a price on my company.

"You have a dress? Something classy but sexy? My ex is a clothes designer."

"I've got a dress, Joe."

"And makeup? You'll have time to do the whole makeup and jewelry thing?"

"Of course."

"Okay, M, you've got a deal. Meet me at the Cathedral

of St. John the Divine in half an hour. You know where that is? One hundred and twelve and Amsterdam. Stay till the reception and I'll give you three-fifty."

"Joe?"

"What?"

"This has nothing to do with your being Jewish, but you actually owe me four hundred." I hung up before he could argue.

I had twenty minutes to make myself look expensive.

joe

I shouldn't have asked her to meet me in front of the cathedral. First of all, it looked suspicious; wouldn't a real girlfriend have been staying over at my apartment?

Second, I felt damn conspicuous, standing around like a waiter with a yellow rose in my jacket lapel, smiling and nodding as all my former friends pulled up in their SUVs and minivans, unloaded their wives and kids, and then drove off in search of parking. My presence was supposed to indicate to out of towners that they were, in fact, at the right place—I figured Lurch hadn't known what role I should play and this was the social equivalent of the outfield.

"How are you, Joe?" "Nice to see you, Joe." "Joe! I didn't realize we'd see you here!" I was kissed and patted by three different blond matrons, each wearing a version of the same boxy silk dress, each tugging two or more sulky children by the hand. Juan Garcia, Lurch's best man, appeared with a drooling baby on his hip.

"Man! Have you seen Lurch yet? He was up way too late last night."

155

"Working or playing?"

"Working, man. The case is about to crack wide open. The brothel's looking to get in a Texas cowgirl so they'll have something fresh to offer a very important visitor. And you know Big Daddy likes his horses."

I made a skeptical sound halfway between a snort and grunt. "Yeah, sounds real solid, Juan. So what was Lurch doing, auditioning ropers?"

Juan laughed politely, but I could tell he didn't get it. "Hey," he said, "speaking of the mob, you look like a made man in that suit. Very stylish."

"You, too, man." I was lying. Like most of the guys on the force, Juan was wearing a wide-shouldered suit that looked like it was purchased back in 1988 and standard issue cheap black shit-kickers on his feet.

There was a moment of awkward silence between us.

"So," I began, at the same moment that Juan said, "Damn. Where's Dolores? She said take the baby for a minute and then she ran off."

Which made me wonder where my ex-wife might be lurking. I realized I had no idea whether she had planned on arriving early to help the bride arrange the dress or was going to swan in late like a celebrity. Well, at least Paolina wouldn't be able to find fault with the way I was dressed; I was wearing the suit and shoes she'd picked out for me for our own wedding. Or maybe she would find fault—maybe it was tacky, my wearing my wedding suit. Shit. I glanced up at the great, gray, Gothic façade of the Cathedral, silhouetted against an equally gray sky, and wished myself on an island in the Caribbean, about to dive under sixty feet of water.

"Here, man, can you hold Talisa for a moment?"

"I've only got one good hand, Juan." I held up the removable cast on my right hand: So sorry, find another babysitter.

"So hold her with that one." Juan pushed his daughter into my arms, along with something that looked like a pink knapsack with a baby bottle in the side pocket. By the time I shifted the baby so she wasn't resting on my cast and got out a "Hey!" he was already charging up the stairs. "Yo, Juan, what am I supposed to do with this kid?"

Juan flashed me a quick grin over his shoulder and then darted inside the church, presumably to find Lurch and the other guys sharing one last shot of whiskey and cigarette before the service.

The baby looked at me with dark, unblinking eyes. I looked back at her, and it was like looking into the eyes of a snake: alien creature, alien thoughts. It did seem to me, however, that her smooth, plump little arms were being pinched by the cuffs of her frilly yellow lace dress.

I sat down on a step and unbuttoned her sleeves with my left hand. Her skin was impossibly soft and fragile. How was it possible to go around in the world wearing skin like that? She stuck her hand in her mouth and chewed on it while staring at me some more. Then, after due consideration, she extracted her hand and patted my face with her moist fingertips. Something about the gesture struck me as being almost a kind of benediction.

I'd always thought children didn't get interesting until they were five or so—old enough to throw a ball, ride a bike, eat junk food and not throw up. But suddenly I could see the whole attraction of babies—they were kind of like human lapdogs, simple and approving and surprisingly pleasant to hold. It struck me that if I wanted one of these, I really needed to do something about having one, and fast, otherwise I was going to be one of those decrepit dads doddering around the playground, too out of it to know when his kids had started screwing around or doing drugs.

Maybe I should let my mother fix me up with some Rachel or Rebecca and let it all happen. After all, when you stripped all the pretty packaging off of marriage, what you got was a partnership to make and raise a kid. In my opinion, marriage wasn't about undying love or even undying lust, it was about creating a family. Why couldn't people accept that simple fact, instead of lying optimistically to each other about how they were going to behave in a few years' time and then splitting up the minute she gained ten pounds or he started having a love affair with the television set?

As for gay marriages, all I could say is, if they wanted it, they could have it. What could gays do to the institution of marriage that straights hadn't already been doing for time out of mind? Till death do we part used to make sense, back when people dropped dead at thirty; these days it was a lie nine times out of ten.

At least Paolina and I had only lied in a judge's chambers. I couldn't imagine getting married in a building that had been under construction for the past century. Lurch had told me they were using authentic medieval methods to construct the cathedral, which meant that by the time they completed it, I was going to be dead. In fact, my kids were also going to be dead, assuming I had kids.

These were morbid thoughts to be having with a baby in my lap. I tried to crack a smile at Talisa and she glanced away, clearly worried about the state of my mental health. "Da?"

"So, Joseph, is this the girlfriend you were talking about?"

I looked up and there was Paolina, looking distractingly voluptuous in a flimsy red ruffled dress and three-inch heels. She was holding hands with a man and I glanced at him, momentarily disconcerted; his face seemed familiar, but after a moment I realized that was just because I'd seen him on TV.

I got to my feet, noticing that Talisa was now staring at Paolina with the same owl-eyed absorption she'd previously trained on me. "I've decided to start seeing younger women."

"I think I'll just ignore the feeble attempt at humor. Joseph, meet Mario. Mario, this is Joe." I realized she'd changed her hair, straightened it or something.

"So you're Joe. I've heard a lot about you, man. Now, just remember, my guns are just props, so just don't shoot me, all right?"

I smiled at Mario just like I was supposed to and shook his hand. I heard a little shriek behind me and turned; it was one of the blond wives, hysterical at the sight of Paolina's actor.

"Oh my God," she was saying, "oh my God, oh my God, it's you. It's you!"

"It's probably me, but I'm never completely sure without a script," said Mario with a smile that creased his left cheek.

"Oh my God," said the wife.

In front of me, Paolina touched the lapel of my jacket. "Nice suit."

Ah, crap, so it had been a mistake to wear these clothes. I tried to think of something to say, but standing this close to her was doing my head in. I kept wondering, had she rewritten her past so that, instead of a starring role, I barely warranted a footnote, or had she never really loved me the way I thought she had?

Not that it mattered anymore. "About your phone call, Paolina . . ."

"Yes?"

"You don't need to worry about me. I'm really doing fine."

Paolina frowned a little, and I sensed that I was missing something. "That's great, Joseph. Maybe later, after the wedding, we could talk again . . ."

"Sure thing." But I said it like I knew we wouldn't. Shit, now she was frowning again. "Now, you're not going to ream me out for not communicating, are you? I thought that was the whole point of being divorced—no problems left to work out."

She gave me a strange look and I thought, what the hell did I say now? Back when I was eight or so and there wasn't much evening TV for kids, I used to watch the Newlywed Game, laughing as the grooms discovered they didn't really know their new brides' favorite movie, most embarrassing moment, secret turn-on. Now I realized it was always the men getting it wrong; the women were usually on the money.

"So," said Paolina, "where is this girlfriend?"

As I started to speak, my eyes cut up and to the left, a classic liar's mistake. And then I glanced over my shoulder again, and there was Marlowe, striding toward us.

"Actually," I said, "that's her now." I'm not sure what

I was expecting my date for hire to wear, but it wasn't a forest green gown that looked like something out of a Robin Hood movie. I felt a rush of embarrassed heat in my face as everyone in visual range turned and tracked her progress.

"What's she got on, Joe, a costume?"

I glanced at Paolina. "Don't ask me. I don't understand the first thing about fashion, remember?"

"Well, clearly, neither does she."

"And thank God for that." I said it to be loyal, but the truth was, Marlowe looked pretty amazing. As she came closer, I could see that she was wearing one of those old-fashioned boned things that push the breasts together and cinch the waist in. I kind of liked the fact that her hair was so short and red; it had that sexy, Annie Lennox, I'm-fucking-with-your-head attitude.

When she was close enough, I called out, "Hey, M." I couldn't put my arm around her, because I was holding the baby, so I leaned over and kissed Marlowe lightly on the mouth, as if this was how I always greeted her.

"Hello, Joe," she said, and I remembered why I'd first liked the sound of her on the phone. She had a voice for late-night radio: deep, warm, slightly amused. "Who's this little girl?"

"My friend Luis's kid. I think she needs a change, but I don't see her folks anywhere . . ."

"You might want to locate them, because from the expression on her face right now, she's about to test just how absorbent those diapers really are."

Oh, man, so that was why Talisa had started grunting. "I don't suppose you'd want to . . ."

Marlowe smiled. "I don't know what her parents look

like, and there's no way I'm changing that baby's diaper in this outfit." Then she turned to my ex, and I mumbled an introduction. "So, Paolina, Joe tells me you're a dress designer."

"Yes, I made the bride's gown." My ex-wife might not care whether or not I had a girlfriend, but I could tell from the expression on her face that it was killing her that she was having to meet Marlowe on her own, while the actor boyfriend was off being mobbed by cops' wives.

"I can't wait to see it. Now, how does that work—do you come up with ideas on your own, or do you consult with the bride first on what she has in mind?"

Clever move, Marlowe. Clearly, my date knew how to ask the kinds of questions people like to answer—which, as any cop knows, is really the first step to getting people to answer the kinds of questions they don't like.

While my ex-wife started thawing, I moved off in search of Talisa's father. "Where's Daddy gone, huh, kid?" I stepped into the cathedral, which seemed vast and shadowy and ever so slightly sinister, but maybe that was because I wasn't used to churches. The guard didn't know where anyone from the Connolly wedding might be, unless they were already in the chapel. He indicated straight back and to my left and said a name that I promptly forgot—Saint Answer? Saint Aspirin? Something like that.

Talisa had begun to smell like something riper than fruit, and I hurried along the dark corridor, sticking my head into one small room after another, whispering "Juan? Dolores?" Nothing but candles and shrines and people wearing sneakers and cameras slung around their necks.

I turned another corner and discovered a corridor that looked like the hallway of an old office building. I walked through and saw a bathroom and was about to yell out Juan's name when I heard a squelchy sound.

Now, I don't know about anyone else, but squelchy sounds in bathrooms always give me pause. This one was coming from the large, handicapped stall and was followed by a fleshy, slapping sound, then a moan, a whisper, a giggle, more slapping, more squelchiness.

Oh, lovely, I'd nearly walked in on some couple who'd decided to get in a quick screw before the ceremony. With my luck, it was Juan and his wife, which meant another good, long stretch of me holding a stinky baby.

I was about to retrace my steps when I caught a glimpse of something in the bathroom mirror. The fine hairs went up on the back of my neck, and I felt a sort of crime-scene residue of wrongness about the scene. I thought for an instant about drawing my .38, remembered in the next instant that I had only one good hand and was holding a baby, and then my feet were carrying me out of there in the time it took "fuck me" to turn into "yes, yes."

I ducked into one of the shadowy corners and willed Talisa to be silent as the slapping sounds picked up momentum. My peripheral vision had registered something in the shadows; a moment later, my mind supplied the details. What I'd half seen in the bathroom had to have been a man in a dark suit, standing in the corner. I wasn't sure how I knew the third person in that room had been there, let alone that he was a man, but I trusted my instincts. He'd been too still to be someone who'd just stumbled along, like me. Even though he hadn't been jacking off—I hadn't seen any movement—I felt pretty damned sure this guy wasn't just investigating to see who was doing the nasty.

Okay, so not a danger, just a peeping tom. Now I was curious. The moaning increased and then there was rustling, the sound of water running, and—holy shit—Juan and the goddamn bride stepped out into the hall.

Jesus Christ. At least Paolina had waited a year before cheating on me. At least I thought she had. What the hell was I supposed to do now—tell Lurch he was about to marry the biggest slut in the five boroughs? I looked at the baby in my arms and realized how similar her name was to the bride's. Talia. Talisa. How long had this affair been going on? Did Lurch not know because he didn't want to know? And if so, who was I to force him to confront the fact that his dream girl was really hot for his best friend?

While I was debating the ethics of my situation, the mystery man stepped out into the hall, head down, walking briskly back out into the main part of the cathedral.

And suddenly all thoughts of Lurch's sad fate were replaced by shock, recognition, and a dark kind of satisfaction.

Well, well, well. No wonder Davie liked wiretapping the brothel so damn much.

marlowe

It was the kind of wedding I'd seen in the movies, but had never actually attended. A full, incense-swinging, kneeling and praying ceremony. Blue-collar bridesmaids in bright pink dresses that didn't conceal the matching unicorn tattoos on their left shoulder blades. The bride had one, too, which made me think that getting permanently inked had been a prenuptial activity. There was a lot of angry whispering in Spanish behind me and I got the impression that the father of the baby Joe had been holding had been doing something he shouldn't have.

I glanced at Joe, who was looking extremely ill at ease. I remembered that he was Jewish and wondered if being in churches made him uncomfortable. It certainly made me uncomfortable; my parents had never been very religious, if you discounted my mother's worship of all things equine.

The reception was held in a pretty garden behind the cathedral, and one of the ushers kept chasing one of the resident peacocks with a fork, saying that he was hungry already. The best man, who looked like a Sinatra type at the midpoint between skinny, endearingly awkward youth and stolid, belligerent middle age, made a drunken speech with a lot of veiled references to things I didn't understand, but which made everyone else laugh. Well, everyone except for Joe.

Mario what's his name, Joe's ex-wife's boyfriend, vanished into the men's room for a while and came back happy and completely indifferent to the pigs in blanket and shrimp toast that waitpersons in black livery were passing around.

As for Joe, he said an extremely brief congratulations to the groom, who was tall and gangly and lantern-jawed and made a strange contrast to his bride, who had the haughty look of an Aztec princess. My guess was Lurch was going to wind up the human sacrifice in that marriage.

Still, she did look beautiful in her strapless white dress. "So, what do you think their chances are?"

"Chances of what?"

"Of catching the plague. Of happiness, Joe, of making it work."

"My money would be on the plague."

I couldn't get Joe to elaborate on why he thought the newlyweds' marriage wouldn't succeed. I assumed he was speaking out of a general distrust of women, which was a little off-putting, to say the least. More off-putting still was the way he kept ignoring me. He seemed distracted, and if this had been a real date, I would've been insulted by Joe's lack of interest in me, despite the fact that I'd worn my Renaissance courtesan dress and was displaying fully half my breasts.

But I was here in a professional capacity, and Joe was

going to pay me for my goddamn time, even if all I did was stand around, sipping champagne from cheap plastic glasses and listening to one middle-aged keyboardist, two teenage guitarists, and a soccer mom on drums murder "Mysterious Ways."

"Marlowe."

I turned, and Joe was looking at me, an amused, assessing cop look in his dark eyes. He leaned in close, and I could smell a hint of some sharp, masculine scent heated by his skin. "What do you know about voyeurism?"

"Well, it's human to be aroused by certain images. We're a very visual, social species, but if the act of observing takes over, then it becomes a fetish."

Now I had Joe's complete attention. "So how do you know when it crosses the line?"

I pondered. "Well, one thing that distinguishes fetishists is the specificity of their desire. We all have some particular traits we tend to find attractive, but fetishists have to have their specific requirements met—a red-toenailed foot with a high arch in a strappy sandal, enormous breasts, elaborate rituals of bondage and domination."

Joe was frowning, either in concentration or disbelief. "I remember that when I first met my ex-wife, all it took was watching her brush her hair, and I got turned on. Is that a fetish?"

I felt a small pang of jealousy. "When you're in love, all kinds of things can get invested with erotic significance. This is a more impersonal kind of specific. It's also non-negotiable—I mean, you could still get turned on even if your wife didn't brush her hair, but a fetishist would fixate on that event like an alcoholic fixates on getting the next drink."

"Okay, I think I get it. I wonder if you'd be willing to do me a favor." Joe didn't whisper, he said the words low and soft, and suddenly all I could think about was kissing him.

"Depends," I said, dragging my gaze away from his mouth.

"I have a theory and I need you to help me test it."

I took another sip of champagne from my cup. "I'm listening."

"There's this FBI guy who got me flopped from the Organized Crime Task Force. And I happen to hate his guts."

"And he's here? Where?"

"He's kind of hunkered down in a corner. I'm not going to tell you where, because then you'll look straight at him and he'll catch on to the fact that we're talking about him. Okay?"

I nodded, thinking that Joe had certain paranoid personality traits I hadn't noticed before.

"Okay, so I've just happened to discover that our boy was listening to Juan nail someone in the bathroom outside the chapel. I think he might be a peeping tom."

"Uh huh."

"So, I'd like to find out if I'm right."

"And we care whether or not this guy's got voyeuristic tendencies because . . ."

Joe looked exasperated. "Because it would affect his judgment, as in his firing of me."

"Because you said you wanted to catch real bad guys and not naughty girls."

Joe dragged his hand over his face. "Shit. Forget I told you that."

"Don't worry, Joe. I keep secrets."

Our eyes met, and I felt again that prickle of awareness. I looked at the civilized fit of his Italian gray jacket, so at odds with the predatory glint in his eyes, and ran my hand lightly over the silk of his tie. "It's part of the job requirement."

"Oh, yeah?" His voice had roughened, and the air between us shifted, warmed. I remembered the feel of his shoulders, padded with muscle, under my hands. Somewhere in the background, there was the hum of conversation and the first few notes of some unidentifiable pop song. All I could think about was the little scar bisecting Joe's left eyebrow, the quirk of a smile playing over his strong mouth.

This was like being a teenager again, this quick, hot, carnal yearning. Whatever he was saying was suddenly as incomprehensible as calculus; all I wanted to do was sit on his lap and grind.

Unfortunately, the last time there had been grinding, he'd gone into emotional shut-down and only the threat of humiliation at the hands of his ex had prompted him to call me again. So what if I felt intoxicated by the very smell of him? He obviously didn't feel the same.

Joe was regarding me with a kind of playful avidity. "So, we going to do it?"

"Do what?"

"Execute my plan. All I want is for you to dance with me, Marlowe. Over there. Real sexy, okay? And then I'm going to take you over into those bushes, okay, just out of sight, and I'm going to act like I'm about to fuck you into next week."

What? "What?"

"Don't worry, we won't really do it. I'm just testing a theory here. I want to see if this guy is really the perv I think he is, okay? Come on, Marlowe, it's important. National security might be at stake here."

He wanted me to pretend we were fucking at a wedding party? Was he crazy? "Listen, Joe," I began.

"Hang on a sec." Joe leaned in and, cupping my chin in his hands, slanted his mouth over mine and kissed me. Hard. The champagne tasted better on his tongue than it had in the glass.

"Sorry," he said, leaning back in his folding chair again. "Had to do that. Now, you were about to say?"

"Why did you just do that?"

Joe took my hand in his and brought it under the table, onto his lap.

"Oh." I thought about it. "When did that happen?"

"When I told you that bit about fucking you into next week."

My breath caught and I felt the twist of desire low in my abdomen. So this attraction wasn't all on my side, although he seemed to have a lot less trouble keeping himself in check than I did. If not for our previous experience, I would have asked him to take me into the bathrooms. As things stood, at least if I went along with this subterfuge, I wouldn't have to risk exposing how very much I wanted to feel his body against mine again.

"Okay," I said, throwing back the last of my drink. "Let's dance." I stood up with a wobble in my unfamiliar dressy boots.

Joe put his hand on my waist and followed me closely out onto the dance floor, where two other couples were already doing a kind of clumsy hustle to an old disco song. Joe started moving, surprisingly well for a straight man with a cast on his right hand, and I did my best to make my side to side Snoopy dance look seductive by raising my arms over my head.

I looked down—woops, breasts spilling out of the top of my corset—and whipped my arms down.

Joe looked at me as if he were puzzling something out. "Hang on a sec." He loped off to the keyboardist and whispered in his ear, and then the keyboardist nodded and conferred with the two teenage guitarists.

I had stopped shuffling and was now standing there, not quite knowing what to do. Suddenly I caught a glimpse of a short young redheaded man and my heart stuttered in recognition.

"Okay, M, we're set." Joe stepped in to me, about three inches closer than I had expected, and moved so that one of his muscular thighs was between mine. His left hand rested on my waist.

I tried to think of where I might have seen the man before. He wasn't a client I'd seen on his own, but I'd had some professional dealings with him. At school? During my stint working at a hospital clinic? Then it came to me: I'd done some critical incidence stress debriefings with cops immediately after September 11. He must have been in one of my groups.

"Joe, I can't do this." But the band had just struck up the first few notes of the lambada and Joe was maneuvering me around a tight turn.

"Please let me go," I said, as Joe draped my right hand over his neck.

"Just relax and follow my lead."

"Joe! I've got to get off the dance floor."

"Why?"

I realized that the simplest way to lie was to tell the truth. "Because I just recognized someone!"

Joe leaned in and lightly bit the outer lobe of my left ear. "Okay, calm down, I hear you. Don't panic."

I opened my mouth to reply but then Joe pulled back and rotated us so that we were turning, still pressed tightly together at the waist. "Listen, Marlowe, so someone recognizes you, then so what? You're not in that business anymore, you're with me, and I don't care what anyone thinks. I'm not about to go off and compare notes."

I stared at Joe, nonplussed. "But . . ."

"Relax, M. You're my date."

I glanced out at the crowd. Everyone was watching us. I had no idea how to move—every time I tried to move my own hips to the sinuous rhythm of the music, I bumped into Joe in an unmistakably embarrassing way.

"Easy, Tiger. Try just looking into my eyes. Forget about your feet."

Dear God, I was living Rita the transexual's Dirty Dancing fantasy.

I looked into Joe's sardonic dark gaze, and his firm grip on my waist cued me when I was supposed to rotate my hips left or right. That, and the long, muscular thigh nudging me every time he moved.

I was beginning to perspire with the effort, but I was getting it.

"That's better." Joe stroked his fingers down my right arm, which was holding onto his shoulder.

I stumbled. "Sorry."

His hold on my waist and hand tightened. "I got you."

Dry-mouthed, I looked up again. I could feel the length of his arousal against my stomach. But at least I had no room left to take a wrong step.

"That's it, Marlowe, you're doing great."

I no longer had to look at my feet; all I had to do was move my hips along with Joe's. I was really getting into it when the music stopped without warning, making me lose my balance. Joe gave my waist a squeeze as he leaned down to whisper in my ear.

"Well, isn't that interesting?"

"Isn't what interesting?" I said it looking out from under my eyelashes, assuming he was flirtatiously referring to my pebble-hard nipples, or to the fact I was still hanging limpet-like onto his neck.

"Somebody just left the party a bit early."

It took me a moment to understand that the incredible sexual tension between us had been pretty much one-sided. While I had been focused on thoughts of what Joe's incredible hip control could mean in bed, he'd been keeping tabs on some guy in the audience.

Clearly, what had been one of the most intensely arousing moments in my post-adolescent life had been a fairly commonplace occurrence for Joe. And while he had kept his wits about him, it was only belatedly occurring to me that at least one witness to my public display of choreographed frottage knew me as a psychologist.

"That's great," I said to Joe, already turning out of his embrace, "and I think that means our work here is done." I snatched up my purse from our table, and was about to make my getaway when the red-haired man cornered me between two side tables and a tray of shrimp.

"Hey. Hey, I thought it was you!" He had a round, snub-nosed, heavily freckled face, and although I could remember him, pale and anxious in the weeks following the attacks on the World Trade Center, I could not for the life of me recall his name.

"How are you doing?"

"Better. So much better. A lot of it thanks to you, as a matter of fact."

I felt Joe come up beside me. "That's great," I said to the young cop, trying to ignore the looming shadow of disapproval on my left.

"Hello, Kevin." Joe's voice was a degree or so north of friendly.

"Hey, Joe, bet you'll never guess how I know this lady."

"I'm not interested."

"Aw, go on, I'm not embarrassed and she sure as hell won't be, 'cause otherwise she wouldn't do it for a living, right?"

"Kevin, really, we don't have to discuss . . ."

"But the thing is, you really helped me with a number of different problems I'd been having. I mean, before I saw you, I couldn't sleep, I couldn't relax, I had a tremor in my hands, and I sure wasn't doing my girlfriend any good . . ."

"Kevin." Joe made the other man's name sound like a warning.

"No, wait, man, I need her to hear this. Because I kept saying, No way, I'm not going to some professional, and then my friends kind of pushed me into seeing this lady here, and let me tell you, she changed my life."

"Jesus, Kevin, have a little respect."

"But I do! I have so much respect for her! I mean, there

are a lot of people doing what she does but how many of them really have a god-given talent? She's not just someone you pay by the hour. She's a healer."

During the course of this conversation, I had gone from experiencing cold chills to hot flashes. Now all I could think of was, what on earth could I have done that made such an impact on this man? All I'd done was see him in a group with . . . oh, dear god. I had to stop him before he mentioned the nine others.

"Kevin, I'm so glad that I was able to help you at a difficult time. I wish I could stay longer right now but I have a pressing appointment."

"It wasn't just me, you know."

"Kevin, you heard the lady." Joe took my arm. "She has to go."

"You helped a lot of people. I mean, you were tireless! The way you dealt with us for hours and hours . . ."

Joe was looking as if he might explode at any moment. "Thank you, Kevin."

"And these were guys who swore they would never even talk to someone like you. I mean, I wouldn't be surprised if you'd seen half the guys here and they were just too ashamed to come up and say hello in front of their coworkers and wives."

Joe froze, a muscle visibly jumping in his jaw. "Christ almighty, Kevin, don't you know when to fucking shut up?"

"No, Joe, I fucking do not." Now Kevin's face was flushed with anger. "I'm not embarrassed anymore about getting help and no one is going to make me feel like I should be." He turned back to me. "You still seeing clients privately?"

I tried to think of an equivocation that would satisfy both men. "That's not something I can discuss here, but if you give me your number, we can talk over the phone."

"That's great, because my girlfriend and I were hoping to see someone before we get married." Kevin leaned forward, lowering his voice. "She's Catholic, you see, and has a few issues about . . ."

"Right. Okay, Kevin," said Joe, stepping in front of me and tapping the shorter man on the chest with one finger. "Let's just get one thing clear. No, she is not seeing clients anymore. She's with me, okay? So if you and your girlfriend can't manage to get it on, you're just going to have to deal with it in some other fashion. Can I suggest cunnilingus? In my experience, it works great on women of all faiths."

"Joe!" I tried to think of something to say to Kevin, but Joe had already grabbed hold of my arm and was dragging me off, while Kevin shook his head and shouted, "You're too good for him! Even if he's the goddamn world champion of oral sex!"

I broke away from Joe and started walking as fast as I could toward Broadway. "Well, that sure made a lovely impression. Next time you want to humiliate me in public, give me a little warning."

Joe caught up with me beside the cathedral steps. "Marlowe, wait. Wait!" He stepped in front of me, trapping me against the wall.

"Marlowe, I'm sorry, I didn't mean to embarrass you."

"You mean you thought yelling out explicit sex terms in Latin was acceptable wedding behavior?" I tried to duck under Joe's arms, but he was too quick and blocked me. "Let me go."

"I was trying to keep that little shmuck from telling the whole wedding that you're a call girl!"

"How, by telling them yourself?"

A deep crease appeared between Joe's eyes. "Shit. Listen, Marlowe, I'm sorry. I lost my temper, I screwed up. But I was thinking about you."

"Bullshit." I shoved hard against Joe's chest but he just ignored it, his good left hand braced on the wall beside my head, his mouth coming down over mine. "Marlowe, please, I really am sorry."

I stamped on his foot.

"Ouch. You mad at me or you saying no, here?"

"I'm furious!"

"Okay, then, hit me some more." I hit him halfheartedly on the back while he kissed me, and then forgot to hit him and wound up tangling my hands in his hair instead. I could feel his good left hand moving up, encountering the boned stiffness of the corset. "Jeez, that thing looks good but it feels like fucking armor."

Okay, this was going way too far. At what point did he think I'd agreed to being felt up in public? "Joe, stop trying to get under my clothes."

Joe patted me down, presumably in a search for fastenings. "How the hell did you get into that thing?"

"I'm not in the mood for this."

Joe's head came back as if I'd slapped him. "You're not?"

Something about the vulnerability in his expression made me reach out and touch the side of his face. "It's not that I don't like you . . ."

"Aw, Christ, Marlowe, I am so sorry, what can I say except that I'm a complete asshole and . . ."

And just like that, I wanted him again. Without pre-meditation, I grabbed Joe's tie and shut him up with another kiss, and now his fingers were dipping into the top of my corset, finding my right nipple. I groaned into his mouth.

He pulled back. "M?"

"Yes?" I was panting, too embarrassed to look in his eyes.

"You acting?"

I stared at him, shook my head.

"Okay, screw this, we're leaving here. Now." He grabbed my hand and I began to totter after him in my boots.

"I don't understand. Where are we . . ."

He yanked me along at a near-run until we were on Amsterdam. "Taxi!" He threw his hand up just as a low rumble sounded somewhere to the west of us. "Shit, if it starts raining, we'll never get a cab."

"Joe, slow down. Where are you taking me?"

He turned. "Back to my apartment."

I'm not sure what I would have said, because at that moment, there was one more ominous boom of thunder and then a gypsy cab stopped right in front of us.

Joe got in. "You coming?"

I stood there, staring at him. A fat drop of rain fell on my head, then another. "I'm not sure."

He held out his hand. "Please."

It was hard to think this out fast enough. He was paying me for this date; if I went home with him, we would wind up in bed. I wouldn't be pretending to be a whore anymore. I would actually be one.

"I can't do this."

To my surprise, Joe didn't look impatient or exasperated or even confused. He just sat there, looking a little sad, and smiling. The rain had started falling faster and I was getting wet now.

"I don't suppose there's some simple answer that will convince you to get in here?"

I shook my head.

"Then how about you get in here and I leave? You need to go home, and the chances of your catching another cab are pretty slim."

I nodded, miserable. "What about you?"

"I don't mind getting wet." Joe got out of the cab and I scooted in, my wet skirt sticking to the backs of my thighs as I slid awkwardly into the backseat.

I watched him stand there in his good gray suit, dry one moment, drenched the next. He slicked the wet hair back from his face and stepped back to the curb. "Joe, this is ridiculous. You're getting your cast wet. Why don't I drop you off at your apartment?"

He leaned his head down. "You go first. I'm all the way uptown."

The driver turned around. "I don't care who goes where," he said, "but close the damn door or get the hell out."

Joe slid in beside me, and for a moment, our thighs were plastered together.

"Where to?" I said.

"I'll drop you off at your place, then carry on to mine."

"How do you know I don't live all the way downtown? We're probably closer to you."

Joe smiled. "Hey, I'm not cheap. And I like the company, for as long as I've got it."

I turned to the driver. "Seventy-ninth Street and Central Park West."

We sat in silence. I could feel Joe's warm, wet body beside mine. After a moment, his hand reached out to cover mine, and I leaned my head down into his shoulder. We rode like that, the rain shielding us from the outside world, listening to the regular squeak and click of the windshield wipers.

The cab driver stopped in front of my building and I could see my doorman, Paris, hurrying over with an oversized umbrella to open the taxi door.

I turned to Joe. "Thanks."

"Nah, it's me who should thank you." He leaned in, almost embracing me, and pressed something into my hand. I glanced down at the four hundred-dollar bills in my palm.

"I don't want your money, Joe." I handed it back to him and he looked at it, then at me.

"So why am I heading home alone? I thought it was about this. If we're really on a date, Marlowe . . ." A lock of dark, wet hair had fallen into his eyes and I reached out to push it back.

"Because it's complicated and not . . . not quite clean. Because the issue of money came into it at all." I waited for him to get out so I could leave the cab. "Because you don't want anyone to go with you to the emergency room. Because even if all I want is a passionate affair, there has to be more going on than just sex."

Outside the cab, my doorman looked confused. His shoes were probably getting soaked.

Joe followed the direction of my gaze, saw him, and understood that Paris's job was to stand there until we sorted out who was getting out. "Okay," Joe said, stuffing the money into his slacks pocket. "All right."

He stood up, stepping out of the way of Paris's umbrella. I faced him for a moment. "Bye, Joe."

I couldn't read his expression. "Bye."

I walked away, glad that I wasn't going to sleep with anyone who looked as large and brooding and unreachable as Joe did with his hands in his pockets in the pouring rain.

I rode the elevator up, shivering in my wet clothes. Back in my apartment, I stepped out of my skirt and was trying to wrestle my way out of the corset when the intercom buzzed.

"Who is it?"

Paris answered. "It's Joe. He says he forgot something."

"Put him on."

"Hey, Marlowe?"

"What did you forget, Joe?"

"I forgot I have to go to work in half an hour."

"You're working today?"

"You have to know this about me, I never forget things like that. Except for today, I got a little distracted by . . . but, uh, the thing is, since I need to leave in thirty minutes and I'm just so friggin' wet, I was wondering if I could just dry off a little . . ."

"Tell Paris to buzz you up to the twenty-second floor."

I looked down at myself; my efforts to unhook the corset had pushed my breasts even further over the top, and my little black panties were visible from below. I ran into my bedroom, slipped my red robe on and then glanced in the mirror: disaster. Raccoon eyes of streaked mascara and eyeliner, hair matted down like a sick child's.

I was just beginning to make repairs when the doorbell rang. Looking myself in the eye, I realized I had absolutely no idea what I was doing.

The doorbell rang again and I opened it. "Hi."

"Hi."

And then I was in his arms and we were kissing.

joe

When the little man stands, my father used to say, one's good sense is in one's ass. It sounds better in Yiddish, but it's true in any language.

In any case, it went a long way toward explaining why I was back with my tongue down Marlowe's throat, against her better judgment and mine.

God, this woman knew how to kiss, and in my experience, the kiss told you everything about how a woman was going to act in bed. Paolina always kept her lips tight, each time, like it was our first kiss and she wasn't sure if she was going to let me do anything so crude as stick my tongue in her mouth. Gina, my old Air Force Reserve friend, used to make me feel like I had a wriggling, teething puppy slobbering and nipping at my face. But Marlowe kissed as if she were trying to get inside my head, and when I pulled away, her pupils were huge and dark and unfocused.

I tried to take a deep breath, to slow myself down, and instead found myself pulling the sides of her red silk robe apart and discovering that her breasts had almost popped out of the top of that green body armor she was wearing. "Jesus, Marlowe." I was moving her backwards, into her apartment as I said it. She shook her head.

"Joe . . ."

I kissed the objection out of her mouth, then made my way down the side of her neck, my good left hand on her tiny waist, holding her still so I could breathe in the scent of her. When I reached the top of her breasts—God, her skin was smooth—she inhaled sharply. I darted my tongue down, over her right nipple, which sprang free.

"Joe, the door . . ."

I slammed the door shut, then backed Marlowe up against something—a table—that wobbled when I leaned my weight across her.

"Ouch, wait . . ."

I sucked her nipple into my mouth and she grabbed the back of my head, which I took as license to go ahead and suck harder. She made a sound and I turned my attention to her left nipple, and this time I let her feel the edge of my teeth, which would have made Paolina complain, but Marlowe was a whole different kind of woman. Her hands were kneading my shoulders now, and not gently. I bit her, softly, and she cried out and dug her nails into me.

Okay, this was new territory for me. I was shaking a little, and I could feel all the muscles down my abdomen tightening as if I was about to get into a fight. There was a kind of violence to this desire that I had never experienced before; it was like I'd been swimming in a lot of pools and lakes, and here I was, on the edge of a goddamn ocean.

I looked at Marlowe, and she looked at me, and there was none of this I'm-so-turned-on-I-can't-think-straight bullshit between us. We had our eyes wide open, acknowledging that we were both perfectly aware of what was going on: That I was fully clothed and soaking wet; that we were moments away from me fucking her up against the wall, even though she'd had some serious reservations about letting me in her front door in the first place.

And probably had reservations still. Which reminded me that I had less than ten minutes before I had to hightail it out of her apartment if I didn't want to completely mess up my professional life.

There had to be some way to make this right. Do her in five minutes or less? Not if I ever cared to have a hope in hell of a repeat performance.

Say, shit, there's no time for this, can I take a cold shower? Call in sick at work at the last minute?

"Marlowe." My voice was a rasp, unrecognizable.

She looked dazed. "What?"

"I feel like I'm going to die of a thrombosis if I don't get inside you."

"Oh." The way she said it let me know how close I was to being where I wanted to be. Her breasts were on the verge of spilling out of their confinement and I could see the tops of her nipples. I half reached out a hand to touch them, then realized getting ourselves more worked up would only make things worse.

Unless she really just wanted to make this first time a quickie and wouldn't mind my charging out the door right afterward. Yeah, that would be fine with her, and I could just slap some money on the dresser to make her feel like a complete whore. For a second I thought about Kevin, then forced the thought away.

She didn't want to be that person anymore. She wanted me, and she'd still want me in eight hours, unless I blew it by being an asshole. I pulled the sides of Marlowe's robe together. "I have to go now."

"Oh." Same word, whole different meaning. Shit. "What I want to do with you, Marlowe? It won't take just five minutes."

She smiled at that, and suddenly I realized her eyes weren't brown, like I'd thought; they were a deep olive mixed with gold. "I didn't know your eyes were green, M."

"They're not. You're just overcome with lust."

"That explains it." I kissed her mouth, this time careful not to press my body against hers. When she pulled away from me, I realized what had me notice the color of her eyes; they were bright with unshed tears.

Whatever was going on here, it sure wasn't business as usual. "Hey, hey. Listen, I'm not going into full emotional retreat here, but I am about to be seriously late for work."

"But your clothes are still soaking wet." Marlowe sounded fine, but she had her arms wrapped around her middle.

"I've got a change of clothes in a locker there. Come on," I said, taking her hands in mine, "relax. Don't you think that merry widow Kevlar vest is protection enough?"

"It's a corset, actually."

"Yeah? Well, it looks great."

"Thanks, it feels like a straitjacket. Do you think you could undo it before you go?" I didn't have the time, but she turned around, and damned if the thing didn't actually lace up the back like a straitjacket. "Jeez," I said, tugging at the laces one-handed, "how do you breathe in this?"

"It's not easy."

"There, I think that's . . ." She turned to face me, and the corset fell away from her body, giving me my first full look at her breasts. "Oh, Jesus."

"Sorry." Marlowe tugged the material up, covering herself. The thing was, she actually looked embarrassed. "I know, you have to go."

I cupped her face in my left hand. "I'm not running away. You know that, right?"

"I know."

I kissed her again, and this time, for some reason, my eyes were stinging. Could sexual frustration actually make a man cry? "I've got to go, Marlowe."

She ducked her head into the space between my neck and my shoulder. "I know."

"I don't finish till one A.M."

She rubbed her face against my neck. "I understand."

I lifted her chin. "Can I come back here and crawl inside you and stay that way for a very long time?"

"How long?"

I laughed with the pleasure of anticipation. "You'll find out."

marlowe

Joe walked in the door looking altogether too relaxed, his black leather jacket slung over his shoulder, a big, confident grin on his unshaven face.

He was on his way, he'd said when he'd woken me up at half past one. It was now ten past two. Since when did it take a cop forty minutes to drive one city mile?

"Hey, Gorgeous. I brought us some Chinese food." He kissed me and I caught a whiff of garlic sauce from the plastic carrier bag on his arm.

He'd stopped off for takeout. Knowing that I was here, waiting for him to finally make love to me.

I, on the other hand, had spent frantic moments in front of the mirror, changing out of my torn nightgown and into my sexiest bra and thong set, wondering if I should also wear my red silk robe or whether he'd seen the damn thing too many times. I'd brushed my hair, moisturized my elbows, filed a rough nail, gargled, and applied perfume to my throat, wrists, and inner thighs, which had been a mistake, as I must've spilled a drop, and was still experiencing a slight burning sensation down below.

And that was all in the past thirty minutes. Earlier in the evening, I'd washed my hair, shaved my legs, straightened the apartment, painted my toenails, and done sixty sit-ups and forty squats in a last-ditch attempt to tone my stomach and lift my butt. After that, I'd had to take another shower.

And he'd stayed late at work and stopped off for takeout.

Joe set the bag of Chinese food down on the table. "You hungry?"

"Not particularly."

He slipped one hand inside my robe and I stiffened. "Okay, what am I missing here? Moving too fast? Not fast enough?" His dark eyes were filled with good humor and the gleam of carnal certainty. Had he been one of my previous boyfriends, I would have explained to him that there is nothing that douses a woman's desire so effectively as a man's casual assumption that the deal's already been done.

And, like my previous boyfriends, he would apologize in the short term and resent me in the long. Or else he'd fade out of the picture, like Ethan had, and I'd assume it was a friendly, mutually agreed upon split. But I'd begun to wonder if there was any such thing as an amicable breakup. After hearing Savannah's revelations about her clientele, I'd begun to wonder if behind every failed relationship lay a host of hidden identities, secret fetishes, missed clues, and failed connections.

And here was an early turning point in my relationship with Joe. What would a Renaissance courtesan do? Bite back her irritation and head for the bedroom? Seductively coax him into the bath? Throw a chamber pot at him and send him packing?

It had been fifteen months since I'd last had sex, and that had been fairly mediocre at best. I did not want to kick Joe out. I wanted him to want me so badly he couldn't control himself.

"Marlowe?" Now he was looking at me assessingly, with a hint of concern. I realized that, like me, he was constantly observing people's behavior, examining their sentences for hidden meanings.

"Put down the food."

"Shit, you're mad at me. Listen, M, we had a situation and I haven't eaten since I had one of those tiny toast things at the wedding . . ."

Well, that did make me feel somewhat better. "Now put your jacket down."

The expression on his face was priceless; somewhere between apology, confusion and the faint beginnings of desire. "I know it may not seem romantic, M, but if you and I are going to do what I hope we're going to do for as long as I hope we're going to do it, I either need sleep or food."

"Stop talking. Now take off your shoes and socks."

"Can I sit down while I . . ."

"Yes. Now be quiet." He pulled out a chair and removed his shoes. They were the same ones he'd worn to the wedding, somewhat the worse for all that rain.

Joe looked up at me. "Now what?"

"Silence. Your shirt." He unbuttoned his rumpled white cotton men's work shirt and pulled the tails out his waistband, revealing the kind of chest I hadn't gotten close to since I'd been a teenager. No, correction—I'd never touched a chest like this. Leanly muscled, but broader than a boy's, the shoulders more filled out. He wasn't as hairy as I would've expected—just a small patch, darkly curling, leading down in a line to the waistband of his navy slacks.

I pointed to the slacks.

Joe looked at me with a faint smile playing around his mouth as he unbuckled his belt. He removed a small gun, which I hadn't been expecting, and placed it carefully on the table before slipping out of his pants. He let them drop to the floor, and there he was, wearing nothing but a Timex watch, a cast on his right hand, and a pair of tight, dark blue boxers that left nothing to the imagination. He was feeling the want, all right.

"Did you bring the handcuffs?"

"I thought you were joking."

"I wasn't."

"Well, you wouldn't like them. Real handcuffs are pretty damn uncomfortable. Don't you have some furry kind that you . . ."

"They weren't for me, Joe."

He looked at me. "Marlowe, I'm getting the feeling that I've seriously pissed you off here, and I . . ."

Smart man. "You need a shower." I took his hand and led him into my bathroom.

Joe whistled. "Nice marble."

I leaned in to turn on the water and Joe ran his hand under my robe and up my thigh. I slapped his wrist. "It's warm. Get in there."

He hesitated. "I need a plastic bag for my cast."

Of course, it had gotten soaked once already today. I went into the kitchen and found an old supermarket bag to tie around his right arm.

"Thank you, Mistress." Joe pulled down his shorts and

I sucked in a breath. God, he was a beautiful man. And, interestingly enough, his penis curved sharply to the right, something I'd never seen before. He stepped into the shower and I watched the water cascade down the firm muscles of his abdomen. He found the soap and lathered his chest, and then, briskly, his fully engorged erection.

Our eyes met, and something inside me contracted.

He stepped out, body streaming with water, the shower still running, and grabbed my hair. "Wait, I didn't give you permission to . . ." his kiss slanted over my mouth, swallowing my words. "Wait . . ."

I could feel his slick hardness sliding over my stomach, and then he was kneeling at my feet. "So you like to be in charge, huh?"

I didn't know. Did I? I remembered what Savannah had said about men in authority wanting to be tied up, and men without power wanting to subdue their partners. I'd been trying to figure out the key to throwing him off balance.

Now I was thrown.

"Am I your slave, Marlowe? Is that the name of this game?" Joe nipped at the fabric, then let me feel the moistness of his tongue. "What do you want me to do next, Mistress?"

"I don't know." Okay, so there was my answer; I wasn't a dominant. Even with his breath hot on the front of my panties, I didn't want to order him to give me pleasure.

"Well, I think I know, and what you really want is to . . . to . . ." Joe threw back head and suddenly sneezed three times in quick succession. "Jesus, woman, how much perfume do you have on down there?"

"I was rushing and some spilled." And just like that, all the blood left my erogenous zones and flooded back into my brain, replacing lust with embarrassment.

Joe stood up. "I put aftershave on my balls once, when I was sixteen. Burns like a mother, doesn't it?"

I nodded. Joe was no fool. Clearly, this was the moment when he would realize that he wasn't dealing with an experienced courtesan here.

"Okay, Missy, off with those panties." I rested my hand on his shoulder as he stripped them off.

"What are we doing?"

"Off with this bra, but can you wear it again for me next time?" I let Joe help me into the shower. "Rinse that stuff off . . . there you go, that feels better, doesn't it?" He turned of the faucets.

"Perfect. Now you smell of girl."

"Joe . . ." I hesitated, unsure how to tell him that I wasn't sure I wanted to do this anymore. I hadn't realized it until just now, but I'd been really looking forward to not being myself in bed. To not being my analytical, honest, communicative, inhibited self. I'd wanted to be some other self, a self that knew how to explode.

While I was searching for words, Joe scooped me up into his arms.

"Joe, your hand . . ." I could feel the cast on his right hand against my back.

"I'm okay. Which way to the bedroom?"

"That way. No, not there, I locked the cat up in the office."

Joe quirked an eyebrow at that, but didn't say anything. He placed me gently down on the bed and bracketed my face with his arms. I touched the tuft of his armpit hair, which was still damp from the shower. For some reason, I had an urge to sniff him, which I did. He smelled clean, like soap, but also a little musky, male.

"Marlowe."

I looked at Joe. "Next time, you want, you can make me your slave."

I shook my head. "Listen, I didn't really want . . ."

"You want handcuffs, I'll bring handcuffs. You want me to play cop, I'll arrest you." He laughed, reading the expression on my face correctly. "Frisk you. Strip you. Put you in lockup . . ."

Oh, God, he was going to think I was some kind of police groupie. "That's not what I . . ."

"But Marlowe, this time? This first time?" I could feel him slipping down my body until he was kneeling between my spread thighs. "No games."

"Okay."

"No pretending." He was looking into my eyes.

"Joe, I have something to . . ." His tongue flicked over my clitoris, and all rational thought ceased for a while, and then I was shouting his name and dragging him up by the hair. "Please!"

He slid the first little bit inside of me and the feeling was so intense that I felt my internal muscles contract around him.

"God, you're tight." He pushed a little deeper inside me, and my legs came up around his waist. His third thrust rocked me back against the headboard, and sank him all the way inside of me. I made a strangled sound.

"What?"

I couldn't speak. He was angled so that when he thrust

hard, he bumped against something inside of me that shorted out my brain.

"You in pain? I'm sorry, but you're the smallest woman I've ever . . ."

"Harder!"

His fourth thrust made stars burst behind my closed eyelids. "Oh, fuck shit." For a moment I thought he was cursing with passion, but then he started to withdraw. I grabbed him with my heels, holding him in place.

"Marlowe," he said into my ear, "we got to stop now, or I won't be able to pull out."

"Pull out?" I could feel his heart pounding in his chest. "What for?"

"I forgot a condom."

Oh, God, so had I. I was on the pill to regulate my periods, but Joe and I weren't in a monogamous relationship. He started to leave me and I put my hand on his arm. "Have . . . have you been with anyone since your ex-wife?"

"No. And to my knowledge she didn't cheat. It's just . . . no offense, Marlowe, but it's not my sexual history that's worrying me here."

"Excuse me, but I haven't had sex in over a year and when I did, I was extremely particular." Now Joe was looking at me very strangely.

"I'm sorry, but when you say particular . . ."

I felt a flash of anger, then thought, of course he's concerned. The man thought I'd been a prostitute. "Joe, what I've been trying to tell you? I'm not a call girl."

"I know you're not."

"I mean, I never was."

"I think I understand what you're trying to say here."

"No, Joe, you don't, because you're not letting me finish my—"

"I'm not clueless, M." His face, only inches above mine, was soft with compassion. "That Swinburne ad, that was to screen potentials, right? You were being selective, probably seeing a few regular clients, not lowlifes, smart guys, well-educated." Joe raised himself up on his elbows, and the change in position bumped him up against that spot again, and set up a vibration inside of me. "I do get it. And I'm not making a judgment about you when I say that I don't . . ."

I clamped my legs around his butt, grabbed his hair in my fists and kissed him with a mixture of pent-up frustration and desire. When he slammed into me for the fifth and final time, he shouted my name and I came so hard that I started to cry.

joe

Since Sunday was my turnaround day this week, I had to be back at work by eight A.M. Which really meant there was no point in trying to get any sleep, so we made love two more times. With a condom, because as I pointed out, we should both probably play it safe and get tested.

"I'm going to be sore tomorrow," Marlowe said when I left. She'd made me coffee and offered me the use of her toothbrush, which I'd accepted. Her sink was white marble and all the taps looked like pieces of modern art.

"Tell me about it. Plus I'm wearing the same clothes."

Marlowe wrapped her arms around my neck. "So the guys will know?"

I kissed her neck. "They'll suspect something when I keep smiling." There was a framed painting on her bedroom wall. Not a print, a painting of someplace green and peaceful, with horses that were just brushstrokes of warm reds and browns. Her bed was made from solid maple, and all her chairs and tables matched.

She pulled back, frowning at me a little. "Are you worried?" In daylight, with her face free of makeup, I could see the faint freckles on her nose. I reached my hand into her robe and cupped one of her small, perfect breasts, just because I could.

"Not exactly." For a second I forgot about how much her apartment cost, and the fact that she had a book on her bedside table called *Those Are Bad Thoughts: Understanding Atypical Sexual Ideation*. I even forgot about asking her anything about clients who were partial to Saran Wrap. Instead, I just thought about how soft her sheets were and how much I wanted to burrow back inside them with her. "Actually, I'm getting hard again."

She leaned in and bit the tip of my nose. "Idiot."

"Can I come back in eight hours?"

"At four? I have a . . . dentist's appointment. Can you come at five?"

That slight hesitation threw me, and I nearly said, Let's leave it for another day. I mean, how smart was getting involved with her if she was still seeing clients? And how the hell could she afford this place, if she wasn't on the game anymore? But then there was a low howl of pain from the other room, and Marlowe said, "Oh, my God, I forgot Burt's still locked up."

For a second I thought she meant she'd had some guy chained up in the other room all night, expecting Mistress Marlowe to set him free so he could pay for his session. But then she came back with a lanky brown ratlike feline that sprang to the top of a bookcase and yowled.

"He do that a lot?"

"Well, he's not used to being in the office so long, and he hasn't had his anti-anxiety pill yet."

I looked up at the cat, and he jumped onto my shoulder and started vibrating.

"Wow," Marlowe said. "He must like you." I wasn't sure how I felt about that.

I kissed her good-bye and went to work, where someone had left a package of Saran Wrap on my desk along with a typed note: Why not just try it yourself?

Having been screwed senseless all night, I actually found myself relaxed enough to laugh as I chucked the note into the garbage. In any case, I wasn't investigating Tony Russo's death anymore, because I'd become convinced that he'd died by his own misadventure. Knowing Marlowe better, I was sure that she'd turned him down when he called.

I mean, sure, she was guilty of mixing business with pleasure, but there were different levels in every profession. You had your fast food workers who spend all day operating deep fryers, your short order cooks who flip burgers and eggs, and then you have the folks who know how to make meals that get written up in magazines.

I figured that Marlowe had been the equivalent of a personal chef. And I could live with that, especially since I was now the happy recipient of all her skill, which was something I needed to not think about because Lili Gonzales was already looking at me strangely.

"Is that like a baby's gas smile or are you really so happy you can't stop grinning, Joe?"

I pounded myself on the chest. "Indigestion."

By the time four o'clock rolled around I was done in. I hadn't slept in twenty-four hours; all I wanted was to eat a sandwich and roll into bed.

With Marlowe.

I killed time at a pizza shop and arrived at her door at ten past five, dizzy with exhaustion. "I'm not good for anything," I told her. She smelled nice, citrusy. "Do you think I could just lie down with you?"

Without a word, she took me into her bedroom, removed my shoes and jeans, and lay down beside me. I fell asleep curved around her small, lithe body, and when I woke up it was midnight and I was already moving against her bottom.

I put my mouth next to her ear. "Can I?"

"Yes, yes, yes."

The next day at the precinct, I opened a letter addressed to Detective Joe and removed a Polaroid of a Caucasian female in her mid-forties wearing thick, plastic framed spectacles, bright red lipstick, a pair of high heels, and not a damn thing else. She looked as if she weighed in the vicinity of three hundred pounds; her breasts were the size of suckling pigs. "Okay," I said, holding the photo up, "anyone know anything about this?"

"Oh, yeah, Janine Masterson is on the prowl again," said Denny, looking over my shoulder. "She's one of those police groupies, comes to all the community meetings."

"Let me see," said Kito. "Oh, man, that's a lot of love for one man. You sure you're up to the job?"

There was a wave of laughter around the room, and then all of a sudden people were talking to me as if I was part of the team.

"Give the lady a break," said Lili. "It's clear she's got a few mental difficulties. I mean, why else would she be interested in Joe?"

I threw an eraser at Lili's head, not sure what had caused this change in my coworkers, but guessing it had something to do with my post-Marlowe good humor.

I'd never met a woman who liked sex as much as she did. After I left work we made love on all fours on the living room rug, then again standing in the shower, then on top of the frigging kitchen counter, her legs wrapped around my waist, while waiting for the microwave to ping.

"I'm going to regret this," she said, but we couldn't seem to stop. When I told her I had the next two days off, her eyes got wide. "Oh, no," she said, "we're going to kill ourselves."

But that night we took a bath together, and didn't make love at all, which is how I knew I was in trouble. Because as I sat there, soaping her breasts and discussing whether or not we wanted to go to a museum or a movie or take my car and drive out of the city, I began to suspect that the persistent urge to lose myself in her that I'd been mistaking for desperate horniness might be something else entirely.

marlowe

We drove up the Taconic in a Ford Escort that smelled faintly of coffee and dust, watching the newly budded trees racing past us as Joe shifted gear, then replaced his hand on my thigh.

I'd managed to reschedule my three Wednesday clients so that I could spend Joe's day off driving to Hyde Park to see Franklin D. Roosevelt's house. We would have gone farther and spent the night at one of the country's oldest inns, but I hadn't been able to reach Savannah, whom I was supposed to see the next day.

Joe was disappointed. He'd kept asking, "Where do you want to go?" and "What do you want to do?" I got the feeling he'd wanted more of a challenge than a day trip. He wanted to surprise me with a grand gesture, but I couldn't think of any outlandish requests.

The truth was, I didn't particularly care where Franklin and Eleanor had slept in their separate bedrooms. I didn't care whether or not we got a table at the nearby Culinary Institute, despite Joe's insistence that he had connections there. I didn't even care that I was being driven at nearly ninety miles an hour by a man who kept only one hand on the wheel.

All I knew was that for the first time in my life, I was in on the big secret. After living thirty-six years in a society where everything is sold with the promise of glorious sex, I had finally seen glory.

And just like the lambent ladies in late medieval paintings, glory had transformed me. Suddenly my skin was clear, my eyes were bright, my hair glossy and obedient, falling in soft, reddish waves around my face.

Inspired by this sudden sensual renaissance, I had decided to wear a pair of low-riding jeans that flattered my bottom but usually languished in the back of the drawer, as they were only truly comfortable when I was standing. I paired the jeans with a long sleeved expensive T-shirt made of a very thin, soft cotton, and thought how ironic it was that I was dressing seductively for a man who would probably have found me enticing in old army pants.

Which, as a matter of fact, was what Joe was wearing, along with a T-shirt and his ubiquitous black leather jacket.

Joe caught the direction of my glance and grinned. "Why do you keep looking at me?"

"I think you know."

"I've got ketchup on my cheek?"

"No, Joe, because I've never been overwhelmed with lust like this before. I keep wanting you to pull over and kiss me. I keep remembering what we were doing half an hour ago and wanting to do it again."

"You're kidding me, right?"

I realized that he probably thought I handed this line to every man I slept with as a kind of professional courtesy.

"I'm being completely straight with you, Joe. I mean, when it comes right down to it, sex is an awful lot like pizza. There's a lot of it around, but very little of it's good."

Joe kept his eyes on the road as he negotiated a curve. "That's interesting, but I don't think guys think about what kind of pizza they're getting."

"Are you telling me there's no difference to a guy whether he's getting incredible, you must be telepathic, rule-breaking sex from the woman of his dreams or whether he's getting a quick screw from a handy stranger?"

Joe shook his head, laughing. "No, I'm saying guys do not know or care what kind of pizza goes into their mouths. We do get more selective about sex as we get older, or at least I did. So keep talking. I want to know what I'm doing right."

"Well, um, first of all there's the physical aspect of things . . ."

Joe grinned, still intent on the cars ahead of him. "You mean, the fact that I list to starboard?"

Heat rushed to my cheeks. "Well, yes, that's . . . a bonus, definitely. But I meant more generally that you're a very tactile person. And more than that, you, I don't know, pay attention. And you have a lot of patience."

I glanced at Joe to find him looking at me with an expression of mild bemusement on his face. "You think I'm patient, huh? Okay, I'll take it, but I'm not sure how you'd figure that one out, because frankly, I haven't been in control a single time yet."

And then he smiled at me in a way that felt almost unbearably intimate, his injured right hand moving back onto my left thigh.

Not since the earliest days of my childhood had I been touched this much, watched this much, adored this much. Joe told me I was charming when I performed the simplest daily tasks—brushing my hair, cutting up a melon, putting on my brassiere. I felt more comfortable with him after two days than I'd felt with other lovers after six months.

And the strangest thing was, I discovered that when sexual desire infuses everything, even a tour of a president's historic home, then sex itself becomes infused with other things.

I had never been more carnally aware than I was walking obediently behind a small group of middle-aged and elderly tourists, inhaling the smell of wood polish and holding hands with Joe.

"This was the living room and library." Joe leaned in to me, pressing himself against my back while we peered at the formal, dark-wood–paneled room with its over-stuffed chairs, Persian rug, and built-in bookcases of leather-bound books. His mouth grazed my ear, his hand resting lightly at my waist, pressing into the underside of my breast as if by accident. In front of us, a phalanx of visitors stood at attention, listening to the guide's pronouncements.

"This is the Dresden room, so named for the finely wrought chandelier and mantel set purchased by Roosevelt's father in 1866." Joe's finger traced over my nipple, setting up a vibration in my entire body.

"And this was the bedroom Roosevelt used as an

adult." Joe moved to the other breast, and suddenly the whole crowd turned. He dropped his hand as the guide led the group out. I looked down; my nipples were clearly visible through the white cotton of my T-shirt.

"I think I have to wait a moment."

"I had a similar thought." I glanced down to the front of Joe's army pants and laughed. "Or, on the other hand, we could just make it worse . . ." We were making out, with Joe's hand just beginning to creep under my shirt, when the guard interrupted us.

Embarrassed, I left the room while the guard was still talking, leaving Joe to follow me outside. It took him a couple of moments—I had the feeling he must have told the guard he was a cop—and as I watched him walk toward me, something about the easy purposefulness of his stride sent a shiver of possessive pleasure down my spine.

"He didn't mean we had to vacate the premises, M."

I just smiled and tipped my head back; a strong breeze was pushing the clouds through the clear, cool sky. Joe put his warm hand on my bare arm.

"You've got goosebumps."

"I shouldn't have worn this shirt. It feels almost like fall." I'd noticed before that there was an eerie similarity between early spring and late autumn, between the time when everything begins and the time when it's winding down. A wave of November wistfulness hit me unexpectedly, and I had to remind myself that this was the end of winter, not the beginning.

"You look a little sad." Joe draped his leather jacket over my shoulders and gathered me in against the solid muscularity of his chest.

"I'm not unhappy." But I was. It had just occurred to me that it was a little dangerous, wanting Joe this much. In the past, I'd tended to see men who had a date stamped on their passports, a built-in escape clause, a ready-made ending. Or else I'd cared less for them than they had for me, and it was my "no" that defined the relationship. But what I felt for Joe was addictive; each time I made love with him, it seemed harder to imagine living without the balm of his touch.

"So how come you're so quiet all of a sudden?"

I didn't say anything. As observant as he was, I felt sure he could read me far too accurately, but saying the words out loud—I think I'm falling for you—would grant them a degree of finality.

"I was just thinking that the guide was leaving out all the interesting stuff. The fact that Franklin was messing around with Eleanor's secretary. Eleanor's hot and heavy letters to a female newspaper reporter."

"You're shitting me. Eleanor Roosevelt was a lesbian?" The breeze blew Joe's dark hair into his eyes, and for the first time I noticed strands of silver in the front.

"I certainly hope so. I mean, she wasn't getting it from Franklin."

"And he was doing other women? I thought he was paralyzed and they just had a kind of platonic marriage."

"I don't know the exact details, but in general, sex is more about desire than it is about mechanics. Even Stephen Hawking managed to find a way to have an affair."

Joe looked thoughtful. "Shit. I guess you can't trust anybody not to cheat. You know, my mother always said that Paolina was probably seeing some other guy toward the end, but Paolina said the breakup was only about us."

"I used to have a professor who said that one kind of truth can hide inside another."

"You used to have a professor?"

I took a deep breath. This was it, the time to come clean. "I have a Ph.D." Even if he got royally pissed off at me for lying to him and using him to sex up my dissertation, I needed for Joe to know me as I really was.

"You have a doctorate?" Joe looked utterly baffled. "In what?"

"Not in fucking men for money, if that's what you're thinking. In psychology."

"Wow." Joe gazed off into the distance for a moment, taking it in. "I can't believe it."

"I know," I said, "but when you think about it, you'll see that . . ."

"I can't fucking believe it," said Joe, still looking off somewhere to the left of us, where a Hummer was pulling out of a parking space. "Hey! You! Asshole!"

"Joe?" But he was off and running toward the car, which was now making a three-point turn.

I watched as Joe gesticulated at the Hummer and then pointed at another car. As I approached, I realized the cause of Joe's outrage: The car next to the Hummer had been hit hard enough to dent the rear door, and the convertible behind it had lost its grill and headlights.

I guessed they didn't teach tank maneuvers in most urban driving schools.

". . . so why don't you come on out of there, sir, and we can start by assessing the damage you've caused and alerting the owners of these vehicles . . ."

"Fuck you, man, I don't got to do nothin'," said the

driver, who, from the look of his beefy young face and arms, was fairly tanklike himself.

"Oh, yeah, tough guy, I'm afraid you do. I'm a police officer, and . . ."

"You ain't the boss of me!" The Hummer screeched into reverse as the driver yanked the wheel left, clearly intending to make a break for the highway.

"Asshole!" Joe spun and ran past me again, this time heading into his own car. He gunned the engine, drove up beside me and barked, "Get in!"

We were tearing up the Taconic before I'd gotten my seat belt buckled; as the Hummer came into view three cars ahead, Joe flipped open his cell phone: "Yes, I'm a police officer in pursuit of a black Hummer heading northbound on the Taconic after leaving the scene of a crime."

I stared at Joe. "You're calling 911? But no one was hurt. Yet! Oh, my God, watch out for that car," I said, as Joe passed a white sedan, only his left hand on the wheel.

"That's right, the Hummer hit two parked vehicles in the parking lot of Hyde Park . . . uh huh . . . NYPD, Detective Joseph Kain . . . great." Joe turned to me with a grin. "Highway patrol's on the way."

We'd caught up with the Hummer, and Joe was keeping a respectable car length behind. The sick feeling in my stomach subsided for a moment, and then I saw the Hummer's brake lights come on. "Shit! Look out, Joe, what's he doing?"

Joe switched lanes, bringing us up along the Hummer's left just as the bigger vehicle's wheels began to inch over the white line. "Seems like the asshole's about to try something truly stupid, like running us off the road."

"Okay, that's it! Get me out of this! I don't want to die because you can't stand being a witness to property damage!" A flood of adrenaline had me light-headed and trembling.

"Don't worry, M." Joe floored the gas and we shot ahead. "I think they're playing our song."

I listened, and suddenly I could hear it, too; the droning whine of police alarms, growing louder. The highway patrol pulled up behind the Hummer; a voice through a loudspeaker ordered it to get to the side of the road.

I sat, huddled in our car, while Joe pulled up and conferred with the other cops. In a few minutes, when my knees had stopped shaking, I got out and walked over to where the beefy young man was standing, his wrists handcuffed behind his back.

Seeing me, Joe reached out and put his arm around my shoulder. "You okay? Seems this joker had about a kilo of coke on him. No wonder he was in a hurry."

"Hey, don't you recognize him?" One of the highway patrolmen gestured to the young man, who had a doughy, unfinished look about him. "That's that heavy metal rock and roll guy's kid."

The other patrolman looked at the kid from behind mirrored sunglasses. "You mean Ozzie?"

"No, man, not that one, the good one."

The three men started discussing the comparative merits of seventies rockers, and I suddenly became aware of how alien a creature Joe was. He was hardwired to find conflict, or, more accurately, to create it, and whatever brief moments of connection and intimacy I felt with him, they were sure to be fleeting.

"Joe." I waited for him to notice that I was still shivering with cold and reaction, but he was busy talking with the highway cops, and I knew that if I kept repeating his name, he'd exchange a look with them: Women, what can you do?

It hadn't been more than ten minutes since I'd tried to come clean to Joe about who I really was, but standing on the side of the parkway, it was suddenly abundantly clear to me that our relationship was doomed.

Not because what we had was based on a purely physical attraction and his mistaken belief that I was an exclusive sexpert.

No, I realized as I walked back to Joe's car, wishing like hell that I'd learned how to drive back in high school, our relationship was doomed because Joe was a complete fucking narcissist.

joe

By the time we reached the Sawmill, I figured it would be better to have her yelling at me. Besides, I didn't know whether I was heading for my place, her place, or hitting an early dead end in the relationship. "Okay, let's have it. You're pissed off at me."

"And why do you think that might be?"

"Because you've been sitting across from me without saying a word, looking like you've got leeches stuck to your backside."

Oh, she didn't like hearing that. "No, Joe," she said carefully, "I meant, what has happened that you think might have caused me to feel upset?"

"You didn't want me interrupting our date to go chase down some shithead. You wanted my undivided attention, but what you don't understand is that I can't just shut the cop part of my brain off whenever I . . ."

"Wait. No. Stop. That is not it. I don't need for you to hang on my every word. But I was in the middle of telling you something fairly important, and you just decided to hare off after this guy, putting us both in danger . . ."

I got into the left hand lane and passed an old fart in a BMW convertible. "Marlowe, I'm one of the best damn defensive drivers on the force. You were never in danger."

"Joe, you're not getting the point. You didn't halt a kidnapping. You didn't stop a robbery. This was a relatively minor incident, which you jumped into because you wanted to. You like the adrenaline rush."

"He was driving recklessly."

"At ten miles an hour! Lots of people scratch cars in parking lots and don't leave a note—he just happened to be driving an armored vehicle!"

"And I'm just supposed to assume he's going to become more careful once he's on the parkway?"

Marlowe narrowed her eyes. "Yes, Joe, I think you should pay more attention to what's going on in front of your nose and less attention to trying to solve the world's problems."

"Well, honey, I think maybe you shouldn't be dating a cop."

"Well, honey, I think maybe I shouldn't."

I looked out my window at the Hudson River, where a few sailboats were scudding across the water's sparkling surface, taking advantage of the pleasantly balmy day. Inside the car, though, the atmosphere was less than healthy. I drove past the exit to my place and turned off at the boat basin. By the time I'd pulled up in front of Marlowe's building, I was feeling slightly sick to my stomach. It was occurring to me that if I went home like this, I'd have nothing left to look forward to—no hot date with Marlowe in the evening, no companion for my next day off, no one to ask along when I took my vacation in August.

And yes, I had already been thinking about Marlowe and me in August.

"This is stupid, Marlowe."

"I agree, it is stupid." Uh-oh, I knew what that tone meant. I put my hand on her arm and she still refused to look at me.

"I mean this fight is stupid. Look, when you come right down to it, most fights are stupid. I mean, you walk a beat and come across two friends whaling on each other, chances are they're not arguing over anything important. No, it's more like, one claimed the other owed him a tenner and the other said, You don't trust me to pay you back, and before you know it, Pow, they're breaking each other's bones."

Marlowe met my eyes, and I realized that she wasn't upset, she was furious. "I think this is about something fairly important, Joe. It's about your finding an excuse to check out of intimacy. And it's not just today, you've got a pattern going."

I let my hand fall away. "Yeah, but the trouble is, stupid fights don't seem stupid when you're in them. No, when you're in the thick of it, it seems like the stupid thing is really just the tip of a big, fucking important iceberg. And if you keep hammering away at the stupid things, you can make an iceberg happen."

Now Marlowe touched my arm. "I'm not just going to dismiss this as a stupid fight. You're not looking at what you're doing, Joe. Have you ever sat down and thought about why your marriage ended in a way that didn't just lay all the blame at Paolina's feet?"

Oh, please, how much crap was I going to have to take before she let me come upstairs? "Okay, now who's trying to solve the world's problems? You sound like a shrink."

"Well, there's a reason for that, as you would know if you'd been paying attention to me earlier." Marlowe stepped out of the car while Paris the doorman hustled out of the building to help.

"Dr. Riddle," he said, "someone's been waiting for you." He looked worried.

"A man or a woman?" She was already walking into the building before I had a chance to say anything. I waited for a moment, thinking. Had she forgotten an appointment? Were some of her clients refusing to take no for an answer? I turned off the ignition and followed them inside the dimly lit lobby.

"I don't understand," Marlowe was saying. It took me a moment for my eyes to adjust to the low light, and at first all I could see was the shadowy figure of a suited man standing beside her.

"Neither do we, but since your voice was the last message on her answering machine, we thought maybe you could help us figure this out."

I stood there for a moment as recognition dawned, trying to make sense out of what my least favorite person was doing here using the official "we." And then Dave turned to look at me and there was nothing left to do but play it by ear.

"Okay," I said slowly, "mind telling me what's going on here?"

marlowe

It was an interview, not an interrogation. An interview, I was informed, was simply a means to obtain information, as opposed to an interrogation, which was a means to obtain a confession.

No one thought I was actually guilty of anything, which made it all the more ridiculous for me to be nervously sipping a gin and tonic, wishing Joe were holding my hand instead of just standing there next to my chair, silently gathering information. But Joe, who had heard me called "Dr. Riddle" for the first time, had gone into some mode I hadn't seen him in before: He looked cynical, almost amused, as if we were bad actors and he was humoring us with his attention.

Clearly, he knew I'd been lying to him, and he was pissed off, although he wasn't going to confront me while his nemesis was in the room. I remembered all the comments he'd made about Dave, and I had to say, there was something about the man that was vaguely unsettling, something besides the fact that he was an FBI agent.

Oh, sure, Agent Bellamy knew how to maintain eye

216

contact and intone the correct, reassuring phrases, but there was something about him that seemed disconnected. When "just call me Dave" suggested I might need a drink, I felt sure that this was not indicative of any personal empathy; he'd probably read an article somewhere about the advisability of proferring alcohol to subjects exhibiting signs of emotional distress.

But the alcohol wasn't doing much to soothe my nerves. My client, Savannah LaBrecque, was dead, a possible suicide, although foul play had not yet been ruled out. This was every therapist's nightmare, and I kept wondering if there had been some clue in her sessions that I should have picked up on, some warning that she was capable of harming herself? Or had her mystery lover become her murderer?

Of course, that was what Agent Bellamy was here to find out. But I didn't like the man, Joe clearly distrusted him, and most damning of all, the agent clearly disliked my cat.

I had some theories about cat haters, and so far, Dave Bellamy, perched on the edge of my most comfortable chair with his back to a corner wall, had done nothing to disprove them.

"So, Dr. Riddle, Savannah didn't say anything to you about who she was going to see today?"

I shook my head. "I was supposed to see her tomorrow. What . . . how did she die?"

"The exact cause of death won't be known until the coroner releases his report." Dave cleared his throat. "We are trying to ascertain if she might have been with a client."

Joe made a derisive sound. "Why don't you just roll

Alisa Kwitney

back the tape, Dave? Or weren't you bugging her at the time?"

"Is that meant to be cute?"

"No, but it's nice to know you think of me that way."

"Listen, either you keep quiet or take a hike until I'm done talking with Dr. Riddle."

Joe held up his hands. "I'll be good. I'll just save all my comments up for later."

I took another sip of my drink, my own familiar living room somehow made alien by the presence of these two men, one of whom I had slept with, both of whom were concealing guns and, I suspected, a few other things as well.

"Dr. Riddle, your message said something about changing an appointment. Did it have anything to do with a man? Did she mention a particular boyfriend?"

"Yes. Savannah was talking to me about someone she . . . oh no. I've just realized something. I can't just disclose information without permission. I mean, there are privacy laws governing this."

"Not unless the Mayflower Madame got elected to office," said Joe.

Dave ignored him. "I understand your caution. But Dr. Riddle, your client is deceased. Nothing you tell us can hurt her."

I shook my head. "I can't. Even after death, there are clauses regarding client confidentiality. I have to get permission from Savannah's next of kin."

Dave did not appear to be perturbed. "You do that. I'm sure that Savannah's mother will want all to know every possible detail pertaining to her daughter's demise. And I'm going to have to speak to you as well, Joe, to determine the nature of your involvement in this case."

"What the hell are you talking about?"

"That was a dumb move, bringing Marlowe to the wedding. Or am I supposed to think this is all sheer coincidence, your seeing Marlowe, Marlowe seeing Savannah? Have you informed Marlowe that you were on the task force investigating Savannah's brothel?"

"I might have done so. Seems that she was the one keeping secrets from me."

"I never actually lied," I said to Joe, trying to guess what emotion was going on behind his clamped-down face. "I just let you believe what you believed about me."

"Gee, I feel so much better."

"Well, I guess that's enough for now," said Dave, watching us the way you'd observe animals at the zoo. "Marlowe, I'll be in touch after speaking with Savannah's mother. Joe, you and I are going to do some serious talking at my office one of these days."

"Yes, Dave, we will talk. And I'd be careful where you cast suspicion, because we all know that the best defense is a good offense."

If Dave was rattled by Joe's insinuation, he didn't show it. "I don't need a good defense, Joe," he said as he picked up his briefcase. "You do."

And then the door slammed and Joe and I were alone.

I didn't say anything. I just sat there and waited. Usually, that was enough to get most people talking, particularly average, law-abiding citizens with a guilty secret. But Marlowe just sat there across from me. Clearly, she'd also had training in the uses of silence and thought I might have something of my own to confess.

I broke first. "Okay," I said, "am I going to hear it?"

"Hear what?"

"Your explanation."

"I'd rather you tell me first why you're so angry."

"I'm not angry, Marlowe."

"I'm sensing anger." She sat there on the small, oatmeal-colored couch with her hands folded in her lap, waiting for me to respond. Her face, which I'd kissed clean of makeup earlier in the day, was calm and composed and serious, and completely at odds with the T-shirt that clearly revealed the sharp little points of her nipples and the jeans sliding down her hips.

"I'm wondering why a person with a Ph.D. in psychology would want a guy to think she's a call girl."

"So you were listening to me before." Her face softened as she said it, but I pretended not to notice. I didn't want to notice. I felt like an idiot, because now that I knew, it was obvious. How could I have failed to notice the titles on the bookshelf behind her? *Psychotherapy of the Borderline Adult. Surviving Sexual Contradictions. The Dark Side of Love. The Dialectic of Sex.*

"What the hell is *Oral Sadism and the Vegetarian Personality*?"

"What? Oh, you mean the book. Well, it's an ironic commentary on . . ."

"Never mind that. What I want to know is, was this some kinky, fuck a blue-collar-guy experiment? Were you doing research? Oh, whoa, that got a reaction. You writing a book, Marlowe? Am I a guinea pig?"

"Joe, I'm not going to sit here and recite lines from your script. Yes, you're very astute, but you're acting as though I were the only one here with a hidden agenda."

"Fuck the doubletalk, M. Just tell me, were you playing me all along?"

Her brows came together. "You're so eager to make this whole situation conform to some preconceived notion you have. What's the title of your drama? . . . How women aren't to be trusted? Or is this just a footnote to your marriage?"

"My marriage has nothing to do with this."

"Of course it does. You're obsessed with being rejected. Well, get over it, Joe. Why not tell me all about Dave, the agent who kicked you off the task force when you told him you thought he was spending too much time watching a little brothel?"

"Shit, how do you know all that?"

"You told me! Was I a part of your investigation from the beginning?"

"No," I said, and Marlowe went quiet. "I was looking into something else. Another case. But I dropped it, because after I got to know you, I realized you weren't the type to just kill a man and then leave him to rot." Marlowe flinched, and I had a sudden urge to touch her, reassure her.

I resisted it.

"I was getting wrong numbers," Marlowe said, her voice so soft that I had to lean in to hear it. "You just dialed a digit wrong."

"Not me—I dialed the right number." There was a sudden flare of hope in Marlowe's eyes, and I knew she half-expected me to add something romantic, like, It was the right number because it led me to you.

I wasn't about to say anything of the kind. "I mean, I dialed the number off some guy's cell phone, to see who he'd been talking to. And you were it."

"This man died?"

"Yeah, Marlowe, he died and it was ugly and pathetic and I don't want to talk about it anymore. So this book you're writing? What's it about—pretending to be someone you're not? Lying your way to a successful relationship? The sexual habits of working-class men?"

She held my gaze. "The central idea of my dissertation is that it's possible to be more honest pretending to be someone you're not than when you're in your everyday life pretending to be yourself."

I stood up, walked over to where she was sitting on the couch. "So what are you saying, that deep down, you're really a whore? I'm not one of your goatee-wearing intellectuals, I want it plain and simple."

Marlowe tilted her chin back to look at me. "That's not simple, Joe, that's simplistic. But if you need me to Dick and Jane it for you, fine, here goes. My lying to you about my identity was the reason I was able to be as honest with you as I was."

I made a rude noise. "If you ask me, sounds like the shrink needs a shrink." I had to admit, I was a little stung by the Dick and Jane comment. Did she think I was stupid?

"You're probably right. It's a known fact that people tend to be drawn to working on what gives them trouble in their personal lives."

"Meaning what?" Shit, maybe I was stupid. What I needed was a written transcript of this conversation, so I could study it later and figure out what we were really talking about.

"You figure it out."

For the first time, I heard the slight thickness in her voice. "You're drunk."

"Not drunk. Tipsy. That was a strong drink you gave me."

"I'm a beer drinker. I don't know how much gin to pour." I took in the slightly glazed look in her greenish-brown eyes, the flush on her cheeks. With her short red hair curling loosely around her face, she looked like a high school student. For some reason, I found myself offering to make her something to eat. It was five o'clock and we'd never really had lunch.

"I didn't know you could cook."

"I can't." But I could make an omelet. At least I

Alisa Kwitney

thought I could; I'd taken the medical tape off my fingers, but my right hand was still a little sore. "Want some eggs?"

"All right." She perched on a stool and watched me as I cracked the eggs. "Joe?"

"Yeah?" The smell of frying butter made me realize that I was hungry as well.

"Aren't we going to talk about Savannah? What do you think happened to her?"

Marlowe didn't have any beer, so I poured myself a glass of white wine. "Impossible to say without more information. Could be some guy she knew. Could be mob-related, which is what Dave wants to hear. Did she give you any clues?"

"I can't talk about what she told me."

"Of course, patient privilege. So tell me about being a shrink. Do you find yourself constantly observing people? Trying to sort out what they say from what they mean?"

Marlowe nodded. "And men find me cool and off-putting and if they don't, then I find them . . . I don't know. Unappealing. The ones who are smart enough aren't . . . I don't know . . . and I just haven't met anyone I wanted until I met you."

I handed her a plate with omelet and salad. "Do you want some, what is this, Chardonnay?"

"Pinot Grigio. I shouldn't."

I poured her a glass and refilled my own. I wanted her to remain as she was, tipsy but not drunk. Disinhibited. "Sounds like we have a lot in common, Marlowe. Put me in an interrogation room, and I can be so damn smart about people. Put me in a room with my ex-wife, I'm a complete asshole. I figured, Hey, my wife

224

doesn't cook dinner anymore, she's probably having an affair, she doesn't care about our marriage, she's wanting out."

Marlowe left her plate to walk around the table and stand behind me, draping her arms around my neck. "And was she? Cheating?"

"I think she was just getting fired up about her career. I think . . . I think maybe I just wasn't ready to be married. Shit, I don't know."

"I think you do," said Marlowe. I turned so that I could see her face.

"What do you think I know?" My arms came around her waist, and I rested my head against her flat stomach. I could feel where the cotton of her shirt had ridden up, exposing the warmth of her flesh.

"I think you know why you told me that story about not trusting Paolina right after you cooked me dinner. I think you're telling me something here."

I turned my head and pressed my lips against her belly. "So what am I telling you?"

A moment of silence stretched between us, as dense and meaningful as a declaration. I felt I had just committed to something without meaning to, and I felt a momentary panic. This day had gone from one extreme to another, from Marlowe's cold anger at me to mine at her, from the possibility of our breaking up to the feeling that I was on the verge of becoming part of a real couple, with all the usual expectations and demands.

And I didn't even know who she was. Before, I'd been a little intimidated by her wealth, but I'd thought she was someone I could help climb out of a self-destructive life-style.

Instead, I'd just discovered that she was a fucking triple threat: smarter than me, richer than me, better educated than me.

On the other hand, all those comments she'd made about how good I was in the sack were starting to make sense. If all she'd known were tweedy academics, no wonder I'd managed to rock her world. Not to mention the exotica factor—cops were probably as rare as white tigers in her world.

And then it all clicked, and I knew what I needed to do.

"All right," I said. "Let's try something." I left the kitchen and went over to my jacket, took out a pair of handcuffs. "Still trust me?"

Marlowe had followed me into the living room. "I think so. I mean yes, I do."

I lined the inside of the cuffs with the silk handkerchiefs I'd brought for the purpose. "Sit back down on the chair."

She glanced at the huge, east-facing windows, which looked out onto the park. "Should we . . . can we close the blinds?"

I didn't see the point, but didn't want to argue it, either. When the room was shaded from view, I helped her remove her shirt and then cuffed her wrists to the back of the chair. It probably wasn't what you'd call comfortable, but if she didn't sit all the way back, it wouldn't be too bad. "Joe?"

"Yeah?" I tugged off her jeans.

"Should you be using your hand so much? I thought the whole purpose of a cast . . ."

"I changed my mind. You'd better be silent. Anything you say can and will be held against you . . ." I pulled down her underpants. "All right, let's begin."

"This is a game, right?"

I just looked at her with a blank face until she shivered. "Does it feel like a game?"

"Not exactly."

"Good." Always, in the past, I had sensed that she'd gotten turned on by the idea of my being some kind of an authority. Of course, she'd always treated the whole thing ironically, as a little campy in-joke between us: Bring your handcuffs. Yes, Officer. And I'd never had any real interest in dominating her or any other woman.

Until now. She'd manipulated me with what she knew of male psychology; now I was manipulating her with what I knew about stress, pleasure, and the use of control on a subject.

"What do you want from me, Joe?"

"You'll figure it out." I bent my head, inhaled the unique, womanly scent of her, which nearly undid me. Pressing her thighs apart, I tasted her.

"My God that feels good. Oh, that's incredible. But I'm too tense to come like this. I just didn't want you to think . . . what are you doing, Joe? Joe, I'm not sure I . . . I . . ."

I did something with my tongue that is still officially illegal in quite a few states, and then did something else with my good hand that I believe is forbidden by at least two of the world's major religions.

Marlowe screamed, and I was betting it wasn't in pain. Not when she opened her eyes and looked at me as if I'd just brought enlightenment. With a last kiss on the sweet curve of her inner thigh, I stood up, still fully clothed.

"Joe?"

"Yeah?" I removed my shirt.

"What are we doing here?"

I released her wrists from the handcuffs. "Stand up."

"I'm not sure if I can. My knees are still a little wobbly . . ."

"Bend over the table."

"You're not going to spank me, are you?"

Hmm. I hadn't been planning on it, but . . . I gave her bottom a light smack. "Joe!" I considered the tone of her voice for a moment, then smacked her again, a little harder. "Joe?"

"Too rough?" I rubbed her tush, which had turned slightly pink.

"Er, no, I think I'm kinkier than I realized."

I stood right behind her, pressed up against her bottom, and ran my hand over her breasts. "That's useful information, but it's not what I'm after." I gently pushed her down so that she was leaning across the table.

"Um, Joe, not that I'm complaining or anything—I really liked everything you've done so far—more than liked, but if you're planning on going where no man has gone before, I'm not sure that I'm ready."

"I'm not going to hurt you."

"Yes, but . . ." She was so nervous that her legs had started trembling.

I sighed. "No virgin territory, okay?"

"Well, in that case . . ." She bent over the table, presenting me with her delectably round tush.

"Good." I leaned over and lightly bit one rounded cheek, which made her squeal. "Spread 'em."

She was so wet that I was able to enter her in one, quick, deep thrust. Marlowe made a soft, animal sound. "How does that feel?"

"Mmmgh."

"Excuse me?"

"Please move!"

I moved, a very little. "Like that?"

"Harder?"

I thrust into her. "Like that?"

"Harder."

I grabbed her shoulders and slammed into her as hard as I could, then did it again. I saw stars behind my closed eyelids, just like in a cartoon. I paused for a moment and Marlowe moved in a way that made me slide out of her. She turned around to face me and I lifted her up on the table.

"Joe." She reached for my shoulders, and I entered her again. "I wanted to see you." Her eyes were moist.

"Did I hurt you?"

"Not hurt, it felt . . . too good. Joe?"

I began moving inside her, then stopped abruptly. "I can't hold on anymore."

"Look at me. I want to watch you come."

My hands clenched her hips and I felt sensation ripple up from the soles of my feet to the top of my head. Marlowe's eyes fluttered closed as her internal muscles began to contract, and for a moment, I could not have said where one of us ended and the other began.

I came back to myself, struggling for breath. Marlowe's arms were still linked around my neck and I bent to press a kiss to her perspiration-dampened collarbone, overcome by tenderness and something that felt oddly like regret.

And then she whispered in my ear.

"I love you, Joe."

Which, of course, was just the confession I'd been hoping for.

marlowe

It took me twenty-four hours to understand that I had been dumped. Even then, I kept coming up with excuses for Joe's not calling.

He'd been kept for questioning by the FBI.

He was hot on the trail of a murderer.

His mother was in the hospital.

Gangsters had him hanging suspended from his feet in a warehouse in New Jersey.

I obsessively reviewed his parting words to me on Wednesday night. He'd promised to go to his parents for dinner; he might have to work a little the next day, but he'd call me. Love you, he'd said at the door.

Without a personal pronoun, was "love you" a question, an injunction to himself, or merely an emotional balloon that, untethered from any I, had floated off to become impaled on the nearest sharp object?

But Joe was not a poem, and it was impossible to unpack his statements and be sure of their intended meaning. Perhaps the words held no clues at all. I'd often counseled my clients that we tend to assume that every-

231

thing revolves around us, but sometimes we are merely bit players in someone else's drama.

Maybe Joe had reunited with his ex-wife. Maybe there was another woman, unmentioned, whom he'd been eyeing in the local coffee shop, someone he barely knew but who had a greater grip on his imagination than I did. Maybe they'd only exchanged a few flirtatious words before now, but she'd been hovering in the wings, a possibility more mysterious and enticing than myself.

Maybe she was French.

At first, I fought to remain open to the possibility that he was just acting a little flaky, the way many men will when faced with deepening intimacy. On Thursday, which was supposed to be his second day off, I left a deliberately chipper message on his machine: Hey, what's up, any news about Savannah? Of course, the real, unspoken message was: Aren't we getting together later?

By Friday morning, I had faced the fact that there was a perfectly good reason that Joe hadn't contacted me.

Because I'd been dumped.

And, intelligent, experienced thirty-six-year-old woman that I was, all I could think of, with astonishment, was that I had learned absolutely nothing about men in the past twenty years.

I was shocked that he had lied. I was astonished that he had made love to me with such fierce intensity and then disappeared. I was stunned to realize that the intimacy that had made me feel helplessly consumed with the desire to be near him had made him want to hightail it as far as possible away from me.

I understood denial and reaction formations. I was aware of all the myriad of strategies that people use to protect themselves from intimacy and hurt. Christ, I'd already pegged the man as hopelessly self-involved back when he decided that what our date was lacking was a high-speed car chase.

But I was also strangely incapable of grasping how Joe could have touched me in such a stunningly intimate fashion and then withdrawn so completely. How could he have been so focused on my pleasure and then proved to be so insensible to the fact that he was causing me pain?

Making matters worse, I couldn't seem to access any righteous anger over his vanishing act. Instead, I vacillated between fantasies of calling Joe and insisting that he talk with me and explain himself, and equally shameful fantasies of revenge.

I'd cite him with a citizen's complaint; I'd send him a care package of self-help books at work; I'd barrage his answering machine with a selection of Alanis and Gwen Stefani man-bashing songs, which would be doubly irritating to him because of the fact that the bastard didn't seem to listen to anything written after the Berlin wall came down.

Joe was an asshole. He was an immature, egocentric, emotionally constipated idiot. Who happened to have shown me a side of myself I hadn't known existed.

Of course, I wasn't the only one in my apartment going through an anxious depression.

Burt, who had been locked in my office for the duration of the FBI agent's visit and had remained incarcerated during the omelet and sex fiasco, was pissed off at me. Literally. He had revealed his pissed offedness by spraying my white linen couch with pungent tomcat urine, and no amount of cleaning or disinfecting could remove the acrid aroma.

At first, preoccupied with my love life and with thoughts of Savannah, I'd tried to disguise the problem with a lemon scent, but Nancy, my elegant East-side client, kept sniffing and complaining. Carl, my twice-monthly actor, actually searched the cushions in a successful bid to postpone discussing his continued Vicodin use. Worst of all, a new referral turned out to be pregnant and so acutely sensitive to bad odors that she had to cut her session short.

I figured it was probably for the best. I wasn't exactly feeling at the top of my game. Who knew what clues I'd missed with Savannah. Not to mention the fact that I was under the lingering threat of a lengthy interrogation—or was that an interview—by federal agents.

On Monday, my fifth day living without Joe and with the smell of cat urine, I decided to visit a trendy Soho furniture store, where everything was elegant and whimsical and hand-crafted in Europe.

It was a perfect early May day, soft and fair, and the apple trees in Central Park were all shedding pink and white blossoms. I, on the other hand, had a huge stress pimple on my forehead which my short hair could not conceal, and had mysteriously gained three pounds despite not having eaten anything in the past few days besides rice pudding, strawberries, and an occasional sushi roll.

In short, I was in a perfect mood to treat myself to something outrageous, so long as it did not require my having to remove clothing to try on.

The store was called Down, Boy and was staffed by a

slender Englishman who managed to make buying a sofa sound like a fun and slightly naughty enterprise. Caught up in the salesman's seductive patter, I found myself wanting more than just a couch. All the chairs and tables had yielding curves and sensuous contours but seemed to be teetering on tiny little heels, and suddenly I thought of my apartment's austere, pale décor and wanted radical change.

I wanted to be colorful. I wanted to be luxurious. I wanted walls of rich mango and a hot pink love seat and I wanted to throw out the damn chair that Joe had handcuffed me to and replace it with something from the store's Retro Modern collection.

I wound up spending a small fortune at the store. I had the money, of course—I was a trust fund kid who'd grown up at a time when it was still fashionable to be poor in New York, and the habit of pretending not to have money had stuck with me into adulthood. Still, I had a strange, light-headed feeling as I took the subway home, as if I'd just lost a lot of blood all at once. The furniture was due to arrive in about two weeks.

When I got back into my apartment, I had three messages on my answering machine. The first was from Savannah's mother, returning my phone call and telling me we needed to talk. The second was from Dave, the FBI agent, informing me that he had a subpoena granting him access to my appointment book.

The third was from Joe, telling me in a flat, completely emotionless tone of voice that I should probably consult my doctor.

"Oh, Burt," I said, and tried to bury my face in his soft fur, only to discover that he had just urinated on my bed.

joe

I couldn't believe it.

Just couldn't fucking believe it.

She'd given me the clap.

Okay, so as it turned out, not the clap, but some new venereal disease that made taking a piss a whole new adventure in pain.

At first, I'd figured I'd just been a little too enthusiastic with the rough sex shtick. I'd made my excuses so that I could go home and soak myself in a hot bath. By lunchtime, it was clear that I was in no shape to get together with Marlowe. Not knowing what to say, I'd said nothing.

Friday, at the precinct, things went from bad to worse. People kept dropping by my desk to tell me things—they were on my side, Dave was an asshole, nobody believed the rumors about me going vigilante and messing up the whole three-year FBI investigation by dating the key subject's shrink.

Despite the fact that the coroner had ruled Savannah's death an accidental suicide, reporters had started sniffing around, and we knew that when they got wind of a story involving a beautiful call girl, a high-profile gangster, and the FBI, there was going to be some pretty unhappy people on high.

We'd had not one but two visits from Dave and a plump sergeant from the organized crime bureau. We all pegged the sarge as being about two minutes from retirement, since he spent most of his time telling us how much he hated these new nontraditional organized crime groups, so many Latino and Russian and Asian gangs that he couldn't keep straight, not like the old days when the Italian mafia ran the show, and you got to order pasta puttanesca at really nice Sicilian restaurants.

I figured Dave was keeping him around like a ventriloquist's dummy, in case he needed to pretend he was getting opinions from the NYPD.

Lieutenant Franks had started keeping a bottle of antacid on his desk. I wondered what Dave was telling Franks about me. Probably that I was a loose screw, and should not be involved with the investigation.

I could barely muster the appropriate response. I'd never been sick much, before; now I discovered that when you're in acute discomfort, your physical distress is pretty much all you can think about. I felt like apologizing to my mother for all the times I'd told her she was a hypochondriac. I wished I could ask her for the name of her doctor, but the guy was probably a family friend who went to temple with my father—no way was I yanking my poor shmekel out for a guy like that. He'd probably just shake his head and tell my folks that this was what came from messing with *shiksas*.

On Saturday morning, I weighed my options and decided to head back to the emergency room. I got there at nine, and had to wait two hours before I was seen.

Naturally, I got a female intern: an attractive young Russian woman with suspicious eyes and a distractingly dark mole on her cheek. Her badge said she was Dr. Irina Markovna.

"Is it your hand?" She was looking at my records.

"No, they said I could take the temporary cast off this week, and it feels fine. Look, can I see a male doctor? This is kind of . . ."

The look Dr. Markovna gave me wasn't what you'd call sympathetic. "If you'd like to wait another couple of hours . . ."

"It's a guy problem."

"Excuse me?"

"It's . . ." I gestured at the general source of my discomfort.

"Ah. What are your symptoms?"

This had to be divine punishment. I swore to myself that if I got through this without permanent damage, then dear God, I was swearing off sex until marriage.

Which would be with some nice girl of my mother's choosing.

Dr. Markovna snapped on some latex gloves and told me to remove my pants.

Goddamn Marlowe. I haven't had sex in a year, she'd said, and when I did I was very particular. Yeah, right. She'd probably researched her way through Columbia, Hunter, N.Y.U. and five boroughs of fire departments before I'd met her. Not that it was ever going to work out between us, anyway. I mean, first of all, she was loaded, second of all, she was a fucking braniac, and third of all, she was obviously a complete career woman, no desire for kids. And she wasn't Jewish. And . . .

Dr. Markovna said two words in Russian that made me look where I'd been trying very hard to avoid looking. I got the feeling that she'd made some Slavic exclamation, as in, Dear Lord, we never saw degenerate diseases like this back in Minsk. "You may pull up your trousers," she told me, peeling off the gloves and dropping them in some kind of biohazard container.

"How bad is it?"

"It is treatable with antibiotics. I took a swab and we have to test to make sure, but my guess is chlamydia."

"What the hell is chlamydia?"

She told me some Latin term, then added that I should inform any and all bed partners, past and present.

By Monday the diagnosis was confirmed and I had a little bottle of pills to see me right. I called Marlowe after I got home from the precinct and tried to tell myself it was better ending things this way. The chlamydia had been a blessing in disguise, preventing me from getting into yet another doomed relationship with another unsuitable woman.

But it was four-thirty in the afternoon on a beautiful spring day, I had the next two days off, and I had nowhere I wanted to go and no one I wanted to see. Remembering the little ratlike cat of Marlowe's, I suddenly missed the way the little guy would wind in and out of my legs when I walked in the door, the way he would howl miserably if you left the house for five minutes, the way he would jump on the table and try to snatch the Teriaki chicken out of the container and then still purr when you picked him up.

Burt. That was his name. I needed a Burt. Grabbing my wallet, I headed down to the A.S.P.C.A. to find myself a neurotic companion of my own.

I came back home two hours later with a year-old Siamese named Mai Tai who had something vaguely Burtlike about the shape of her head and the sound of her yowl. The minute I let the cat out of her box, however, the phone rang and she scurried under my bed.

I was about to pick up the phone, but the caller hung up after the third ring. Probably my mother. She'd phoned earlier in the day and left a message saying she just wanted to know if I was alive or dead, because she hadn't heard from me in over a week. She also wanted me to know that she was still alive, in case I was wondering.

I spent half an hour trying to lure the Siamese out with a tin of sardines and a lot of "Here, kitty, here puss, nothing to be scared of, pretty girl," but eventually I figured out that the last person who'd handed her that line had scooped her up and dumped her at the animal shelter. Why should she trust me to be any different? I left her to eat the fish in her own sweet time.

The phone rang again and I considered answering it before deciding that the cat had the right idea; there was nothing wrong with hiding out for a while.

The machine clicked on: It was my father. Clearing his throat, he started to say something about my mother going into the hospital.

My mother never went to the hospital. To the doctor's, yes, constantly. To the hospital?

"Dad? It's me. What's wrong? What happened?"

"She was having chest pains, I thought it was heartburn again, or maybe she was just saying it because she didn't think I was paying enough attention to her."

"What happened?"

"She had a heart attack, Yossi. The paramedics had to come with an ambulance."

A wave of cold fear washed over me. "But she's alive, right? She's not dead."

"She's alive, of course she's alive. Listen, could you come over here? I left the store in a hurry and I haven't told Itzik where to put the new deliveries." And then my father started to make a terrible sound; for a moment I thought he was choking.

"Dad? Are you all right? Dad?" And then, in a calmer voice, I said, "You're at Columbia Presbyterian? I'm on my way."

"Hey, Ma. How are you?"

My mother was lying quietly in a semiprivate room in the cardiac ICU, one arm attached to an IV and the other to a blood pressure band. There were little black pads on her chest that hooked up to a heart monitor and a bunch of other machines I didn't recognize. An oxygen mask dangled near her face.

She looked tired and drawn and about ten years older than the last time I'd seen her. "So this is what it takes to make you come see me?"

I lowered myself into the chair by her bedside and took her hand, which felt cool to the touch. "Heard you gave Dad a bit of a scare."

My mother met my eyes. "What did he tell you?"

I stroked her dark hair back from her face. "That you had a heart attack."

"Not a full one. A sort of warning one. Angina, they told me." She closed her eyes for a moment. "It's not your fault."

"I know that, Ma."

"I'm going to be fine."

"Of course you are." I turned away from the sight of the IV needle taped to her pale arm. The veins on her hands seemed more prominent than before.

"Do you know exactly what it means, angina?"

"A sort of charley horse in the muscle of the heart."

"I don't understand half of what they're telling me."

"When I leave here, I'll talk to the doctor."

"She's a woman."

"That's good, isn't it?"

My mother made a little shrugging gesture. "Your father is useless. Is he at the store?"

"No, Ma, he's just outside."

"Well, make sure he eats something."

"Don't worry, Ma."

"Yossi, if anything happens to me . . ."

"What are you saying that for, Ma? Nothing's going to happen." I rubbed her cold hand in both of mine. "I'm going to take care of you."

"Of course you will. But who's going to take care of you? I'm not going to live forever."

"Don't talk like that, Ma."

"You know the incidence of suicide among cops?"

"I'm not going to kill myself."

"And when I die, when your father dies, what then? What's holding you to life then, Yossi?" My mother put her hand on my arm. "Go find a girl, someone with a brain, not just a nice tush like that ex-wife of yours. Because that tush won't look so hot in ten years, my son, but a good brain, that'll keep you on your toes."

"What if she's smarter than me?" I was joking, but my mother looked at me sharply.

"Then she'll make you smarter."

I kissed my mother and promised her to start looking for a nice, Jewish girl as soon as she got better.

I bought my father some yogurt and canned peaches from the hospital cafeteria, where I naturally ran into Dr. Markovna from my humiliation in the ER earlier in the day. She gave me a sardonic, very Slavic look, smiled and then turned back to the sandwich selection.

"She looks nice," my father said, rallying. "Is she Jewish? Ask her out."

"Not really appropriate under the circumstances, Dad." I stayed with him for the consultation with my mother's doctor, who told me that with a change of diet and a gradual introduction to some mild form of exercise, my mother could look forward to many healthy years of life.

And then, tired and shaken, I went home and decided that what I really needed to do was anesthetize myself completely. I tried getting drunk, but two beers didn't even begin to take the edge off. I hadn't been stoned since my senior year of high school, but as I recalled, it did a pretty decent job of slowing higher brain function.

I didn't care if it was illegal. I didn't care if anyone saw me scoring some weed and had me reported. All I knew was that I was going to get high enough to escape gravity and hover above everything for a couple of hours.

As soon as my hands stopped shaking.

marlowe

Faced with not one but two difficult meetings, I spent half an hour in front of the bathroom mirror, blending foundation, applying blush, even brushing on a hint of eye shadow before accidentally poking myself in the eye with the mascara wand, which meant rinsing out my eye with water and washing all the makeup off.

Turning my focus to clothes, I hesitated for a while in my closet while Burt sniffed at my shoes and batted an odor-eater ball around. Of course it didn't really matter what I wore to confront Savannah's grieving mother and Dave the disgruntled FBI agent; regardless of how I presented myself, I assumed both people would be predisposed to feel sharply critical, and possibly even openly hostile toward me.

But I thought I might feel marginally more composed if I looked put together, crisp, elegant, clean. Because I didn't feel clean; Joe's message had implied that I was now the kind of woman army sergeants warned their troops to avoid. Still, no reason to advertise the fact.

I wound up selecting khaki capris, a white shirt with a

large, open white collar, black ballet style flats. My hair, which had begun to curl from humidity, provided the only bright color.

A mournful howl, followed by frantic scrabbling, alerted me to the fact that I had just trapped Burt inside my closet. I opened the door and he shot out, racing twice around the bedroom before streaking away.

Shit. I went to the kitchen and poured a healthy splash of vodka into my orange juice—I figured I drank screwdrivers at brunches, and this one counted as medicinal—and had just picked up the phone to dial my doctor when the intercom buzzed.

"Yes, Paris?" A surge of adrenaline washed over me. Was it Joe? The police, to confiscate my appointment book? The FBI?

My doorman's voice crackled back through the intercom. "Ms. LaBrecque to see you."

"Let her up, thanks." I took a long sip of my drink and poured the rest down the drain.

My first thought when Savannah's mother walked in the door was that she was much younger than I had expected, maybe as young as forty, and a youthful forty at that. I had gotten the impression of a nervous, somewhat clingy older woman who needed her daughter's constant attention. In person, Marie LaBrecque looked like Savannah's more buxom older sister. She was dressed in a fitted black blazer, slacks, and high heels, and in her arms, she held a teacup Yorkshire Terrier, its silky black and tan fur held back from its face by a red ribbon.

"I have a cat," I said, but when I saw how she was holding the puppy, I added, "let me shut him in the bedroom."

"Thanks," she said when I returned. "Peaches and I are sticking together right now."

"Where do you want to sit?"

"Anywhere."

I decided on the kitchen, feeling it might be upsetting to Marie to be shown into the office where I'd seen her daughter. It was only when she sat down near the window that I could see the lines and shadows of age and grief around the faded green eyes, and another, subtler difference.

This woman, who must have given birth to Savannah in her late teens, was harder and more experienced than her daughter. I knew, without a word exchanged between us, that this was not Marie's first tragedy, merely her worst.

"So you're the psychologist," said Marie, pulling a cigarette out of her elegant red leather handbag with shaking fingers. Her Southern accent was flatter than her daughter's, less refined. "Savannah never told me she was seeing you. I guess she was embarrassed, don't ask me why. If she wanted to spend her hard-earned money telling her problems to a stranger, who am I to object? Although God knows I would've listened, and maybe been able to give her some advice that didn't come out of a book." The puppy, Peaches, shivered in her lap.

I considered a few possible responses before settling on, "So, you don't think that sometimes you appreciate what you're getting more when you pay for it?"

Marie gave me a reluctant smile. "All right, point taken. And God knows everyone needs a little something on the side. It's just that I thought she told me everything, and now . . ." A shadow crossed her face. "Damn. Sorry. Mind if I smoke?"

"Normally, yes. Today, no."

Marie flicked her lighter off and took a deep drag of her cigarette, one of those long, thin kinds that are targeted at women: You've come a long way, Baby. "Do you want something to drink? Coffee? Juice? Water?"

"Whiskey would be nice." The smell of tobacco followed us into the kitchen, reminding me of long-ago nights spent clubbing, making unexpected connections with strangers, or, on occasion, bumping up against unanticipated dangers—barfights, strange parties, getting lost in a desolate part of town. I offered my guest a small plate to use as an ashtray and wondered if what I was experiencing was truly déjà vu or a premonition that something bad was about to happen.

I handed Marie the whiskey and she took a long swallow before speaking. "Dr. Riddle, the feds keep telling me I'm supposed to give you permission to tell them whatever my daughter told you."

"But you have reservations?"

"I just don't see why they're so damn interested." Marie exhaled a final plume of smoke before stubbing out her cigarette. "What'd Savannah tell you, anyway? She mention this guy she was seeing? She tell you his name?"

I shook my head. "She referred to him as Brad, like the movie actor, but that wasn't his real name. All I know is that he was doing some sort of research project, and that he wasn't actually intimate with her."

"She tell you what I had to say about him?"

"She said you didn't approve of him."

"Damn right. I told her there's two kinds of men—the ones with visible vices, like they want to do it with two girls at once or they want to be diapered and spanked, and the ones who pretend not to have any vices at all. Those are the dangerous customers."

I thought about Joe and tried not to look like someone who enjoyed being spanked. "But you don't know who this man was?"

Marie took a deep swallow of her whiskey. "Savannah thought he was a writer or a professor working on his dissertation, but I always suspected . . ."

The intercom buzzed again. I was very aware of Marie's eyes on me as I pressed the button. "Yes, Paris?"

"Man here to see you, Dr. Riddle. Dave Bellamy."

I held Marie's gaze. "Tell him to give me a moment. I'm not dressed."

"He says he can wait upstairs."

Seeing that I really didn't have much choice, I told Paris that would be fine. Marie stood, shifting the puppy to her other arm. "Who is it?"

"A federal agent. He's subpoenaed my appointment book, because I told him I couldn't speak to him without your permission."

"Huh. Well, the way I figure it, never say yes until you know the real worth of what you've got. That's why I wanted to talk to you before you went and told the feds anything. You know that my house is being bugged?"

I cast my mind back. "Savannah told me you thought you heard clicks on the phone."

Marie huffed a laugh utterly devoid of humor. "She

tell you I was paranoid? Well, I have reason to be paranoid. In my life, I have been stalked by two ex-husbands, and I know when I am being spied on."

"Marie, Agent Bellamy is going to be here any moment. I need to know what you want me to do."

"I don't know yet."

"Well, he's going to ask you."

The doorbell rang. Marie patted the puppy, which was making low, unhappy growling noises and looking at the door with its ears pricked. "Hush, Peaches, it's all right."

I let Agent Bellamy inside.

"Dr. Riddle." He looked so blond and Midwestern and sincere in his pale gray suit and navy tie, the type you see with kids and golden retrievers in life insurance commercials. He took in the fact that Marie was standing next to me, the puppy now trembling violently in her arms. "I didn't know you had company." I couldn't swear, but for a moment, I thought Dave Bellamy had a moment of slight discomfiture.

I wasn't sure whether he was feeling uncomfortable interrupting me with a client or whether he recognized Savannah's mother, so I simply said, "Do you want to have a seat while I get you the appointment book?"

Dave glanced at Marie. "Or perhaps Ms. LaBrecque has decided to allow you to supply me with any pertinent information regarding her daughter's therapy?"

Well, he knew who she was, all right, but boy, that was one awkward, impersonal appeal to a mother who has just lost her child.

"Well, I don't know," said Marie, giving Dave a challenging look. "How about you start opening up first by telling me why you were bugging my house?"

"You're not doing yourself or your daughter any fa-
vors by playing games with the FBI, Ms. LaBrecque."

"Is that a threat? If so, it won't work on me. My daughter is dead." Marie's eyes were cold and bright. "I don't
think it matters what I do anymore."

"Are you saying you have no interest in seeing justice
done?"

The puppy gave a sharp squeak of pain; Marie must
have gripped it too tightly. "Justice?" Her voice was very
quiet. "That's your game."

I walked over to Dave, who looked a little lost, as if
he'd just wandered into a foreign country: the land of
emotion. "Why don't I just get you my current appointment book so you can be on your way?"

"I'd appreciate it."

I went into my office and Dave followed me. I felt a
moment's embarrassment that the room wasn't perfectly
tidy. I'd been going through my notes on Savannah's
therapy, and hadn't had time to put everything away in
the file cabinet. I spotted a copy of my book, *The Woman's
Medical Guide*, left out on my desk open to the section on
Sexually Transmitted Diseases. Just look natural and relaxed, I thought, no reason for him to suspect I'm reading
it for myself.

"Here it is." I'd copied over my next week's appoint-
ments already.

"Thank you." Dave took the fake leather-bound book,
and I tried not to think about strange men reading my
personal handwritten notes in the margins regarding
"full leg waxing, Tues" and "Must buy tampons."

"Dr. Riddle, I was wondering if . . ." Dave glanced

down at the appointment book. "If I have any questions regarding handwriting or abbreviations . . ."

"Agent Bellamy, I don't think you're going to find the answers you're looking for in there. I only saw Savannah twice, and there's a lot about her life I didn't know."

"Still, if I have any questions I need to ask you . . ." Dave cleared his throat. "You will be available for further questioning?"

"Of course, but I won't tell you anything Ms. LaBrecque hasn't authorized."

"Understood. By the way, I would think that a health care professional would be aware that second-hand smoke is a leading cause of—"

I shut the door on his medical concerns. Marie sank down into a chair. "God," she said, "I need another smoke." She lit a cigarette for herself, and the puppy whined. "Hush, Peaches, we'll go in a minute." After a moment, Marie looked at me and said, "Thanks."

"I wish I could do more. Ms. LaBrecque, do you think there's a chance that by cooperating we could help the FBI explain the cause of Savannah's death?"

"I don't need explanations." At my surprised look, Marie added, "My daughter was one very unhappy girl, and every time she'd stage one of her suicide attempts, I'd think, next time, maybe you'll take one pill too many, maybe the man won't come home in time to find you."

Astonished, I could only say, "Suicide attempts?"

"You didn't know? The first was six years ago. Always over some idiot who said he was going to leave his wife. If you ask me, the big difference between sex for free and sex for money is that sex for money usually costs a lot less."

Marie shook some ashes off her lap and stood up, holding the squirming puppy in her right hand like a small, furry football. "All right now, let's get going, Peaches."

"Ms. LaBrecque, if Savannah's death wasn't a homicide, do you have any thoughts about why the FBI would want to know the details of what went on in her therapy sessions?"

Marie reached out a hand and touched the side of my face. "You really are just like one of my college girls," she said, making it clear she wasn't paying me a compliment. "And I'll tell you what I tell them. Anyone who wants something is a potential customer. And it's up to the seller to find out what the customer really wants. Because it's not what he says he wants. It's what he's too embarrassed to ask for out loud." I must have looked blank, because she clarified, "He was interested in *you*, Doctor. And not just in your abbreviations."

She left without saying another word and I didn't try to stop her. Looking back, had I picked up any subliminal hints that Dave had been attracted to me? Nope, none. Yet surely Marie was savvier than I was about such things. Was it possible he was interested in me simply because I'd been Savannah's therapist? Or because I'd dated Joe?

Putting Marie's glass and ashtray in the sink, I reflected on what she'd said about men and sex, and realized that Joe had skipped out on me without settling up. When you paid a prostitute, you weren't paying for sex, you were paying for the understanding that you were free to walk away afterward without apologies or excuses.

252

But Joe hadn't paid me a thing, which meant that he owed me a few explanations. He could start by explaining just what sort of a medical condition I might have caught. Then he could go on to telling me what the deal was with Dave.

He could finish by explaining why he'd turned off like a light.

joe

Unfortunately, none of the local dealers wanted to sell me so much as a bud. They explained that they weren't dealers. They didn't even associate with dealers. In fact, they were slightly affronted by my assumption that they *were* dealers, but anyone could make a mistake, so they weren't taking it personally.

Then I was told to Have a Nice Day in such a manner as to suggest an implicit Fuck You, Asshole.

Clearly, I looked like a cop, I walked like a cop, I made street-friendly small talk like a cop. Good thing I'd never had my heart set on working undercover.

Finally, out of desperation, I called Paolina and asked her for a reference, figuring that fashion people always know where to buy the best drugs.

The worst part was fielding my ex-wife's concerned questions. "Are you all right, Joe?"

"No, but I will be."

Two hours later, I was happily flipping around from channel to channel while eating pepperoni on stale matzoh. I spent some time watching a soap opera where a heavily made-up blonde was having a picnic with a guy who looked like a gay stripper but turned out to be a disgraced cop. Now that was one guy the dealers would never sniff out; even if he flashed his badge, they'd all stick around, expecting him to tear off his shirt and start singing "YMCA."

When the made-up blonde began to quiver with what was either lust or indigestion, I switched over to an old *Mr. Rogers* show.

I was a little disappointed when I realized that the trolley had just left the land of make believe and good old Fred was exchanging his puce zip-up cardigan for his leisure suit jacket.

"And I like you, just the way you are," said Mr. Rogers, staring right into my eyes with the same calm good humor he'd had back when I was four. Suddenly I remembered that the real Fred Rogers was dead, had died a year or so ago, and found myself tearing up. Who was going to tell me that I was special, now that Mr. Rogers was gone?

Switching channels again, I found myself listening to an old guy with a huge, bulbous nose saying something about the connection between pretense and desire. I fired up the joint again and took a deep drag before settling back into the couch.

"This is the play where Shakespeare really lays Marlowe's shadow to rest." The next few points did not make sense to me, possibly because I drifted off into thoughts of another Marlowe. "You have the character of Rosalind, pretending to be a boy, teaching the man she loves how to woo her female self, and you have the crude fool Touchstone, who informs us that he has a venereal disease with a pun on the words "hour" and "whore": '. . . and so from hour to hour we ripe and ripe, and then from hour to hour, we rot and rot, and thereby hangs a tale.' "

There wasn't enough of the joint left to smoke without a clip, so I let it burn itself out in the ashtray. When did I outgrow the need for a roach clip? Ten years ago? Twelve? Around the same time that I stopped listening to new music, probably. I was growing older. Bit by bit, I was turning middle-aged.

I noticed that the Shakespeare expert had bristly white hairs growing out of his nostrils. I found myself wondering whether one day this would happen to me, and whether no one would tell me.

"Of course, Touchstone's most memorable line is about lovers and poetry, and how 'the truest poetrie is the most faining' and how lovers 'they do feign.' "

I tried to feel around the edges of my nostrils. When did a man's nose hair start to grow out of control? At forty? At fifty? Women always seemed to keep this stuff in check; when a man lived alone, that was when the Howard Hughes stuff started happening. Long, talonlike fingernails. Peeing in jars.

"And as we all know, 'to fain,' " he said, "is to desire, while 'to feign' is to pretend."

For the first time I realized he was talking to someone else, an older woman with graying hair in a bun on the top of her head and a glazed look of simulated interest in her eyes.

"So all desire is a kind of pretense," said the lady, "and all pretense a kind of desire? Sorry, but I'm afraid we're just out of time, Professor."

All of a sudden it struck me that what I really wanted

On the Couch

was chocolate. I was just getting up to look for some when the lobby intercom buzzed.

"Who the hell is it?"

"The person you least want to see." I tried to recognize the voice through the house phone's crackling, static-filled receiver.

"Mom?"

"No."

"Marlowe?"

"Sorry."

"Dave?"

"Jesus, Joe, are you going to let me up or what?"

Paolina. "I don't think I can deal with you right now," I told her.

"Well, I think you'd better."

I contemplated letting an angry ex-wife up into my apartment, where the pungent sweet smell of weed had slowed my brain down to a crawl. "How about I take a rain check?"

"Okay, listen, Joe. I tried this once before on the phone, and you steamrollered me. But clearly you're going through something, and I figured maybe if I saw you once in private, it would be easier . . ."

Oh, dear God, was this an intervention or was she going to tell me that she'd cheated on me when we were married, like it mattered anymore. "Don't take this the wrong way, Paolina, but please just leave me alone."

"You want to be alone? You want to be alone! Oh, hello, one of your neighbors has just offered to let me in. No, thanks, I'll just speak my peace into the intercom here, what do I care if the whole building finds out that Joseph Kain in apartment 3A has . . ."

257

I didn't know what she thought I had, but I was pretty sure it wasn't a winning personality. "All right, shut it already, I'm letting you up."

I passed Paolina the joint. We were sitting side by side on the floor of my kitchen, which was none too clean, but neither of us could seem to motivate ourselves to move. Besides, we were close to the refrigerator here, which was convenient. We'd already worked our way through half a jar of peanut butter, a box of Passover jellied fruits, and a package of Oreos, but I wasn't convinced we were done yet. I'd forgotten how good everything tasted when you were stoned.

"So it was you, that one time when we met for lunch and—Jesus, Paolina, that means I've had it for over a month?" I flashed on the moment when I'd first made love to Marlowe: What had I said? Something about worrying about her sexual history.

"Sometimes the symptoms don't show up right away. What's that strange grimace you're making?"

"Acute guilt."

"Well, it's not my fault, Joseph, I didn't know that I had it. And when you come right down to it, that cheating prick Lucas probably didn't know he had it, either."

Trust Paolina to assume it was all about her. "I wasn't blaming you, I was blaming me." I looked down at the box of Oreos between us. "You want anything else to eat?"

Paolina thought about it, her dark hair gleaming in the fluorescent light. She looked softer than I'd remembered, curvier, more womanly. She was wearing a pair of old jeans and a light cotton sweater, the kind of stuff she'd worn when I first met her. "Mario broke up with me," she said, wiggling her bare feet, which were long and elegant, with silver rings on some of the toes. I'd always admired her feet. Paolina looked at me, expecting a response. I thought back, realized what she'd said.

"That shithead. Was it because of the, uh . . ."

"I don't know. Probably. Maybe. I think it was just an excuse, you know? At first, he seemed really cool about it, he made me laugh, made me see it wasn't such a big deal. And then—poof! He vanished. Something in L.A., a possible movie deal, then something else, a trip to Monaco to do some awards show, and then he stopped calling so often, and then . . ." Paolina turned to me. "Why do guys pull this shit? Why not just lay it out and say, I'm breaking up with you, and this is why."

"I don't know, 'lina. Because we're jerks?"

She punched me in the shoulder. "You're not. You never ran out on me. I ran out on you."

"That's right. You were the jerk." I located a last cookie in the bottom of the box and offered it to her.

"No, thanks, I've already managed to gain five pounds in this past week."

I glanced at her plump breasts. "You look great."

"Yeah?"

"Yeah." I took her hand, companionably.

"So, how are things with Marlowe?"

"Kind of not happening right now."

We weren't looking at each other; Paolina's head was resting on my shoulder. "Her decision or yours?"

"Mine. I did the jerk thing after learning about the chlamydia."

"Oh." Long pause. "I guess maybe we all have our

moment of jerkishness." Paolina snuggled up against me, and at first I thought it was like last time, she was hoping for me to seduce her, make her feel desirable again. But then I glanced down and saw that she was crying, her shoulders now beginning to shake with it. "Oh, Joseph, I'm sorry."

"What for? As you said, you didn't know."

"Not that. I mean, not just that. For not trying harder at our marriage. For hurting you." She lifted her face to mine. "For not appreciating you when I had you."

I stroked her smooth hair, trying to mask my growing trepidation. "Yeah, well, you weren't all to blame. Maybe part of the problem was that I was so ready for things to go wrong."

"You've gotten very smart."

"That was Marlowe's influence." I said her name to hold up a shield, to stop things from getting complicated, and sure enough, I felt Paolina pull back.

"You're in love with her, aren't you? Even though you broke up with her."

"I don't know what I am."

"I waited too long." Even as she said it, I could see she thought it wasn't too late. Paolina was still hoping for me to kiss her, screw her, remarry her, fold her back into my life. But even if I acted out her fantasy, we weren't ever going to really connect, not the way Marlowe and I connected. Because I wasn't the good guy Paolina thought I was. There was always going to be something a little held back in me, something that sat apart and took notes.

Marlowe recognized it because she had a piece of that in herself, too. And because she had it, she played the same kinds of head games with me that I played with her. Taking on the role of bad girl to my good cop. Researching her theories while I tested mine.

Which should have spelled disaster, because how could you be real with someone when you were acting a part?

Except it was real. What I'd felt with her—what we'd done that last time—I'd never been so turned on. I didn't understand it. But I figured Marlowe would, and maybe, if I was really, really nice to her, she'd explain it me.

Or maybe, I thought, flashing on the memory of the handcuffs, nice wasn't what I should be to her, at least not all the time.

"Joe?"

"Yeah?"

"I realize that you're in love with Marlowe and about to go back to her and all, but do you want to fool around one last time?"

I gave Paolina a hug. "The answer to that one is, I am too stoned to be anything other than flattered."

"I love you, Joe."

It felt safe to answer in kind. "I love you, too, 'lina." And then, just when Paolina was raising her face in hopes of a kiss, the lobby intercom buzzed again.

marlowe

Joe opened the door and I was pleased to see that he looked truly awful: red-eyed, stubbled, his hair and clothes stained and rumpled.

"Marlowe," he said, sounding extremely cautious. "This isn't really the best time to talk."

I walked past him and stood in the middle of his living room as if I were there to serve him a summons. "I'm sorry I can't make this work on your timetable, Joe, but I just can't wait for never."

Joe closed the door and ran a hand through his already disheveled hair. "I was going to call you."

"Well, what were you waiting for, Joe? An all clear from your astrologer? Because it's been five days since you handcuffed me to a chair and asked me to trust you, and the only communication I've received since then has been a rather brusque suggestion to seek medical assistance."

"Look, I'm having a really bad day today. Couldn't we just make a date to talk about all this later?"

"Oh, I'm supposed to sympathize with you? Poor baby, I can see how hard it's been." I cast a withering glance over his apartment, which was littered with the detritus of a junk food fest.

"Marlowe, if all you want to do is have a go at me . . ."

"All right, you know what, let me start again. What exactly did you mean, I need to see my doctor?"

Beneath the five o'clock shadow, Joe's face flushed with embarrassment. "I, uh, felt a stinging sensation, and I went to the ER, and it seems I caught an STD."

Even though I'd been half expecting this, my heart flopped over. "What kind of an STD?"

"A good kind, actually. As these things go. Chlamydia. Completely curable with antibiotics. Caught right away, no lasting damage."

I let out a deep breath. "Okay. Okay." I allowed myself a moment's relief before the memory of his cryptic message fired my temper up again. "And the incredibly sensitive, caring way you let me know? Any explanation for that?"

"I was . . . look, I'm sorry, it was wrong, it was a completely fucked up thing to do. I was just kind of messed up about it, and . . ." Joe met my eyes. "I assumed you'd given it to me."

I folded my hands in front of my chest. "Even though you knew I wasn't ever a prostitute at that point."

"Yeah. I know it sounds stupid. It was stupid. Marlowe, I know I can't explain it well, but nothing like this had ever happened to me before."

"And you were looking for any excuse to bolt. Don't forget that part."

Joe winced a little. "Okay, yeah, maybe there's a bit of truth in that. But I can't be the first guy who's found it a little intimidating, trying to keep up with you."

"You're intimidated by me?"

"If I have to Dick and Jane it for you, well, yes." His grin was a disarming combination of rueful and sly, and it took me a moment to realize he was quoting something I'd said to him.

"Oh. Ouch. But you have to know how smart you are."

"I'm not saying I'm stupid. And it was a little easier when I thought you were a graduate of the school of hard knocks instead of a Ph.D. But you always keep me on my toes, and that's kind of a new experience."

For a moment, I felt a little leap of hope. He was admitting what he'd done wrong; he was taking responsibility, facing up to things. Maybe he *had* been about to call me. Maybe there was a chance for us.

And then I realized something suspicious: He was a little too ready to admit he'd been wrong. "You said you'd assumed I'd given it to you, Joe. Something's changed your mind. What?"

"Paolina." He mumbled her name under his breath. "She, uh, told me she'd given it to me. Which wasn't her fault, she didn't know either."

"You've been sleeping with your ex-wife while you were sleeping with me?"

"No! No, absolutely not, I slept with her about four weeks ago, before I ever met you. Swear to God." He held up his right hand.

"Do you even believe in God?"

"Well, no, not exactly."

"Swear on your mother's life."

"I can't do that." I gave a derisive snort and Joe quickly added, "But believe me, I wasn't cheating on you." Joe came up to me, his eyes on my face. "Look, M, I really was going to call you. I know I messed up."

"Then why the hell didn't you call me? Were you held at gunpoint? Tied to a chair? You just can't bear to be the bad guy, can you? That's what this is really all about. You want to do whatever you want and not suffer the consequences."

"I'm *not* a bad guy, Marlowe." Joe looked a little insulted. "And remember, I'm not the only one here with issues about intimacy. Seems to me that a woman who'd let a man think she was a call girl on the trumped-up excuse of researching a book has a few knots of her own to untangle."

"Oh, please, you're going to analyze me? Don't make me laugh."

"Meaning what? Only guys with advanced degrees need apply?"

"Meaning that you are completely lacking in any psychological insight about yourself."

Joe took a step forward, and then gave me a slow, knowing smile. "Seems to like I had a few insights into what makes you tick." Slowly walking around me like a wolf stalking its prey, he said, "Is that really why you're here? To make me mad enough to lose control?"

I put my hands on my hips, turning my head but standing my ground as he continued to circle me. "You must be joking."

"You're hurt and mad as hell. But you came here because you still care about me."

"No," I said, enunciating very clearly. "I do not. I came because I wanted to have it out with you face to face. I also wanted to ask you why Dave Bellamy wants to find out about Savannah's therapy when her death was ruled a suicide. Marie LaBrecque seems to think he's interested in me romantically."

"I don't think Dave's really your type."

"Is this some one-sided competition between you two, or does he hate you as much as you hate him?"

"Oh, I think the hate is pretty mutual." Joe was standing behind me now, his breath on my neck. I could feel the heat of his body, nearly touching mine. I didn't need to touch him to know he was aroused. "You going to date him to get back at me? I have a feeling you'll be pretty disappointed, M. It's me you want."

"God, you're an egomaniac." I spun around so that I could face him. "I don't have time for cowards, Joe, and you're an emotional coward."

"Trying awfully hard to get under my skin, aren't you?"

"You know, now that we've spent some time apart, I can see that you really are an alien being. I mean, once the human mask comes off, all that's left is lizard thoughts and reptile brain."

"Keep talking like that and I just might have to bite you."

"I'd like to see you try."

He quirked one eyebrow. "I know I'm lacking in any psychological insight, but that would be a challenge and an invitation, correct?"

I tried to hit him, but Joe grabbed my raised right wrist before I made contact. "Easy, Tiger. I'm not quite ready for the rough stuff."

I tried to hit him with my other hand and he grabbed that wrist, too. "Let go of me!" I tried to knee him in the balls.

"Not if you're going to do that." He twisted one of my arms behind my back, forcing me up against him.

"Let go of me!"

"Stop fighting me."

So mad I couldn't think straight, I leaned forward and bit him on the chest, through his shirt. "I hate you!"

"Marlowe . . ." The tenderness in his voice undid me.

"I hate you, I hate you, I hate you." I had no idea what I was trying to do; bite his face? It was as if I'd gone insane. But then the next thing I knew he was kissing me, and I was kissing him back, his hands still holding me prisoner, and I could feel the delicious hardness of him pressing against me, making its own insistent argument that I was, after all, still wanted, still desired. I didn't realize I was crying until Joe pulled back, my face framed between his two large hands. "Marlowe," he said, his voice filled with something like wonder.

And then I heard a woman clear her throat. "Don't mind me."

I wrenched away from Joe to stare at the voluptuous, dark-haired woman standing barefoot in the doorway to his bedroom. "I don't mean to break things up, but if you two are planning on doing it, maybe I should leave. I just need to find my sandals."

I stared at Joe, my cheeks hot with embarrassment and rage. I wiped at my eyes. "Funny how you forgot to mention that your ex-wife was in your bed."

"Bedroom. She was in the . . . we were in the kitchen, talking, and it just seemed simpler to . . . and then I sort of forgot she was there."

"You know what, Joe? I don't need to hear it. What are you going to tell me, that it isn't what I think? Well, I think you used being hung up on Paolina to avoid getting in too deep with me, and now you're using me to hold off Paolina."

Joe got in front of me, barring my way with his arm. "Look, let's not end things like this. I mean, I don't want to end things at all. Can we talk in the morning?"

"What is this, a power thing? You want to be the one who ends it? Okay, fine. You broke up with me. Now, let me out the door."

"Marlowe . . ."

"Let me out!" I left him alone with his silky ex-wife, trying not to think about how long it would take them to pick up where they'd left off.

I decided to go home to my mother for a few days. This would not be my usual reaction to emotional upset, but the way I was feeling, I figured it couldn't hurt, even if I was only exchanging one brand of stress for another.

Most people can't get over the sheer, picturesque beauty of my mother's upstate horse farm in spring— long expanses of rolling green fields, acres of white picket fences, leggy Thoroughbred foals frolicking in the shade of flowering maples and elms.

My friends never understood how I could wind up so tense and miserable in such an idyllic, pastoral setting. Why didn't I drive out every weekend? Why didn't I have my own horse to ride? All the visiting horse owners, who paid for the privilege of spending a night in our guest house, couldn't understand my attitude.

But for me, this was the place where my mother's obsessive compulsive behavior was a way of life, and every glossy, overgroomed horse at Stable Establishment was testament to her anxious, chain-smoking, meticulous attention to detail.

I lifted Burt's cat carrier out of the passenger seat of

my rented car and breathed in a deep lungful of soft, fresh air.

Burt had howled miserably for the first half of the trip and was now scrabbling miserably to be freed. Should I let him out, or keep him safe inside? Out, I decided; knowing his penchant for Houdini-like escapes, he would eventually find a way out of my room, and besides, he deserved a little adventure.

Puffed up like a Halloween decoration, Burt stalked out to confront the grass, shrank back, and then, spotting a chipmunk, bounded out into the great wide open.

Good for you, Burt, I thought. At least one of us has found purpose in life.

But that was just me being pessimistic. This time, I thought, I'm going to do it differently. This time I'm going to avoid getting sucked into confrontations. Instead, I'm just going to concentrate on writing a book: *Sexy Lies and Scary Truths: Keeping the Mystery without Sacrificing the Intimacy*.

Not that I had any idea how this could be achieved, but at least the concept now sounded catchy. There was nothing like a failed love affair for taking you out of the theoretical and into the practical: It was now perfectly clear to me how to sex up my dissertation, and it wasn't simply by adding sex. Because sex, in and of itself, wasn't particularly sexy.

What was sexy was the tension between being honest and holding back, the fine line between tenderness and strength, aggression and affection, resistance and acceptance.

What was sexy was being handcuffed, just for a little while, by someone you felt might really be falling in love with you, but was frightened of what that might mean.

What was sexy was an assurance that your desire was reciprocated, coupled with an uncertainty as to the timing and manner of consummation.

Of course, what was not sexy was the unanticipated fallout of consummation, in my case, an emergency trip to the gynecologist for a pap smear, a chlamydia test and a lecture on condom usage. That was actually the antithesis of sexy, made worse by the fact that my gynecologist resembled the young Ava Gardner, and appeared to be happily married to a Mount Sinai neurosurgeon.

If only I could be as smart in my personal life as I was in my work. But despite everything—Joe's wham bam rejection, my involvement with the FBI, the huge antibiotic pills I had to take for a week while keeping out of the sun—I found myself longing for the sound of his voice. He'd become my friend as well as my lover, and I didn't really have many friends. I'd been able to talk to him, really talk, because he'd been an incredible listener.

And oh, dear God, did I miss kissing him.

As I opened the Corvette's trunk and hefted my suitcase onto my shoulder, three yapping Jack Russell terriers bounded out of a barn, followed by two small, dark-haired children, whom it took me a moment to identify as my nephew and niece. They stopped when they saw me, and glanced nervously back at the barn. The dogs barreled on toward me and ran in circles around the car.

"Papa! Papa!" The children said something else in rapid-fire Spanish, and then my brother came out, carrying a third child, a sturdy, round-cheeked baby.

"Tanner?" Surprised, and more than a little embarrassed that I hadn't instantly recognized his kids, I put down my suitcase and gave him a kiss. Of course, they resembled their Mexican mother, Dolores, and not my slender, balding, blue-eyed brother, and they had grown quite a bit since I'd last seen them, but still. "I didn't realize you'd be here. I can't get over how big Graziella and Tomas have gotten! And look at Jorge! How old is he now, a year?"

"Fifteen months. Graziella, Tomas, say hello to your Aunt Marlowe." He repeated this in Spanish, and something about the way he said my name made me realize the kids had lots of other aunts, on their mother's side, whom they saw all the time and loved.

"Hey, guys." I crouched down on the muddy ground, and the children approached.

"I need to pee," said the girl.

"So do I," I said with a smile, but neither of them laughed. I hadn't seen them since Christmas, which didn't feel all that long ago to me, but must be a small eternity to two- and four-year-olds. "I didn't expect to see you here! Weren't you guys just here for Easter?"

I'd always found it hard to read Tanner's face, but it seemed to me that he was surprised, even taken aback. "Well," he said slowly, "Dolores and I are trying to work out what happens next. We thought it might help to talk things over with Marnie."

"And I thought I was the only one having a run of bad luck. Has Marnie been any help?" Using our mother's name began as a gesture of adolescent rebellion on my part, and then stuck because it turned out she preferred it.

"She's consulting her lawyer."

271

"You're having legal troubles?"

Tanner cocked his head. "We both are, aren't we?"

"I guess so." But I hadn't even told our mother about my situation, I'd just said I was taking a couple of weeks' urgently needed vacation, which was the same thing I'd told my remaining clients. None of them had been in crisis, and their rather tepid response to the news of my departure made me wonder if any of them were planning on coming back to me. "Hey, Grazie, Tomas, want to help me get my bags inside?" I handed Graziella my pocketbook and Tomas my scarf.

Tanner watched me pick up my suitcase, and I had the feeling he might have wanted to say something more, but with Tanner it was hard to tell. He never conversed the way ordinary people do, filling in the gaps with questions or offering information. Back when he was a gorgeous, tousle-haired sixteen-year-old, all my girlfriends had thought he was infinitely fascinating, and argued over what his silences might mean.

In the end, he married an outgoing woman who surrounded him with a steady stream of Spanish-speaking relatives, and my brother's taciturn nature was assumed to be a peculiar Anglo trait.

"So, where's our mother at? With the new foals?"

"She's checking out a stallion someone wants to breed to Singapore Sling."

"Is it going to happen?"

"I guess we're about to find out." I followed the direction of Tanner's gaze and saw our mother walking toward us, leading a large, well-formed, restive stallion. The owners, clearly a city couple dressed up in English horse-riding clothes, walked at a respectful distance from their horse's prancing hooves.

"So," my mother was saying, "are you two going to spend the night while we breed Financial Impropriety to Singapore?"

"I think so, yes," said the man, who was firmly stout and had a meaty, intelligent, handsome face.

"I thought we'd stay at the inn in Rhinebeck," said the woman, who was alarmingly thin in her tan jodhpurs and long boots. At first, I had taken her for a woman in her late thirties, but now I could see that her dark pageboy framed a face of surgically tightened, collagen-lipped agelessness.

"Then we'd miss seeing our boy at work," said the man, who needed to lose a good twenty pounds to get away with wearing the traditional tight-fitting black jacket.

The woman said something disparaging in what sounded like Russian. My mother said nothing; she was used to both kinds of owners, the ones who wanted to watch the spectacle of horses being bred, and the ones who barely liked being around their animals at all.

"Marusa, Alex, come meet my daughter." Next to the Russian woman's smooth complexion, Marnie's skin looked like a piece of leather, and I noticed that her ash-blond hair had about an inch of gray at the roots.

"Hello, you are beautiful, isn't she beautiful, Marusa?" Alex took my hand in both of his. "We have a daughter your age, I think." Although I found the man more than a little ridiculous in his local squire costume, I felt a little thrill of awareness pass from his flesh to mine. A ladies' man, I thought; a sexual opportunist.

"Nonsense, Alex, Sasha is much younger than this lovely lady."

I smiled sweetly at the venomous Marusa and excused myself from joining the group for lunch in town, saying that I was tired from driving and needed to go up to my room.

My bedroom was away from the main house, above the farm manager's office in one of the barn buildings. Despite the utilitarian gray carpeting, everything smelled pleasantly of horses and hay, and my wide picture windows overlooked the stallions' stalls. I wrestled one window open before slipping out of my clogs and jeans and stretching out on the bed in my T-shirt and panties.

Suddenly remembering my mother's poor housekeeping skills, I pulled back the cover to check for dead insects.

Clean sheets. For a long, blissful moment, I lay back and basked in the silence, and then I heard voices drift through the open window from the office below.

"So when will the breeding take place?" Alex's voice.

"After lunch. Will your wife . . . Alex?"

"Sh. Marusa might prefer to visit the shops in Rhinebeck. She does not wish to see the horses mate." Alex made a short, grunting sound in the back of his throat; I wondered what the two of them were doing. Something physical. Moving boxes?

"Alex, I . . . this isn't . . . my daughter is upstairs." She was whispering now, but no less audible.

"But you are almost there, aren't you?" Another grunt, a gasp. Oh, Jesus, my mother was having a quickie downstairs. I wanted to close the window, run some water, turn on the radio. But what if she heard and then realized I'd been listening?

"Your wife . . ."

"Is still putting on her makeup, come on, darling, I'm going to make you happy, that's it, come on . . ." he said something in Russian and then there was a sharp rap on the door.

"You guys in there?" It was Tanner's voice.

"Coming," said Alex, and my mother laughed and there was the sound of zippers being zipped and then the door being opened and slammed shut.

This was just too much. I hadn't expected much in the way of comfort from my mother, she wasn't the maternal sort, but I had expected to take comfort in the fact that hers was a life free of men and erotic ambition. I'd thought that she had displaced all her affection and energy, and that, at least for a while, I might be able to do the same. But a married man had just made a conquest of Marnie in the space of three minutes, and I had the uneasy feeling that the next week would be punctuated by other such furtive attempts at consummation.

Preoccupied with thoughts of my mother's illicit love life, I almost didn't hear the knock on my door. "Marlowe?"

"Tanner? Hold on." I tugged my jeans over my hips. "Okay, I'm decent."

My brother stood there awkwardly, for once not holding a baby. "I sent Dolores to lunch with the kids. I thought maybe we should talk."

"Sure. Um, do you want the bed or the beanbag to sit on?"

Tanner chose to sit on the other side of the queen-size bed. "I guess walking in on them was pretty horrific."

"Walking in?"

"On Marnie and Alex."

Complete look of incomprehension. "Were they doing something? Oh. No. I wasn't thinking about them." Yet another long, Tannerian silence.

"Tanner? Is everything all right between you and Dolores?"

"Yes, we're fine."

"The kids are all right?"

"The baby seems to be a little slow to roll over, but we're not worried yet."

"Everything's okay at work?" Tanner worked as a carpenter and shared shop space with a ceramicist and a weaver in nearby Connecticut.

"I guess."

"Okay, Tanner, I give up. What did you want to talk to me about?"

"About our father, of course."

I stared at my brother, utterly dumbfounded. We hadn't really discussed our father since mid-adolescence, when Dad had made his big book sale and run off with our former babysitter. Initially, of course, there had been some contact—weekend visits at his Manhattan apartment before he moved to England with Jessica, Christmas gifts, the occasional invitation to come stay at their house in Notting Hill. But our mother's bitterness over the divorce, coupled with our father's complete, almost obsessive fascination with his twenty-three-year-old wife, made maintaining the relationship almost impossible.

And Jessica, who had been a great babysitter, turned out to be the worst kind of second wife. It was impossible to have a conversation with our father without her running interference. She was his assistant, his manager, his agent, his nurse.

The last time I'd spoken to either of them was in 1984. I'd been urged by a therapist to work out some of my anger toward my father; Jessica had insisted that he had a heart condition and could not be subjected to any emotional stress. Tanner, as far as I knew, had not spoken to Dad since college, when our father had said something about his son's lack of intellectual acuity.

"You want to talk about Dad?" I took Tanner's hand, trying to think of the appropriate things to say. "That's wonderful," I improvised. "I think it's very healthy to deal with unresolved feelings, particularly now that you yourself are a father . . ."

"I'm more concerned with the financial aspect of things, actually."

"Financial aspect?" To my surprise, Tanner put his other hand on top of mine.

"You haven't heard, have you? I thought . . . it's been in all the entertainment magazines, because of the movie deal . . ."

"Movie deal?"

"*The Princess of Maybe* is being made into a major motion picture, with one of those young girl singers signed on to play the lead. So everyone's been eager to interview Dad, and they're reprinting the book, and that's how Dolores and I found out about the baby."

"Hang on a second, you're having another baby?"

"No, Dad and Jessica just had a baby."

"But she's, she must be too old to . . ."

"She's forty-four, not too old, as it turns out. They had a daughter in March and they're calling her Miranda."

My hand felt clammy in Tanner's. "Okay," I said, "so they've had a daughter. It's not like it really changes anything. I mean, what are we supposed to do, send a pink outfit?"

"There's more, Marlowe." Tanner's eyes were very kind, I realized. I imagined that Dolores must get to sit with him like this all the time, holding his hand, confiding her troubles. "Dad's decided to revoke our trust funds."

"What? He can't do that." Even as I said it, I realized he could. Our father had placed almost three million from the *Princess of Maybe* sale and royalties into a trust for Tanner and myself—guilt money, my mother had called it. My brother and I were the fund's income beneficiaries, meaning that we each collected about $150,000 a year. We weren't rich, but the money meant that we didn't need to work if we didn't want to, and when we did work, we could do things we loved. I got to live in a great apartment and go to graduate school twice; Tanner got to work with his hands and live in a pretty Victorian house with a pool and two nice cars.

I'd been dimly aware that the actual trusts were still in our father's name, and therefore revocable, but it had never occurred to me that he might actually cut our funds.

"But he doesn't need the money! He's set from the BBC stuff and the Viking series, and now with the movie deal, he probably stands to get even richer."

"There's an interview in the back of this week's *People* magazine. He says that grown children who haven't bothered to contact him in over fifteen years shouldn't expect to keep nursing at the financial teat." There was more expression in Tanner's voice than I'd heard since the mid-eighties.

"Oh, so we're supposed to have contacted him! I don't suppose he thinks that maybe he might have tried sending us a birthday card from time to time? I can't believe this. It all boils down to the fact that he's got this new kid so he's just leaving us out in the cold!"

"I've been talking to Marnie about Dolores and my moving into one of the farm houses." Tanner patted my hand, and I realized he was taking my words literally. "And we both have careers to fall back on."

I thought of my handful of clients, the looming specter of an FBI investigation into my treatment of Savannah, and, absurdly, of all the expensive furniture I'd just ordered. "Oh, my God, Tanner."

"Don't worry, Sis, if worst comes to worst, I'm sure Marnie will let you live here for a while, too."

Unable to contain myself, I burst into tears.

joe

"Hello, this is Dr. Marlowe Riddle. I am going to be out of town from Wednesday, May 7 through Sunday, May 11. If this is an emergency, you may call me on my cell phone."

Shit. She'd left the city. Which meant that I had to figure out where she'd gone to before Dave did.

It had taken me what felt like a long forever to get Paolina out of my apartment, and then I'd needed to check in with the hospital to find out how my mother was doing.

Now I was finally free to mull over the whole screwed-up scene with Marlowe, so I could try to understand how my life had gone so badly wrong in such a terrifyingly short span of time.

What was it with me? I'd fucked things up beyond all recognition. Marlowe was the one woman I could see myself happily playing games with for the next fifty years and she was never going to trust me again. Why the hell had I let her up to my apartment in the first place? Because I didn't want to piss her off? Well, she was well and truly pissed off now.

And then it hit me: She'd come to ask me about why Dave was dogging her about Savannah. And the answer was, it didn't make sense. Not if Savannah's death had been ruled a suicide. And I didn't believe for one moment that he was simply interested in screwing Marlowe, not even as a way of getting back at me. I mean, I didn't need a Ph.D. in psychology to figure out that there was something a little wacky about the guy's sex drive.

Which got me thinking about the questions he'd asked back when we'd all been together in M's apartment.

The last thing he'd said before she'd cited patient privilege had been something along the lines of, Did Savannah have a boyfriend? And the answer, now that I thought of it, was yes.

Something about this wasn't kosher. Could Dave have something to hide? Could Dave, the awkward voyeur, have gotten so turned on with all the constant spying on Savannah that he'd lost sight of professional boundaries?

Could he have murdered Savannah to hide a potentially career-damaging revelation?

This was all wild speculation, of course, but if any of it even had the slightest grain of truth to it, then Marlowe just might be in real danger.

I tried her mobile number: She was out of the service area. I called again and again: After half an hour of pressing redial, I finally got her.

"Marlowe?"

"Joe?"

"Thank God. Where the hell are you?"

"What?" Her voice was filled with static.

"I said, where are you? This connection stinks and I need to tell you something important."

Marlowe said something loud and undecipherable. Was she yelling at me? Shit. "Listen, I wouldn't blame you if you wanted to hang up on me, but please, please could you just wait a sec and hear me out?"

"I'm listening."

Okay, that was clear enough. What to start with, the apology or the possible danger or all the emotional shit? The apology would have to go along with the story about Paolina coming over, which would lead to the emotional shit. I opted for danger.

"Okay, first off, I have a theory going about our boy Dave. I don't want to go into detail on a cell phone, but suffice it to say that we're dealing with a man who has a few screws loose. Let me ask you something."

"Okay."

"A guy who's socially inept, no real close friendships, maybe some phobias about touching, how do you think he'd react to his first real sexual relationship?"

"Joe, did you call me to get me to do some sort of psychological analysis?"

"No. Well, yes, and I have to say that I have missed talking stuff over with you, but—" The line went dead. Shit. I should have started with the apology. I called four more times: Bupkis. Nothing.

Time to do some detective work.

Marlowe had sounded distant, almost out of the cell phone's range—maybe she'd been on an airplane? She hadn't told me anything about her family, but I figured that was a good place to start. Maybe she'd gone home to her folks.

It only took me a few minutes on the Internet to learn

that Marlowe was the daughter of one of my favorite childhood authors, John Riddle, currently living in London. I hadn't thought about him in years, but back when I was about thirteen or so, I got into his Viking series, which had just the right combination of blood, broodiness, and male bonding to suit my tastes.

I didn't have much time for the girly book that became his big bestseller, but *Doomstead* and its sequels had been my great escape during the horrible year when my time was divided between school and Bar Mitzvah preparations.

Glancing at my clock, I saw that it was about five o'clock—almost eleven P.M. in England. Too late to call, so I logged onto his website and sent him an email:

To: John Riddle
From: Joe Kain

Am friend and work colleague looking for your daughter, Marlowe. Also huge fan of your Viking series. Any idea where your offspring might be hiding out for a couple of days' R&R?

Within moments, I had a reply:

To: Joe Kain
From: John Riddle

Liar. Any friend would know Marlowe has not been in contact with me in years. A colleague would presumably attempt to find her through business contacts. Who are you?

I pondered this question and the information that Marlowe was estranged from her dad before replying:

I'm her boyfriend.

A message flashed on my screen telling me I had an instant message from JohnRiddle: Did I want to open it? I clicked yes.

JohnRiddle: If you're her boyfriend, why aren't you having the R&R with her?

JoeKain: Because I'm a shmuck.

JohnRiddle: Hm. And yet you seem to think that I should help you locate my daughter? Uninvolved tho I am, that would seem contraindicated.

JoeKain: Well, in addition to my being her boyfriend, I'm also a cop who needs to protect her from an unscrupulous FBI agent. By the way, no offense, but why aren't you two in contact?

JohnRiddle: It all boils down to wives, my boy. We males hold the power until the ring is on the finger; after that, they take the reins.

JoeKain: Okay, now it's my turn: Liar. Your daughter, your responsibility. No passing the blame.

JohnRiddle: Very astute. I am a liar, but not enough people tell me, so I tend to forget. Although you speak with a young man's confidence. When you grow older, and your health fails, you may see things differently.

JoeKain: Listen, Marlowe's health may fail if I don't get hold of her.

JohnRiddle: Indeed? Well, I have no idea where my daughter might go to relax. The last time I spoke with her, she was a boy-crazy seventeen-year-old whose idea of recreation involved dancing to Punk music and being fumbled by young European males.

JoeKain: You're kidding! I got the impression she was this uptight psychologist. Well, that was my second impression, at any rate.

JohnRiddle: I am assuming you have tried her mother's horse farm?

JoeKain: No, but thanks. That'll be my next call.

JohnRiddle: Good luck, Marlowe's boyfriend. This has been diverting.

JoeKain: Thanks. And I really was a huge fan of your work. I liked the way you hinted that the three blond Norns could either show a young boy the great mystery of life, or reduce him to a quivering mound of rendered fat.

JohnRiddle: Such is the power of women. I hope you get to see the great mystery. I am, at present, more at the quivering mound of fat stage of life.

JoeKain: You might try getting to the gym more. Hey, listen, why don't you try tracking M down yourself? Life is short, and she's a pretty amazing person.

JohnRiddle: I think we've traveled beyond the point where I would be of any use to her. I hope to do better as a parent to my baby daughter this time around.

JoeKain: This time around? As in, have new kid, forget the past, start over? You incredible asshole. No wonder you can't sleep. You can't just disown your own flesh and blood like that.

JohnRiddle: You think I have a guilty conscience? I will think some more on this. But perhaps you do as well, young man, or else you wouldn't remark on mine.

And with that, he signed off, leaving me a little surprised by the level of rage I was experiencing. I wanted to punch someone. Why the hell did so much detective work boil down to typing names and phoning people? Right now I probably had a gallon of adrenaline burning a hole in my gut. Maybe I needed a change of profession.

Forcing myself to sit back down at the computer, I located Marlowe's mother's horse farm. Jotting down the directions, I wondered just how much of a head start Dave had on me.

marlowe

In romantic comedies, the heroine's big depression is usually depicted in a relatively charming manner; she lies in her big, comfy, four-poster bed, which is littered with tissues, crying her eyes out over some old black and white film. Or else her misery might be rendered amusing by the technique Voltaire invented, piling misfortune upon misfortune so rapidly that tragedy is transformed into dark comedy.

In real life, however, feeling awful doesn't have much to recommend it. After my brother left me, I went to bed, tunneled under the covers, and settled into a mood of unremitting bleakness.

I'd always thought, in the back of my mind, that I would eventually find a man whose love would heal the parts of me that had gone unappreciated, unfathered, unloved. But I had finally met a man who spoke to my subconscious, and all he'd done was inflict new injuries. In a way, I supposed I was lucky that things had ended so quickly, before I could invest more in the relationship. But I had lost faith that I would find something better.

I knew that I was being shortsighted, self-involved,

and glum. I knew because my mother had used those very words to describe me when she'd come up to bring me some coffee.

She'd advised me to just "Suck it up and just get on with things," an unfortunate Britishism that gave me an all-too-vivid visual of her cavorting with the potbellied Russian. Tanner didn't come to see me again, so I presumed that he'd retreated back into his cocoon of Latins. I tried not to feel sorry for myself, but it was difficult. Even my cat was beginning to avoid me because I kept clinging to him when all he wanted to do was go hunt chipmunks.

It began to occur to me that I was unusually isolated. Every time I turned on the Lifetime channel for women I saw female friends comforting each other over cappuccino or apple martinis or pints of chocolate-chocolate-chip ice cream. I thought about Amanda, who had acquired the married woman's reluctance to reveal too many of her own personal details (although she was only too happy to listen to mine), and Melissa, eternally preoccupied with beating me out in some one-sided competition, and Claudia, who made *me* feel competitive. I didn't want to confide in any of them.

I wanted to call Joe, to tell him about all my other hurts. I wanted him so much I looked him up on the Internet and found a picture of him in uniform, looking very young. I wondered if he was thinking about me at all, and decided he probably wasn't, which sent me deeper into my funk.

I knew that my bleak mood wouldn't last forever. I thought about the future and predicted that I would eventually meet someone appropriately desperate at a single's event, marry in order to produce a child, and have sex with clinical precision at the fertile points in my cycle. No one would ever talk for hours with me on the phone, searching every word I said for hidden meanings. No one would spend hours making love to me as if my body were a glorious new wilderness and he its first explorer.

Instead, my future husband and I would eventually spend all our time talking about our child, which would lead to an amicable divorce at some point. My child would grow up, start dating, kiss me good-bye, and head off to do a junior year abroad.

I would start to breed Burmese cats, and my house would smell like cat piss forever.

Joe would meet someone who loved him, though. Of course he would. So what if he were limited, flawed, emotionally retarded? He was a man. The world would forgive him for being an asshole.

It went without saying that I couldn't write a word of my self-help book. What advice could I offer others? I couldn't find the necessary will to call the furniture store to talk them into canceling my order, let alone locate any creative energy inside myself.

Making matters worse, Claudia's book on European and American sexual mores, released a week earlier, seemed to be climbing steadily up the bestseller lists. I'd been dimly aware of this, but nothing could have prepared me for turning on the television set in my room and discovering that Claudia (her hair newly colored and cut in a chic, shaggy, caramel-and-honey bob) was appearing on both the *Today Show* and CNN.

I decided to get professional help.

Dr. Michael Bergman was a former professor of mine and one of the most highly respected psychiatrists on the East Coast. I'd turned to him several times in the past, to ask him to supervise me on a difficult case or to see a client whom I felt needed medication.

Now that I actually needed him, however, I couldn't get him on the phone. I'd already left three messages with his answering service and hadn't gotten a response. Now it was approaching five o'clock and I was growing desperate.

Maybe I should try a different tack.

"Hello, this is Dr. Marlowe Riddle, calling for Dr. Bergman."

"I'm afraid the doctor isn't available at the moment. If you'd like to leave a message . . ."

"Can you please tell him it's urgent?"

A pause. "Are you a patient of his?" I understood the unspoken subtext as: Are you suicidal, or just really desperate to discuss your feelings of inadequacy with the great man?

"I'm a colleague." Not strictly true, as I wanted to speak to Dr. Bergman for purely personal reasons, but I figured I'd receive more respect if they thought I was calling as one professional to another.

"Hold on a moment."

After five minutes of listening to Pachelbel's Canon, Dr. Bergman came on the line. "Marlowe," he said, sounding quite pleased to hear from me. "What's going on?"

"Well, quite a lot, actually. My estranged father has just disowned me, I'm getting over an unpleasant breakup, and I'm experiencing legal problems." I thought it best not to specify that I was being investigated by an FBI agent, as it might lead to an incorrect initial diagnosis of paranoia.

"I see. That is quite a lot." Pause. "Were you calling to make an appointment with me?"

"I would love to," I lied, "but I'm not in Manhattan right now. The thing is, what with all of these rather unsettling life events converging on me like this, I've been feeling kind of, well, depressed."

"Tell me what you mean when you say depressed. Despondent? Anxious? Antisocial? Are you able to get yourself out of bed and dressed in the morning?"

I glanced down at myself, still wearing yesterday's T-shirt. The panties were fresh, but I hadn't bothered to actually put on pants, as I hadn't left my room all day. "Look, Dr. Bergman, I know the varying clinical degrees of depression, and I know I'm not suicidal," I said, "but yes, I am exhibiting all the typical signs of dysthymia. I wake up feeling lousy. I don't want to take a shower, have a brisk walk, and look on the bright side of things. I keep having negative ideations about myself : I overintellectualize in order to distance myself from people, I defend myself by shutting down emotionally, I don't do well in unscripted social situations. Oh, and I've just spent the last three hours crying because I'm afraid there might be something essentially off-putting about my personality."

"It sounds as if you've been doing a lot of thinking about what you might have contributed to your current situation. I don't think that's all negative, Marlowe."

"Oh, please! What are you telling me, that I'm right to think that I'm socially defective?"

"I'm just saying that the picture you're painting isn't as bleak as you might think. Tell me something. How long have you been feeling like this?"

I thought about it. "I kind of reached full saturation last night, when I found out about my father."

"Last night. I see. Well, Marlowe, why don't we make an appointment for you to see me when you're back in the city . . ."

Oh, no. No way. Dr. Bergman charged $400 for a session, and asked his patients for an initial four-week commitment. I wasn't about to waste the time and money talking about how I had control issues stemming from my father's abandonment, which naturally predisposed me to experience my greatest sexual release in a scenario that allowed me to relinquish control. I already had an intellectual appreciation of my problems: What I needed was to feel better.

I was giving up on happy; clearly, happy was out of my league. But not being miserable, surely that was well within reach? "Actually, Dr. Bergman, what I really want is just to take something that will relieve the immediate symptoms of anxious depression. Just for a little while, until I have time to assimilate all these life changes."

"Uh huh. You were thinking I could just write you a prescription for Buspar and everything would just sort itself out?"

"Xanax, actually. Buspar takes too long."

"Marlowe, what you want is a magic wand." He sounded disapproving.

"I don't. Really, I don't. I just want—I just want to feel better. I want to feel better now." I was crying now. "I'm sorry, I didn't intend to fall apart like this."

"Why are you apologizing?"

I took a deep breath, tried to calm down. "Because I know you're disappointed in me. You probably figure I'm making the same mistakes your patients make, wanting to just get rid of the pain without doing any of the work . . ."

"Marlowe, we all make the same mistakes our patients make, me included. Being a doctor doesn't mean you're never going to get sick. In fact, it can make it harder to get help."

I sniffled. "So, what do I do now? I'm stuck up here in my room at my mother's horse farm, trying not to listen to her having sex with a married man, pretending that I'm not worried about losing my financial safety blanket, not sure if I want to confront my father about any of this, and feeling like the one person I want most in the world to talk to is the guy who just left me in the coldest way possible."

"You really want my advice?"

"I do."

"You're on a horse farm. Go for a ride. Get out in the sun and try not to think too hard for an hour. Make it two hours. Ride until you're sore."

"I could do that, I guess. But I'd rather take a Xanax."

"Try exercise first. And do think about making an appointment with someone when you're back at home. Therapy is a useful tool, you know."

"I know." I hung up the phone, knowing I wasn't going to listen to him about the analysis. When it came right down to it, I wanted someone to listen to me because they cared, not because I was paying them.

Maybe I was in the wrong profession. Or maybe it was

just that my biggest problem was that I didn't have anyone intimate to turn to, and seeing a therapist wasn't going to change that.

Well, at least Dr. Bergman had made one useful suggestion. I pulled on my old jodhpurs and thought about how far into the hills I could ride before sunset.

Most of the horses on my mother's farm were unsuitable for riding: They were either too young, too pregnant, or too loaded with testosterone. Marnie actually only had three pleasure horses—Benedick, Charlie, and Navarra—two gelding quarter horses, and that rarest of creatures, a relatively calm Thoroughbred.

I'd chosen Charlie, the most even-tempered of the three, because I hadn't been riding in over a year and always had to overcome an initial nervousness. Horses are flight animals, and there is always a chance that some real or imagined terror—a snake underfoot, a strange scent on the breeze—can startle them into bad behavior.

Also, that last, unexpected conversation with Joe had shaken me into extreme cautiousness with myself. I'd been about to leave my room when he'd called, and the swift lift in my spirits at the sound of Joe's voice had frightened me. My heart pounding, I'd fought to keep my voice even, to say, Yes, I was listening, as if nothing much depended on what he said next. As if he didn't have the power to crush me again.

But he'd wanted to talk about Dave. He wasn't lying around, despondent, his life empty without me. He was thinking about work, Savannah, my involvement with a murder case. Which meant that what we had was really, really over. It was obvious now that whatever attraction

I'd held for him had been wrapped up in the persona of the professional courtesan. As a call girl, I'd been experienced, mysterious, elusive, desirable. Stripped of that mystique, I was uninteresting to him, except as an intellectual sounding board.

I'd hung up on him, feeling physically ill. I hadn't realized that heartache was a physical sensation; if I ever went back to work as a therapist, it was a useful bit of information.

And then, mostly because I was scared of being alone with my feelings, I'd gone out to the barn where the riding horses were stabled.

The first forty minutes of my ride, I'd been completely focused on remembering to keep my back straight and supple while allowing my weight to sink down into my heels, as well as maintaining a firm but relaxed grip on the reins, which had to have enough contact, but not too much, with the horse's mouth.

My mother was an instinctive rider, not averse to falling off, getting hurt, and getting back on. She was relaxed in the saddle, something that cannot really be taught, only learned. I envied her, because I was an analytical rider, self-conscious and almost always a little on edge. Tanner, like most men I knew, distrusted horses, and didn't ride.

By the end of the first hour, however, I was beginning to enjoy myself. Charlie and I had climbed out of the dense, tree-filled, hilly area just above the farm and had emerged onto a field that a farmer had leased for our use. Charlie's ears were pricked with interest at these new surroundings, and I had unwound enough to let my gaze wander, to take in the deep, wide expanse of clouds and sky, the low, swooping soar of a hawk, the distant vista of mountains.

By that time, I'd worked up enough courage to attempt a brisk trot, which kept bouncing me out of the saddle, and a slow canter, which was perfect, effortless, wildly exhilarating. And then it happened: a hiccup in Charlie's stride, a return to a sort of half-trot, which I handled badly, by pulling back on the reins too hard. I should have kicked him on, back into the faster, smoother gait of the canter, but instead, I only succeeded in getting him into a defiant trot, which my thighs just couldn't handle. Propelled out of the saddle, I landed hard on the rocky ground, twisting my ankle.

My first reaction was to cry. Then, after a few moments, I realized that I had to get it together, because the only person I could count on to come to my rescue was me. I dried my face, got to my feet, and managed to grab hold of Charlie's reins.

It took me over an hour to get back to the farm. By the time I had Charlie untacked and in his stall, dusk had fallen. Hobbling awkwardly out of the barn, I saw the red taillights of a car disappearing down the driveway. I could just make out my mother and Alex standing in the gathering shadows; when the car was out of sight, Alex whispered something in my mother's ear, and she laughed. I presumed that it had been his wife who had driven off, and that he and Marnie were about to tear off each other's clothes in a blaze of late midlife passion.

Climbing the stairs to my room, I had already unbuttoned half my shirt. Once inside, I turned on a lamp and had started to unhook my brassiere when I heard the sound of someone clearing his throat. I gasped, and then, for one joy-filled moment, I thought it was Joe, because who else would wait so long to announce his presence?

But then the figure stepped out of the shadows, a gun in his hand, and I stood half undressed before the deceptively guileless blue eyes of Agent Dave Bellamy.

"I'm sorry," he said in his mild, Midwestern voice, "I didn't mean to surprise you."

I didn't move, taking in the loosened tie, the wrinkled suit jacket, the cowlicks of fair hair no longer tamed to lie flat. "Are you going to shoot me?"

Dave looked down at the gun in his hand. "Shoot you? No, no, absolutely not."

"You wouldn't mind putting the gun away, then?"

Dave shook his head. "I can't. Not yet. That's why I came here."

"You're going to rape me?"

"No! God no, I'm no rapist! I'm just so depressed, and I was planning on killing myself. I thought I'd talk to you, but I'd like to leave the gun out for now, in case I change my mind."

"Oh," I said, finally getting it. Dave was interested in me, all right, but not the way Marie LaBrecque had assumed.

He was interested in me as a therapist.

joe

I got stopped by three different state policemen for speeding, which slowed me down considerably. By the time I found Marlowe's mother's horse farm, it was full dark, and not the kind of dark I was used to in the city, where the constant glow of streetlights and neon signs kept the night at bay. Here it was the kind of dark that meant you had no fucking idea where you were putting your feet.

Walking up the long path to the main house, I discovered that the three likeliest choices were, ditch, hole, and horseshit. Why hadn't I thought to bring a damn flashlight?

Overhead, the stars were brilliant; you could see the constellations as they must have been a hundred years ago, before we smothered them with a blanket of pollution. Off in the bushes, I kept catching flashes of the bright, reflective eyes of nocturnal animals: Cats, raccoons, and with my luck, rabid skunks.

Still, if I hadn't been stumbling around with my hand on my gun, wired from lack of sleep and nerves, I'd have found it all very scenic.

I managed to make my way to the main house, where a porch light had attracted every flying insect in the area. I tried the big horseshoe knocker; no response. I rang the bell; still no reply. In the end, I just opened the door, which was unlocked, a practice I thought had gone out of fashion with leaving your milk bottles on the mat. The moment I got inside, I understood why no one had heard me; someone was making the bed-springs creak loud enough to drown out a herd of stampeding horses.

Of course, the primal grunts of ecstasy were getting pretty noisy, too.

I figured that no mother would make that much of a racket with her kid in the house, even if that kid was old enough to make the bedsprings creak herself. I left and tried looking around outside. There was another build-ing to my left, which turned out to be a barn; there was a smaller house behind it, and a pretty Mexican woman answered the door. She had a baby on her hip and two smaller children at her skirts. She told me to try the apartment on top of the third barn. I squinted, saw a light on the top floor, and thanked her.

As she turned away, I heard her say in Spanish to someone behind her that I was the second gentleman who'd gone looking for Marlowe tonight.

Ah, shit. I drew my Glock and walked up the stairs, making as little sound as possible, trying to keep my mind blank so I was prepared for anything: a scene of vi-olent bloodshed or a situation wound tight and about to explode. After what felt like an eternity of having my guts in a knot, I was finally ready for action.

* * *

What I wasn't ready for was the sight of Dave, sitting on the edge of a bed about two feet away from Marlowe, pouring his heart out.

"So," Dave was saying, looking down at his lap, "it wasn't that I didn't want to talk to girls. I just didn't know how. No one had bothered to teach me, and since I'd always been in a class with kids four or five years older . . ."

"That must have been hard."

He looked up at Marlowe, who was sitting in a chair across from him, dressed only in a gray bra, a pair of tight-fitting black pants, and knee-high boots.

What the fuck were they doing? "What the fuck are you doing?" I said.

Dave looked up at me. "This has nothing to do with you, Joe, so just back off and leave us alone." He emphasized his point with a .40-caliber ATF aimed at my midsection.

I kept my own gun steadily trained on him. "What do you mean it has nothing to do with me? Why else did you pick my girlfriend to be your shotgun shrink?"

"Because I felt a strong connection the moment I met her."

I noticed that this was news to Marlowe, too. "Well, I'm disconnecting you. Put your weapon down, Dave."

"Why should I? I have the advantage. My gun's bigger than yours."

"Dave, you could be carrying a cannon and still not hit the side of a barn ten yards away. Now, be a good FBI agent and put your 'big gun' away. And fix your tie, you're making the bureau look bad."

"You actually dated this man?" Dave sounded more

curious than angry. "What on earth could an intelligent woman like you have seen in a Neanderthal like him?"

"Well, to start with, I'm good with my hands."

"Joe, stop." Marlowe sounded disapproving. "You're making him nervous."

"He should be nervous."

"He was threatening himself, not me. He's suicidal. All he wants is to talk it out."

I kept my focus on Dave. "Then how come you're not wearing a shirt?"

"He's very uncomfortable around women. This made him feel less threatened."

I raised one eyebrow. "Your brand of therapy's a little unconventional, wouldn't you say?"

"He's in crisis, Joe. Also, he said my moving around made him jumpy."

"Right. Move away from him now, Marlowe. If he jumps, I'll kill him."

Marlowe narrowed her eyes. "Oh, no you're not. Listen, Joe, I'm helping him. Unlike some other men I know, *he's* opening up to me."

"Hey, *I* opened up to you! Remember me saying we needed to talk, and you walking out on me?"

"Well, maybe I didn't feel like having your ex-wife in the audience!"

"I did say it wasn't a good time!" I was trying to ignore the fact that Dave was watching us as if we were acting in some instructional video: Arguing with the Opposite Sex 101. "It wasn't my fault that Paolina dropped by unannounced to see if I wanted to take her back, which, by the way, I did not. And this was all on the same day that Mother went into the hospital with a heart attack."

Alisa Kwitney

Marlowe's face softened. "I didn't know about your mother."

"Well, she's going to have another heart attack when she finds out you're not Jewish. But I love you, M. I look at you, I'm not just seeing fun and games, I'm seeing a future, furniture shopping, maybe even a baby or two."

Marlowe made a move as if to come toward me.

"Hold on there. Stay right where you are." Dave gestured with his gun. "I'm glad you're both feeling better, but I still feel pretty lousy."

"Dave," I said, trying to sound reasonable, "you and I both know there's a moment where a drawn gun either gets fired or put away. We're at an impasse here. You really think shooting someone's going to make things better?

Dave gave me a thin smile. "Well, I'm sure my shooting myself would make *you* feel better. You know, it's kind of funny, I always felt like there was some way in which we were two sides of the same coin. Both of us a little smarter than the rest of the guys, both of us not quite fitting in. Of course, I'm smarter than you."

"Yeah, but I don't kill my girlfriends, so that's a mark in my favor."

"I didn't kill Savannah."

"You sure you didn't hand her that little cocktail of Wellbutrin and vodka? Sure solved a lot of your problems. Wouldn't want it coming out that the head of the investigation was seeing the main subject on the sly."

Dave's face flushed. "I didn't kill her!"

"Joe," said Marlowe, "maybe you should let me handle this."

"You handle the patients who don't come armed. I

deal with the ones who are packing. So what was it, Dave, she kill herself over you?"

Dave's shoulders started to shake, not a good thing when a man has a loaded gun in his hand.

"Jesus, man, hold it together. Don't start blubbering."

"No, no, it's good to cry, Dave." Marlowe put a hand on his arm. "It's important to grieve."

"I knew I shouldn't have gotten involved with her. I knew it. But I always found it so much easier to talk to people when it was part of the job, so I just kept pretending it *was* part of the job. I told myself I was investigating her, you know? Trying to get information." He lifted his face, and with the tear marks, he looked about fifteen years old, maybe younger. "As an agent, I've got confidence. Every conversation has a point to it. But what the hell are you supposed to say to a girl when you just meet her out of nowhere? How much information do you give? What kind of questions do you ask her?"

"Jesus Christ, Dave, you just talk to her."

"No, Joe, maybe *you* just talk to her. I just clam up. Or else I say the wrong thing and sound like an idiot." Dave hunched his shoulders and let his head droop down between his arms. "Sometimes I think it's not worth it and I should just find a prostitute. I mean, one I'm not investigating."

There. That was it. My opening. I was across the room in an instant, twisting his wrist back to disarm him when I felt his other fist connect with my jaw. Then we were grappling, rolling off the bed and onto the floor while Marlowe scrambled back.

A shot rang out and we froze. Then we heard two more shots in quick succession, both coming from outside. Holding each other's gaze for a millisecond, Dave and I both rolled away from each other, coming up fast with guns in hand and running flat out for the stairs.

Marlowe was right behind us. "Get back," I yelled as Dave and I fanned out. As we moved into position, a motion-sensitive light flickered on, illuminating the scene perfectly: the stocky dead naked guy on the ground, blood seeping from his abdomen, the hard-faced brunette with a ladylike pistol as tiny as a child's toy, her gaze riveted on the thin, naked woman screaming by her dead lover's side.

"I could handle the whores," said the dark-haired woman, "but if Alex was sleeping with an old bag like you, it meant he had to be in love." She started to squeeze the trigger, and Dave and I fired at the same time.

It would take a ballistics test to determine which of us had killed her. But it didn't take more than a moment for us to realize who she was.

"Jesus Christ," I said, "I think we just shot Marusa Andropovitch."

Dave, kneeling beside the other body, nodded his head. "I don't believe it. Three years of trying to catch Big Daddy, and now his wife shoots him dead at our feet. Do you realize what this means?"

I saw the moment it hit him; this didn't mean anything. He'd gone off the deep end, and I knew it. He'd caught the bad guy, but as soon as word got out he'd been fooling around with Savannah and holding her shrink at gunpoint, he was ruined.

Unless I took pity on him and kept my mouth shut. And like him or not, I had to admit, listening to him spill his guts to Marlowe had made me pity the guy a little. I'd been right all along, there was something weird about Dave, but hearing him admit it made me feel a little guilty for all the times I'd yanked his chain.

"Yeah, Dave," I said. "I know what this means. We did it." I held out my hand; after a moment, he shook it.

"Look, Joe, if you want to come back on the team . . ."

"I'm saying I'm not going to rat you out, I'm not saying I'm about to go walking into the sunset holding your hand. And you need therapy. Real therapy."

"I know."

"But not with my girl."

I walked up to Marlowe, who had her arms around the naked woman and was murmuring soft comforting things. Looking up, Marlowe's eyes met mine, and I tried to tell her without words that I was there for her, that I loved her, that I would do whatever it took to get her to give me a second chance.

I hoped to God she understood, because the next thing I did was step away to call for the local police. All things considered, it didn't seem like the most auspicious time to introduce myself to my future mother-in-law.

marlowe

Two weeks later

"Are you wearing underwear?"

"Joe, come on, we have to leave now."

"This will only take a moment." Joe ran his hand over the back of my thin, black cotton dress. "Hang on— what's this? A thong?" He snapped the back of it.

"Ouch, that stings. It's a compromise, Joe. I can't go out with you in a dress this short without wearing anything underneath."

"That's not the bargain we made. You want me to do this for you, you have to go commando for me. So take 'em off."

"We don't have time for this."

"So stop arguing." He knelt at my feet, grinning up at me with boyishly cheerful lewdness. "Now, lift your leg." He slid the thong panties off me and threw them over his shoulder.

"Okay, satisfied?"

"Not quite." His big hands were sliding up my thighs, over my bottom.

"Joe, if you're feeling ambivalent about going, we should talk about it."

His mouth found the sensitive underside of my knee. " 'If you were April's Lady . . .' "

"Quoting Swinburne isn't going to work this time."

" 'And I were lord in May . . .' " I felt the soft brush of his kisses climb higher.

"We're going to be late."

" 'If you were queen of pleasure, and I were king of pain . . .' " He bit the inside of my thigh and I gasped. Joe looked up, eyes gleaming with dark satisfaction. "Now, who's feeling ambivalent?"

Suddenly, there was an angry hiss from one of the cats, followed by the frantic scamper of claws over waxed wood floors.

"Your cat is terrorizing him."

"They'll work it out." Joe stood up, his hands splayed on my hips, pressing the whole length of his aroused body against mine. I tried to take a step back and wound up falling back onto the hot pink couch that had just been delivered this morning. Joe lifted my dress up. "What do we have, five minutes left?"

"More like two. Joe, not on the new sofa. Do you know how much this thing cost?"

"Please. It's bad enough I have to live with furniture that looks like a giant tongue. Hey, is that meant to be some kind of a hint?" Joe slid down until he was kneeling on the floor at the foot of the couch. "Besides, we can afford it, now that I'm a lieutenant and you've got a big book deal."

"Joe, we have an appointment across town in about twenty minutes. How are we going to get there if we finish whatever it is we're starting?"

"You're forgetting how I drive." Joe lifted my right leg over his muscular shoulder. "So, how fast do you want me to be?" He kissed the inside of my thigh, then slid his hands under my butt to lift me up. He licked me once, a quick, hard flick of the tongue.

"Joe, I can't possibly . . . stop . . . I'm too tense . . . we're going to be late . . . Joe, Joe . . ."

He stopped. "Okay? All done? Should we go?" But he already had one hand on the fly of his jeans, unbuttoning.

"You're really sick, you know that," I said as he joined me on the couch.

"So heal me."

Despite my concerns, we made it to couples therapy right on time.

If you were April's lady,
And I were lord in May,

If you were queen of pleasure,
And I were king of pain,
We'd hunt down love together,

Pluck out his flying feather,
And teach his feet a measure,
and find his mouth a rein.

"A Match,"
Algernon Charles Swinburne,
1837-1909